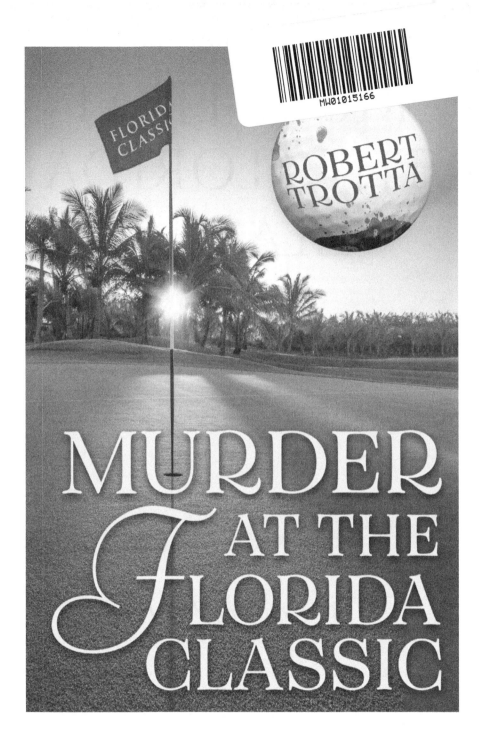

FLORIDA
CLASSIC

ROBERT
TROTTA

MURDER
AT THE
FLORIDA
CLASSIC

MURDER AT THE FLORIDA CLASSIC

By Robert Trotta

ISBN: 9781702322034

This book is dedicated to 72 law enforcement officers and 344 firefighters who lost their lives on September 11th, 2001, and the dozens who have since passed from 9/11-related illnesses.

CHAPTER 1

Fifteen-year-old Jasmin Dollbee awoke early from a restless night of sleep. So excited was the tall, pretty, Dwyer High School junior that she could not sleep—thinking about how lucky she was to be chosen as a standard bearer for this year's Florida Golf Classic at Professional Golfers' Association (PGA) National on the Champion Course.

The pro-am round was today. The pro-am is a pretournament event where big donors or corporate sponsors are paired with a professional golfer in a one-day competition. Usually the group you drew for the pro-am would be the group you would be assigned to for the entire tournament. Adjustments would be made if your group did not make the cut on day two of the tournament. The weather forecast called for clear sunny skies through Thursday with a strong possibility of a thunderstorm and rain on Friday evening and Saturday.

Jasmin would be joining her two older sisters, Megan and Katherine, both of whom had volunteered at the Florida Golf Classic for the past several years. For Jasmin to be selected as a standard bearer, her very first time volunteering, was in itself unusual. Her golf coach at Dwyer High School, Beth Donovan, put in a good word for her with Ann Quick, who was the director of volunteer services for the event.

Jasmin's sisters, eighteen-year-old Megan and twenty-year-old Katherine, both played golf at their colleges, Florida State University and High Point University in North Carolina, respectively. Their dad, Ken Dollbee, and mom, Patty, both played college golf, worked in the golf industry, and supported their daughters' golfing. They were members of PGA National, which helped their daughters secure plum volunteer positions. Both Ken and Pat knew that Jasmin—the better athlete—was the only daughter with the skills, discipline, and desire to play golf professionally. Before being shuffled off to bed by their parents the night before, the girls talked about which group they might get to walk with.

"I would kill for the Ricky Fowler, Jason Day, Webb Simpson group," an exuberant Megan cried out.

"Not me," said Katherine, "I hope I get Daniel Berger's threesome." Berger, a Dwyer graduate, often came to team practices while she was a senior there and sort of flirted with Katherine. She immediately fell in love. Jasmin didn't care who she walked with. She knew this was the chance for her to learn some things from the best golfers in the world. She would watch how they prepared for each shot, what they discussed with their caddies, and most importantly how they approached each shot and lined up their putts.

Jasmin's dad taught her at an early age how important putting is. "Golf tournaments are won or lost on the putting green," was his teaching mantra to a young Jasmin. She had played the Champion Course several times with her parents and sisters. She also competed in amateur and high school team events, so again she felt she would learn a lot by observing the pros.

The Florida Classic, formerly known as the Jackie Gleason Inverrary Classic, moved to PGA National. Under the leadership of Tournament Executive Director George Goll, the tournament grew in prestige among the pros and drew most of the top names in golf to play in the event. The fact that many of the top golfers in the world lived in Palm Beach County also added to the inducement for the pros to play, not to mention the winner's share of the purse was just over one million dollars. Goll's leadership as executive director was the main reason for the tournament's success over the past several years. His background in marketing as well as ability to involve the local community were in no small way part of the success of this event.

In addition to the large purse in the players' pool, The Classic's payout to local charities had reached over three million dollars. Quite impressive for a golf tournament that only several years ago was being considered to be taken off the PGA's schedule. This success fell squarely on the shoulders of George Goll and his team. The American Motors Corporation (AMC), the principle sponsor, was also committed to the tournament, so much so that in the *golf world*, it was referred to as "The Classic," much like "The Masters" or "The Open."

CHAPTER 2

Neither of the older girls were assigned to the groups they hoped for, and Jasmin drew a relatively unknown international player, German Karl Messerschmitt, and three executives from Florida Power and Light (FPL), the local energy company. Most pros do not enjoy these pro-ams, and Messerschmitt was no exception. The three FPL execs were decent players, but Jasmin could see their disappointment in Messerschmitt's attitude.

He barely spoke to them other than to compliment them on a nice shot and spoke German to his caddy. Jasmin knew the caddy spoke English because he introduced himself to her and told her his name was Dieter, a name Jasmin had never heard before. Jasmin's group came in the middle of the field and after the round, Messerschmitt signed golf gloves for the volunteers in his group and politely shook hands with the three execs. Jasmin did observe that Messerschmitt consulted with his caddy on almost every shot. He played well.

CHAPTER 3

On Thursday morning round one of the tournament was set to begin. All three Dollbee sisters were driven to the course by their mom and dropped off at the same entrance as the players, caddies, tournament officials, and other volunteers. People attending the tournament would have to park away from the venue and take a shuttle to the course. Jasmin reported to her volunteer supervisor and was issued her standard with the three player names and was told to be prepared to be on the tenth tee for their 9:18 tee time.

Jasmin was disappointed to learn she had drawn Messerschmitt again, along with Canadian Greg "Boney" Moroney and Englishman Tommy Blackpool. Moroney had a brief career in the National Hockey League but decided he was better at golf and had the teeth to prove it. In his first professional tournament, he was disqualified for using an unauthorized club. Moroney had fashioned a putter head to a hockey stick shaft, which was deemed to be nonconforming.

In addition to Jasmin, the three pros, and their caddies, the group would be accompanied by a scoring official. The gallery following this group would be very small, as none of them were very popular and not expected to make the cut. None of the players introduced themselves to Jasmin. She was put off when Messerschmitt's caddie approached saying, "Hello, Yasmin (Germans pronounce *J* as *Y*). So nice to see you again." Right away she thought the tall, dark, curly haired caddy was weird, his smile was almost sinister, and she made it a point to walk as far away from him as possible.

The round began, and the three golfers went about their business in a professional manner. No one made a birdie or bogey until they reached the Bear Trap—holes fifteen, sixteen, and seventeen. Messerschmitt birdied the par three, fifteen, and seventeen and made par on sixteen and eighteen to go two under. Moroney and Blackpool did not fare so well, and they both made bogey on fifteen, sixteen, and seventeen to go three over. On the front nine, Moroney made bogey on five and seven to fall to five over. Blackpool played even and remained at three over. Messerschmitt birdied one, three, and nine to finish five under.

After they finished the round, golfers and caddies all shook hands as is custom. They would play together again Friday afternoon. Dieter, the German caddie, gave Messerschmitt's signed glove to Jasmin and told her he looked forward to seeing her again tomorrow. Jasmin thought that Dieter, who was probably twice her age, was kind of creepy. She noticed that the fingers on his right hand were bent at an inward angle. He noticed her looking and held up his hand, "Accident. I used to be a pretty good golfer too, better than Messer, but now I just caddy for him." Jasmin just nodded and wanted to get away as fast as she could. This strange guy frightened her.

Back at the volunteers' staging area, Jasmin caught up with Megan and Katherine, and all three girls were talking at once and discussing the groups they were with. Except for Katherine, who had Russell Henley—a past Florida Classic champion—in her group, none of the girls thought they would be around for the weekend. Jasmin did not mention to her sisters about the signed glove given to her by Dieter. She thought, who cares? No one knows Karl Messerschmitt or his creepy caddie Dieter.

CHAPTER 4

Friday's second round proved to be a repeat of Thursday's first round. Once again Moroney and Blackpool had mediocre scores and did not make the cut, which stood at five under. Messerschmitt shot two under for a two-day total of seven under, four shots behind the leader Rory McIlroy. Messerschmitt would play his third round Saturday with Paul Stockall, the talented Canadian.

Although he had won three times in the past four years on the European Tour, Messerschmitt was relatively unknown to the average American golf fan. The TV commentators even joked about his name, as it was the same name as a German WWII fighter plane. In fact, Messerschmitt's grandfather, Wilhelm, was the founder of the airplane-manufacturing firm that bore his name. On the few occasions that Messerschmitt was on TV, analyst Paul Maloy would comment to his TV partner and former pro golfer Lou Schneider, "Is that a Stukker hitting the ball Lou?" To which Schneider would reply, "No, it's a Messerschmitt," and they would both crack up. The show's producers told them to can that comment, as it was getting a bit old after a couple of times.

CHAPTER 5

Back at home the Dollbee girls could not stop talking about the day's events and all the great golfers they had seen. As was their Friday night tradition, Patty ordered pizza from Anthony's Coal Fired Pizza. As they ate the pizza, the girls talked about their day. Megan had been reassigned to the players' wife's hospitality tent and was going on about how beautiful all the top golfers' wives were.

"Sure, if I made five or six million a year, you think I would be married to your mom?" Ken said with a chuckle. Patty reached over and punched him playfully in the arm.

"And if I could chip and putt like Michele Wie, I would not have married a hacker like you." Both Ken and Patty laughed.

"I still love you though, Patty. Look at the three beautiful daughters you gave me."

Jasmin knew her parents loved one another. On more than one occasion, she had heard them making love when they thought all three girls were asleep. On the first occasion, Jasmin was about ten and was having nightmares. She awoke and went to her parents' room, but before entering she heard her mom moaning and whispering, "Kenny, Kenny, oh, Kenny more, I want more," and she could hear the bed squeaking and her parents moaning as they climaxed together. Jasmin ran back to her room not knowing what to think. The next morning, she told Katherine what she heard the night before. Kat, who was six years older, just laughed and said, "You might get that little brother you've been pestering mom and dad about." Jasmin didn't understand but let it go.

After dinner Jasmin asked her mom if she would drive her over to her friend Trisha Maddox's house. Trisha was Jasmin's best friend and once played on the golf team but gave it up. She lived about eight miles from the Dollbee's Palm Beach Gardens home in the rural Jupiter Farms development. Trisha lived with her mom and her older brother in a rented house formerly owned by Trisha's grandfather. Since Trisha's mom and dad divorced, things had been hard on the Maddox's. Tricia's dad, Ron, had left his wife and kids, moved to Louisiana, and worked on an oilrig in the Gulf. He made decent money but was always behind on child support. Trisha's mom, Pam, was a nurse at Good Samaritan Medical Center and worked crazy hours. As a result Trisha was on her own a lot and started to hang out with some other kids that Jasmin did not like to be around. Patty dropped Jasmin off at the Maddox's' house. "Let me know when you want me to pick you up. And if you decide to go anywhere, send me a text."

"Yeah mom, OK." Jasmin was still excited about the events of the previous days at The Classic.

Trisha on the other hand seemed distracted as if something was bothering her. "Is that all you're gonna talk about? That stupid golf tournament?"

Jasmin was shocked at Trisha's comments. "I thought you would want to know about what I did."

"Well, I don't. I don't care about some stupid golf and stupid golfers."

Jasmin could see that Trish was upset and she didn't know why. "I'm sorry Trish, I won't mention it again. Do you want to watch a movie?"

"No, I don't. Let's go out. My friend Mark is having a party at his house. His parents are away, so let's go there."

Jasmin was unsure. She knew the crowd that Mark hung with and they were kids who smoked pot and drank. "I'm not sure I want to do that Trish. I thought we were gonna hang out here."

"Well, I'm gonna go. You can come or not, but I'm going. I called an Uber, and he'll be here in ten."

"Oh, OK then." The Uber drove the girls to Mark's house a few miles away in the western part of Jupiter Farms. When they got to Mark's house, Jasmin could smell marijuana and hear the music being played way too loud. She figured the cops would be called soon. Once inside Trisha went into the kitchen and came back with two beers.

"Here Jas, take one."

"No thanks, I don't much like beer."

"Then try this," Trish said handing Jasmin a small pipe packed with weed. Jasmin did not want to seem uncool, so she took a hit.

"Listen Trish, I'm not comfortable here, so I'm gonna hit the road."

Trisha was getting tired of Jasmin's *attitude* toward her friends and told her maybe it was best she left. "I'll call you an Uber, and you can owe me the money. It was only six bucks from my house, so it might be a bit more to your house."

"OK, I'm sorry Trish, it's just—"

Trisha cut her off. "It's OK Jas, It's OK."

Jasmin went outside and waited for her ride. After about ten minutes and no Uber, Jasmin thought about going back inside to find Trisha and have her check on the Uber. Then she thought, I could call home for a ride, but I can't do that. Mom will know I was here. She thought, I'll just wait a few minutes more.

Before the thought left her mind, she heard a familiar voice. "Vell, I'll be darned. Vhat a coincidence."

Jasmine turned toward the voice, it was Dieter, Karl Messerschmitt's caddy. How in the world did he just show up here now, she wondered?

"I was riding home to where I am staying, and I saw you standing here. Can I offer you a ride?"

"Er, no, that's OK. I am waiting for my dad to pick me up," she lied hoping it would scare him off. She thought to

13

herself, on his way to where he's staying? Out here in the Farms? She became frightened.

"So tell me did you enjoy watching Messer play today? We are still in the running, you know."

Just then, seemingly out of nowhere, dark thunderclouds rolled in and lightning struck. A loud thunderclap startled the already nervous Jasmin. Dieter laughed and, still leaning over the driver's seat, opened the car door. "You better get in or you might get hit with lightning. I've seen it happen on a golf course in Germany. You could get seriously hurt."

Reluctantly Jasmin got in Dieter's car. "My dad should be here soon, and I don't want him to miss seeing me."

"Don't worry. Maybe I drive around the block so we will be behind him."

Before Jasmin could answer, Dieter drove off and locked the doors. Jasmin was about to tell Dieter to stop the car and let her out when she felt something was placed over her head. It became quite dark. She screamed and felt a sharp blow to the back of her head and thought she was going to pass out. Struggling, she grabbed at the object over her head and started to scream. She felt another blow to the back of her head. Fear and panic would be the last feelings she would experience in her young life.

CHAPTER 6

Back at the Dollbee residence, the family was gathered around the television watching the golf channel when Patty noticed it was getting close to 10:00 p.m., and Jasmin's curfew was approaching. She decided to give Jas's cell phone a ring and see if she wanted to be picked up at Tricia's house. Since Jas didn't call early to say they were going out, she assumed that they stayed at the Maddox's to watch a movie. Jasmin's phone went to voice mail and Patty left a message.

About ten minutes later she decided to call again, but this time she did it from her car as she decided to drive to the Maddox's house. When she arrived, she was surprised to see all the lights out and no cars in the driveway. Starting to get nervous, Patty approached the house, a modest three-bedroom ranch with a small front yard, porch, and a fence surrounding a larger backyard. Patty rang the bell and waited with no answer. She rang again and called Jasmin's cell, but again it went to voicemail.

Patty was starting to worry and decided to call her husband. Now they both were worried about their daughter. They were concerned because it was unlike her to not answer her phone or at least let her parents know if she changed plans. Patty drove back to their house, and she and Ken decided to ride around the neighborhood looking for their daughter, hoping maybe she decided to walk home. It was nearing 11:00 p.m., and a heavy thunderstorm was already starting to flood the low-lying streets of Jupiter Farms, many of which were not paved.

Around 1:00 a.m. the Dollbees decided to contact the Palm Beach Gardens Police. The officer taking their call gave them the usual response when parents reported a teenager missing, "Maybe she was staying at a friend's house. Or did she have an argument with one of you and was being rebellious?"

"You don't understand, officer," responded Ken. "Our daughter is a good kid and is not like that."

The cop rolled his eyes. He heard the same thing a hundred times but took the information and told the Dollbees he would file a report. He put out a description to the units on patrol and notified the neighboring Jupiter Police Department (JPD) and the Palm Beach Sherriff's Office (PBSO).

Back at the Dollbee residence, the family waited for word. Both Ken and Patty sensed something was wrong; this was out of character for their youngest daughter.

CHAPTER 7

Each morning Mary Thomas would walk her dogs in the Cypress Creek Natural Area just west of Jupiter Farms off Indiantown Road. Mary liked to walk her two German shepherds, Siegfried and Roy, early and if there were no other cars in the parking area, she would unleash the dogs and let them run, sniff, and do their business. They would always return when she whistled. She noticed it was 6:50 a.m., and daylight was about to break through the clouds. It had rained most of the night and heavy rain was forecast all day, so she was thankful to get her dogs out early. She had tickets to The Florida Classic for today and Sunday and planned to meet a couple of her friends for lunch at PGA.

The Cypress Creek Natural Area is a ten-acre, state-run recreational area and includes Cypress Creek Preserve. Fishing, canoeing, and kayaking are permitted, and the park offers a series of trails for hikers. There are several sitting areas where one can observe the variety of waterfowl that patrol the area looking for a meal.

As she strolled on the trail adjacent to the large fishing pond, she lost sight of the dogs. And when she gave the familiar whistle, the dogs did not respond. Mary continued up the trail and spotted her dogs by the water, sniffing at something laying partially out of the water. Her first thoughts were that they found a dead fish or maybe even an animal. As Mary approached and whistled, both dogs turned to her and barked, as if to say, "Hey, look what we found."

Mary approached the water's edge and was shocked to see what appeared to be a human leg protruding out of the murky water. Now frightened Mary called both dogs back to her and reached into her fanny pack, got out her cell phone, and dialed 9-1-1.

Palm Beach (PB) County Sherriff's Deputy Dexter Nichols responded to the call of a possible body in the Cypress Creek Natural Area. Upon his arrival he was met by a shaken Thomas who related what she had observed. Nichols told her to remain where she was and keep her dogs leashed. He walked toward the edge of the pond. Oh shit, he thought to himself, it's a dead body. So he did what he was trained to do—call for a supervisor and secure the area.

Within ten minutes of his call, Deputy Nichols was joined by Patrol Supervisor John Weisser and several other deputies. Sergeant Weisser notified the JPD, the PB County medical examiner (ME), and the district three homicide division. After hearing the report from Sergeant Weisser, Commanding Officer (CO) Lieutenant Tom Cashin looked at the assignment board and saw that Detective Lydia Martinez was up next. Cashin was new to the unit and liked to work on Saturdays, as it was quieter in the squad room, and he could get his paperwork done without interruptions. Working Tuesday through Saturday fit into his personal life, as he had a regular Monday golf game at Tequesta Country Club, where he lived.

Martinez was the only female and one of his best detectives in his eight-person squad. Even though her cubicle was only a few yards from his office, he called her on the phone and asked her to step into his office.

Martinez had spent the last two weeks at the murder trial of Teofilo Caban and Alvaro Ocasio-Cortez, two local gang bangers who were charged with the murder of a homeless Vietnam vet named Robert Stabins. Stabins, who struggled with alcohol abuse, existed in a makeshift shanty constructed of two or three large cardboard boxes plastered with "Trump for President" and "Make America Great Again" stickers strung together under the Blue Heron Bridge. When the Palm Beach County Fire Rescue personnel extinguished the fire, all they found was Stabins charred body and a red "Make America Great" cap. Both perps were convicted of the lesser charge of second-degree homicide, rather than the original first-degree homicide charge.

Martinez was disappointed but felt that if Stabins had an advocate or family to speak on his behalf, the original charge might have stuck. Both Caban and Ocasio-Cortez were in the country illegally. Caban had been deported twice before. Martinez and her partner, Sergeant Chris Clarkson, broke the case with the help of an informant only two days after the homicide. Both perps joked to their friends how they poured gasoline on the shanty and watched as it went up in flames, burning poor Stabins to death. Word got back to Martinez through one of her many snitches in the Latino community in West Palm Beach. Within forty-eight hours of the crime, Martinez and Clarkson had both perps under arrest.

Martinez asked, "Yeah, Lt., what's up?" (Most detectives referred to lieutenants as Lou or Lt.)

Cashin replied, "Patrol called in a body out at that Cypress Creek Natural Area. Check it out, and if it's ours, let me know and I'll send you some help."

Cypress Creek Natural Area was constructed and managed by the Florida Department of Agriculture and was located within the confines of the town of Jupiter. Law enforcement responsibility was shared by the Jupiter PD and the PBSO. However, if a serious crime were to occur in the Cypress Creek Preserve like this possible homicide, JPD would defer to PBSO.

"Who else is out there?" he said gesturing with his head to the squad room.

"Well, Franks and Beans (Detectives Jerry Nathans and Lee Bush), but they are working on that triple homicide in Boynton Beach. I'll go out there and if it's ours (meaning if it's a homicide), I'll call in for another team." Before Cashin could answer she was out the door.

Martinez's partner Sergeant Chris Clarkson was on sick leave after having back surgery and, truth be told, Martinez liked working alone. As she walked out of his office Cashin shook his head. He had heard that although she was a good detective, Martinez was set in her ways. She liked to do things her way, which was not always in line with department protocol.

Cashin was a decent enough guy but liked doing things by the book. This was his first assignment in the detective division, which was unusual, but he was previously on Sherriff Rick Romain's command staff and wanted an investigative assignment to aid in his career path résumé. Naturally Romain, who thought highly of Cashin, was only too happy to give him this prestigious assignment when the previous CO retired.

Cashin thought about Martinez. Of course, he read her personnel jacket, as he had with all of his detectives, but was impressed with her record as well as her service as an army reserve officer and four years of active duty, including two deployments to Iraq and Afghanistan as a military police officer. He knew she was single but was involved in a relationship with an older guy. The story he heard was that the older guy was a retired cop from New York who worked for an insurance company. And together they solved a couple of homicides last year that involved the theft of a valuable painting, the New York Russian mob, and the Ruggerio crime family. Word was that she and the old guy were responsible for bringing down the Russian crew and forcing big changes in the hierarchy of the Ruggerio's. I've got to read that file one day, he thought to himself.

CHAPTER 8

Martinez arrived at the Cypress Creek Preserve at 8:45 a.m. and showed her ID to the JPD patrol vehicle blocking the entrance. She parked her department-issued Crown Victoria next to the two green and whites. Exiting the Crown Vic, she walked to the area where Deputy Nichols and Sergeant Weisser stood engaged in conversation. Martinez was pleased that yellow crime scene tape was strung around the area, and a Jupiter PD cruiser was blocking the entrance to the Preserve. The ground was wet and soft from last night's thunderstorms, and the drizzle that started earlier that morning was turning into a steady rain. Martinez put on a PBSO hooded windbreaker and covered her head when she exited her Crown Vic, taking along the black attaché case that Dio had given her.

"Detective Martinez. What have we got here?"

"I'm Sergeant John Weisser," said Weisser extending his hand, which Martinez shook. She knew Nichols and just nodded hello. "I responded to a call from that lady over there." Nichols pointed toward Mary Thomas, who was on her cell phone and restraining her two leashed dogs while trying to hold an umbrella over her head. "There's a body down in the water partially exposed. I didn't touch it or try to bring it out."

Martinez nodded and started toward the pond followed by the two uniforms.

"I notified Crime Scene," said Weisser. "They should be here shortly. I also put a call into the Jupiter PD," he said pointing to the cruiser blocking the entrance. "The ME's office was also notified. You think they will want this?" added Weisser, nodding toward the white JPD cruiser.

21

"I doubt it," she replied. "They defer most homicides to us, and I'm assuming that's what we have here or at least a suspicious death."

As they approached the pond, Martinez could see the right leg of the body and the one sneaker that was exposed. She knew by the sneaker that this body was that of a young female, probably a teen. Martinez then asked Weisser to help her pull the body from the canal while handing him a pair of plastic gloves. She took out her cell phone and took a few pictures of the body lying in the water. They pulled the body out of the canal. "Oh my God," was her first response. "Look at this poor girl."

"Holy shit," replied Sergeant Weisser.

The body was that of a young white teenage female. Her jeans and underpants were pulled down to her knees, and Martinez noticed bruising around her anus and the back of her head just below the hairline. She took several additional photos with her cell phone and then she and Sergeant Weisser rolled the body over and observed there were no other bruises on the face or upper part of the body, at least none they could detect. Sergeant Weisser, who had been a cop for over twenty years, was visibly upset having a daughter of similar age. By the texture of the skin, Martinez figured the body had been in the water for several hours.

"Who the fuck could do such a thing?" He was referring to the bruises on the body's anus and assumed (correctly) that she had been anally assaulted. Martinez figured the girl had been dead about ten to twelve hours, but because it was submerged, she would leave that determination to the ME. She probed the body's jeans looking for some means of identification and found a cell phone from the front right pocket. She tried to turn it on, but it had been submerged in the water too long to be of any use at this point. She placed the phone in a plastic bag and patted down the body to look for any ID or jewelry. The dead girl did have a pair of small diamond studs in each ear. Other than that, there was nothing.

Martinez decided to wait until Crime Scene (CS) arrived to do anything further with the body. She asked Sergeant Weisser to stay near the body, as she wanted to interview the woman who found the body.

Mary Thomas told Martinez pretty much what she told Deputy Nichols. She was walking her dogs as she normally did and when they went down to the edge of the pond, they would not respond to her whistle, which was unlike them. "When I went down to the water, I noticed the leg sticking out of the water and called 9-1-1."

"How far down did you go?"

"Only about halfway. I know from watching *CSI* on TV that the crime scene should not be disturbed, plus I'm wearing flip flops and just had a pedicure." Martinez glanced down at her feet and nodded. "Listen, can I go now? I'm getting soaking wet, and I have to feed the dogs and—"

Martinez cut her off. "Yeah sure, just give your contact information to Deputy Nichols up there," Martinez said pointing to Nichols who was on his cell phone. "And Miss Thomas, thank you for your help." Thomas just nodded and walked away. Martinez thought it strange that she did not ask about the body but let it go for now. She figured she or another detective would probably talk to her again.

The ME arrived about ten minutes later, and Martinez gave the responding pathologist, Dr. Debra Widman, what she had. She had worked with Widman before and knew her to be an efficient pathologist. Crime Scene had arrived while Martinez was interviewing Thomas, and they were in the process of conducting their investigation of the body and the crime scene. The rain had stopped for now, but the sky was still overcast. Two officers from the Jupiter PD arrived, one in uniform and the other a detective who introduced himself as Detective Brian Poissant.

"I guess this is yours," he said to Martinez. "Let us know if you need anything. I notified my chief and he concurred that the sheriff's office is better suited for this." He handed

Martinez his card. "I'll leave the uniform officer at the entrance to keep the park closed until you're done." Martinez sensed he was more than happy to let her handle this case. The CS team consisted of Detectives John Whalen and Tom Chisholm, who were two of the more experienced crime scene investigators in the department. Martinez was confident they would do a good job of gathering and cataloging all of the pertinent evidence. They erected a tent to work under and placed the body inside as they assumed the rain would start again. They did not want any forensic evidence to be destroyed by the rain.

Martinez then asked Dr. Widman what the cause and time of death might be and when she would conduct the autopsy. Widman, who was eating a bagel and drinking coffee from a container, was a tall, thin, attractive woman of about fifty-five, noticed Martinez eyeballing the bagel.

"I came right from home, no time for breakfast. It looks like the body has been in the water a while, and there are bruises on the back of the head and anal area. I'll know more when I get her to the morgue and get her cleaned up." Martinez just nodded. The crime scene detectives started to expand their search, taking pictures of the surrounding area, and told the ME they were finished with the body.

"Do you have an ID on the victim, Detective?" asked Doc Widman.

"Not yet, she had no ID on her, and her cell was submerged." Jeez, she thought, I better get to work on IDing this kid. Martinez had been doubting herself these last few months and thought that maybe it was time to *pull the pin*, as they say. Retire and move to London where her boyfriend Dio lived. She met Dio Bosso about a year ago when they met and worked on The *Green Violinist* homicide. Dio was a retired NYPD deputy inspector, working for Lloyd's of London. They had become lovers after they solved the double homicide and the theft of the famous Marc Chagall painting by master theft Rocco DeAngelis, a made member of the New York Ruggerio crime family. That bust all but eradicated the Russian mob in

24

Brooklyn and forced Ruggerio family boss Tommy Ruggerio into an early retirement. Martinez was initially pissed that Dio made a deal with DeAngelis and the state's attorney, stipulating that if the painting was returned or recovered undamaged, he would not be charged. Rocco was never charged with the theft and was now living in Tennessee on Lake Barefield, also in retirement. She knew a weasel like DeAngelis would never be content just fishing or making day trips to Nashville to go to the Grand Olde Opry. No, sooner or later he would get back into *the game*, but that was not her problem.

Martinez knew that Dio deeply cared for her, as he professed each time she visited him in London. She was not sure if she felt the same way. Relationships, the few she had, were not her strong point. Although, she did feel different with Dio. She cared for him but thought, If I retired and moved to London, as he suggested, what would I do? How much sightseeing could I do? Plus, the fact that Dio was fifteen years her senior was of some concern. She cleared these thoughts from her mind for the moment and knew she had to get to work on this latest case. She would call Dio later and let him know she would not be coming to London as planned this next weekend.

Martinez got back in the Crown Vic and called Lieutenant Cashin and let him know what she had. She had asked Sergeant Weisser before he left the scene to check if any recent missing person reports were filed where the missing person fit the description of their victim. She asked Detective Poissant the same. Martinez was in her vehicle no more than ten minutes when her cell rang.

"Hello, Lydia, its John Weisser." She was surprised that he used both their first names but let it go.

"Yeah, Sergeant, whaddya got?"

"Got a call from Detective Poissant from the Jupiter PD. He said they got a report from the Gardens PD of a missing female last night, and it fits the description of your vic. Name is

Jasmin Dollbee. I'll text you the name and address of the parents. They live in Palm Beach Gardens."

"When was she reported missing?"

"Last night around 10:00 p.m. The report was taken over the telephone."

"OK thanks, Sarge. Can you send a deputy to meet me at the address? I'll make the notification, but I think it would be best if they see a uniform."

"Sure thing, I have Deputy Kim Blanshaft working today. She's professional, and I think a female would be good for this purpose."

"Ok, good, and thanks again," Martinez hung up and started heading toward Palm Beach Gardens.

Why didn't Poissant call me himself? she thought. Male chauvinist probably. Doesn't think women belong in policing. Poissant, she thought, what kind of name is that? Sounds like a French pastry chef's name.

Within two minutes, Martinez's cell phone beeped, and she saw that Sergeant Weisser sent her the address. As she headed toward the Dollbee's address on Misty Lakes Drive in Palm Beach Gardens, her cell phone rang again.

"Detective Martinez."

"Hi Detective, I'm Deputy Blanshaft. I'm about one street from the residence. Sergeant Weisser briefed me on your homicide. I thought I would meet you here, and we can drive up in your unmarked car as not to necessarily alarm the parents."

Smart cop, Martinez thought.

"OK, I'll be there in five," and hung up. This was the part of her job that she hated. What cop would like to do what she must do in the next ten minutes? Notify parents that their teenage daughter was brutally murdered. She pulled up behind the marked sheriff's office car. Deputy Blanshaft exited, and the first thing Martinez noticed was how tall she was. Martinez got out of the Crown Vic and extended her right hand to Blanshaft.

"Lydia Martinez."

"Hi. Kim Blanshaft," as they shook hands. Martinez wanted to maintain a businesslike attitude and asked the deputy, "This your first homicide notification?"

"Yes, but I guess you'll do all the talking. I figure I'm just here to make it look official. You know, the uniform and all."

"Yep," Martinez liked her straight away. She seemed to be all business.

They reached the house and Martinez knocked. The door was answered by Pat Dollbee and, as soon as she saw the uniform, she knew this could only be bad. Before Martinez could introduce themselves, the woman started to scream, "No, no please don't tell me something happened to my baby."

With that, a man appeared from inside the house. He went to his wife's side but before he could say anything, Martinez said, "I'm Detective Martinez and this is Deputy Blanshaft. Mr. Dollbee?"

"Yes, please, have you found my daughter?"

"Not sure, sir, we recovered the body of a young girl earlier today and unfortunately she matches the description you gave us last night. I am very sorry for your loss, but we need you to come with us to make a positive ID."

Pat Dollbee was now hysterically weeping, and two other young girls came to her side also crying. "Is it Jasy? Did you find our sister? Is she dead?" Blanshaft stepped into the house and tried to comfort the two sisters.

"Please, Mr. Dollbee, I know how hard this is for you."

But before Martinez could continue, Ken Dollbee said, "What happened? Can you tell us what happened to our daughter?" He was shouting and holding back tears. Martinez decided not to show them the photos she took of the body. She would wait until a proper ID was made at the ME's, where the body would at least be cleaned up.

"Please, sir, I know this is difficult for you, but I need to ask you some questions and have you come with me. Deputy Blanshaft will stay here with your family."

27

"OK," said a somewhat subdued Ken Dollbee, "just give me a second with my wife and girls." He then hugged his wife. "Maybe it's not Jasy. Maybe they made a mistake. I'll go with the detective and I'll let you know if it's her."

Martinez and Ken Dollbee got into the Crown Vic. She could see he was visibly shaken, but Martinez had to ask some questions and proceeded to do so. She called Doc Widman who informed her she and crime scene had completed their preliminary investigation and the body was on the way to the morgue.

"I'll make sure the body is cleaned up as soon as possible."

"Thanks, Doc."

"Mr. Dollbee, can you tell me when you last saw your daughter?"

"As we told the police last night, it was about 7:00 p.m. She finished her day at The Classic and Pat, my wife, drove her to her friend's house. They were going to hang out and watch a movie. Can you tell me what happened?"

Martinez did not connect The Classic reference but let it go for the time being.

"We don't know yet. What's your daughter's friend's name and where does she live?"

"Trisha Maddox. I'm not sure of the address, somewhere in the Farms. My wife would have it." Locals referred to Jupiter Farms as *The Farms*, just like they called Palm Beach Gardens *The Gardens* or Palm Beach *The Island*.

They were getting close to the ME's office, and Martinez thought she would hold off any questions until a positive ID was made. She pulled into a parking spot marked PBSO, and they both entered the building. Martinez showed her ID to the deputy on security duty and gave him Ken Dollbee's name.

The anteroom to the actual morgue had a couple of soft chairs and a drawn curtain where Dollbee would make the ID once Martinez made sure the body was ready. She entered the morgue and was met by Dr. Widman.

"Hey, Lydia, how you doing?"

"I've got the vic's dad outside. Is the body ready for ID?"

"Yes, it's a slow day so I was able to clean her up and make a partial exam, but I haven't logged her in for the autopsy yet."

"Good, let's get her by the viewing window, and I'll bring the dad over."

Outside Mr. Dollbee was sitting on the chair nervously biting his fingers.

"Mr. Dollbee, we're going to stand by that curtain, and I want you to tell me if that is Jasmin."

Martinez stood by his side and tapped on the window. The curtain was pulled back and as soon as Dollbee saw the body, he let out a sob. Martinez did not have to ask him if that was his daughter.

"My baby, my baby," he cried and then he suddenly turned and hugged Martinez. She was taken a bit aback by this but just patted him on his back and said how sorry she was, and she would do her best to find who did this to his daughter. Her cell phone rang, and she saw it was the office and realized she had not reported back to Lieutenant Cashin since she found the body.

She pulled away from Ken Dollbee, "I have to take this call."

"Martinez," she said answering the phone.

"Where the hell you been, and what's going on?" an annoyed Lieutenant Cashin asked.

"Oh, sorry Lou, but I was just going to call you. The body was that of a Jasmin Dollbee, female, white, about sixteen years old. I'm at the ME's now with the father who just made a positive ID. I'm going to need some help here. I want to interview the father, and I also want to be here when the ME does the cut. Anybody around who can help?"

"I'll send Kiers and Telmany over there. They're on the day shift and have no open cases. Nathans and Bush are out of the office on their case."

"Good, thanks boss," Martinez knew Cashin liked it when his detectives called him boss; it was like a sign of respect among detectives. Although she would prefer to have Franks and Beans work with her, as she didn't know Frank Kiers or Ed Telmany that well. She knew they were both seasoned detectives and would be an asset to her investigation. Telmany was still referred to as Fat Eddy, even though he lost sixty-five pounds about ten years ago while still a patrol deputy and kept himself in shape. Frank Kiers had been on the job over twenty years and a detective for about half that time. Martinez asked Cashin to have them meet her at the morgue where she would bring them up to speed.

Moving back toward Dollbee she asked, "Mr. Dollbee, we found Jasmin's cell phone, but we will have to send it to our Data Forensic Unit to see if we can retrieve any useful information from it. Jasmin was wearing diamond studs in her ears. Did you know if she had other jewelry when she left home last night?"

"I'm not sure, but she always wore the anklet my wife and I gave her for her last birthday."

"Can you describe it?"

"Well, it was gold and had a small golf club charm attached. The plan was to add a charm each year on her birthday or if she won a golf tournament." With that, he broke out sobbing again.

Martinez was pleased that she had asked Crime Scene to search the pond area and call in a diver to search the pond. She then told Dollbee that two detectives would be there shortly to ask him some additional questions and drive him home, but he could call his wife if he wanted to. She went back inside and asked Dr. Widman if she had any idea when she might do the autopsy.

"Not right now, I need to get something to eat. I haven't had anything since breakfast."

Martinez thought, my God, how can she think about food when she is about to open the victim's body and remove all her organs. They're a strange breed, these pathologists, she thought and realized she was hungry too. She thought about calling Kiers and asking him to stop and get her something but then thought better of it. She went out to the anteroom. Dollbee was on his cell softly crying, probably talking to his wife.

It wasn't long before Kiers and Telmany arrived at the morgue. Martinez greeted them and filled them in on what she had so far and wanted them to interview the Dollbees and find as much about the vic as they could.

"This isn't our first homicide, Martinez. Do we look like rookies to you?" asked Telmany sarcastically.

"I know that, but I'm just trying to let you know what I need and what direction I want this investigation to go. Sorry if I offended you, Ed."

"No problem," chimed in Kiers. "Is that the father?" he asked, pointing to Ken Dollbee.

"Yeah, he's pretty shaken up and I think his wife will be worse. I got a uniform at the house in The Gardens babysitting." She gave the address and introduced them to Ken Dollbee. The two detectives shook Ken's hand and extended their condolences. Martinez told them the detectives would drive him home but needed to ask him some questions. He nodded but appeared to be in such pain. Martinez's heart went out to him, and once again was thankful that she never had children. She could not imagine the pain one must feel losing a child, especially the way Jasmin Dollbee appeared to have died.

As the two detectives walked Dollbee out of the anteroom, Martinez could not resist getting back at Telmany for his wisecracking earlier. He was still sensitive about his weight. "Hey, Ed, is that an old suit? Looks like you're putting some weight on." Kiers smiled and Ed flipped her the bird behind his back as they walked out the door. Martinez went back inside the morgue. Dr. Widman was sitting in her office eating a sandwich and reading something on her computer. She must have seen Martinez look at her sandwich.

"It's ham and cheese on rye. I have another one in the fridge if you want it. This is plenty for me." Martinez was famished but knew that if she ate now, she would only puke it up during the autopsy. Although she witnessed dozens of autopsies, she would never do it just after eating. The telephone rang in Dr. Widman's office, and she picked it up on the second ring.

"Hi, Michael, must be a slow day in New York," she chuckled. R. Michael Widman, Dr. Widman's older brother, was the police commissioner of the NYPD, and Martinez remembered how Dio thought highly of him during the *Green Violinist* case.

CHAPTER 9

Detectives Kiers and Telmany drove Ken Dollbee back to his home and on the way asked some basic questions. They learned that Jasmin would turn sixteen next September 5 and was a junior at Dwyer High School. She was on the golf team and played in many junior golf tournaments both locally and as far away as Indiana. She was by far a better golfer than her sisters, both of whom played college golf. He told the detectives that Jasmin was a volunteer at The Florida Classic and was scheduled to be working there today. He continued saying that the heavy rain would probably delay or postpone today's round, but he would call them just to let them know Jasmin would not be coming in today.

"Heck, she would beat both me and my wife, and we both played amateur golf for years. Jasmin was being recruited by several big named schools plus all the state schools. She was a good student too. Who could do such a thing?" He broke down crying again and Kiers glanced over to his partner. Telmany read him well and stopped the questions for now.

While at the Dollbee house, Deputy Blanshaft did her best to be supportive of the Dollbee women. She was relieved when several neighbors and family members arrived, and she was relegated to opening the door. Next to arrive was Mr. Dollbee and two men Deputy Blanshaft knew were detectives. She was relieved when one of them told her she could resume her patrol duties.

Neither Kiers nor Telmany wanted to stay at the Dollbee residence longer than necessary, so they asked both Mr. and Mrs. Dollbee if they could ask them a few more questions and then they would let them get back to their daughters and family. After about thirty minutes they completed their questioning, offered their condolences once again, and gave the usual, "The PBSO will do everything in its power to see that the individual(s) responsible will be caught." With that, they left. Both of these seasoned detectives felt truly sorry for the Dollbees.

"What kind of low-life scumbag could do such a thing?" Kiers mulled. Telmany, who was more cynical, just looked at Kiers and said, "Common Frank, you've been doing this shit how long?"

CHAPTER 10

It was close to 1:00 p.m. when Martinez arrived back to the district three homicide office and met with Kiers and Telmany. Lieutenant Cashin joined in and inquired about the direction of the investigation. Martinez brought him up to speed as to what she had so far. She then started the necessary notifications and written reports that would go into the case file. She had also called Crime Scene and was informed by Detective Chisholm that he and Whalen completed their work and submitted what they had to the lab. He added that the dive team did not find any jewelry or objects that might belong to the victim in or around the pond. He would email her his report as soon as it was completed. Next up: get out and interview Tricia Maddox and find out what they did last night.

She arrived at the Maddox home at a little past 2:00 p.m. It was still raining, and the doorbell was answered by a woman about Lydia's age who opened the door with a cigarette and a cup of coffee in her hand.

"Detective Martinez," Lydia said while showing the woman her ID.

"Which one of my kids is in trouble now?" asked the woman as if this was routine.

"Is your daughter Tricia here? She's not in trouble. I just want to ask her some questions."

"About what?"

"Is she here?"

"Yeah, I guess. Let me check her room. She came in late, so she's probably still in bed." She turned and walked away offering Lydia entry with her arm. She walked up the stairs and

35

Lydia could hear her say to her daughter, "Get up. There's a cop downstairs who wants to talk to you. What the fuck did you do now?"

Classy lady, Lydia thought to herself. Mrs. Maddox came back downstairs. Lydia noticed she was wearing those silly, pink, furry rabbit slippers.

"You from the youth squad? Tricia is only sixteen. What kind of trouble is she in now?" Lydia wanted to ask what kind of trouble she was in before but didn't.

"I'm with homicide. Do you know your daughter's friend Jasmin?" She purposely said *do* rather than *did*. Just then a tall, young, blonde girl came down the stairs.

"What about Jas, is she OK?"

"Why would she not be?" asked Martinez.

Looking at Mrs. Maddox she asked, "Is there some place we can talk?"

"Yeah, sure, this way. You want some coffee? I'm gonna get some."

"No thanks, I'm good."

"I'll have some," said Tricia. Mrs. Maddox just gave her a look and shuffled off into the kitchen.

"Tell me, is Jasmin ok?"

"Jasmin is dead, Tricia," she paused wanting to see if Tricia's response would tell her something.

"Oh my God, what? It can't be. I just saw her last night," she started to cry—sob, actually.

Mrs. Maddox came rushing back in. "What? Jasmin is dead? How can that be? Weren't you two together last night?" Tricia was crying, and it was Martinez, not her mom, who put a soothing hand on her back and gave her a gentle rub.

"Tricia, I need you to tell me everything you two did last night from the time she got here until whenever you saw her last. Do you understand?"

Now Mrs. Maddox sat down on the sofa and took over the soothing role from Martinez. Tricia stopped crying and looked at Martinez with red eyes.

"This is all my fault. I should have never let her go home by herself. I swear this is all on me," she cried.

Mrs. Maddox looked at Martinez but said nothing.

"Tricia, let's start at the beginning, OK?"

Tricia stopped crying enough to tell her story.

"Well, we went to this party and at first she didn't want to go. All she wanted to do was watch a movie, and I insisted that we go to the party. It's all my fault." She started to cry again.

"Where was the party, Tricia?" Lydia asked in her most motherly tone.

"It was at my friend Mark's house."

"What's Mark's last name, and where does he live?"

"Van Hooey, and he lives on 136 Terrace, here in The Farms." Jupiter Farms is a subdivision west of the turnpike of mostly two- to five-acre homes—horse country—not too far from where Jasmin was found.

"Go on, Tricia, did anything happen at the party? Who did you and Jasmin talk to? Were this Van Hooey boy's parents there?" Lydia assumed not but wanted to hear it from Tricia.

"No, his folks were away. That's why he had the party. Jas wanted to leave right away. She's not into that scene."

"What scene is that?" Martinez asked, but knew.

"You know, some kids were drinking beer, and some had some weed. The music was loud," she looked at her mom who started to say something but stopped when Martinez held her hand up toward her.

"Go on, Tricia, you're doing fine."

"Well, she told me she wanted to go because she wasn't comfortable, and she had to work at the golf tournament early the next morning. I guess that would be today," she paused and started to cry again. "If I left with her, she would be alive. It's all my fault."

"No, it's not." But then she thought why she hadn't asked what happened to her.

Just then, "What happened to her? Was she killed in a car accident? Did the Uber crash or did the driver do

37

something? Those guys can be scary, especially the foreign ones."

"Hold on, Tricia, lets back up. You're at the party and Jasmin said she wasn't comfortable. What next?"

"Well, I called her an Uber to take her home. The driver said it would be twenty minutes, so she wanted to wait outside."

"What time was that, and why did you call the Uber?"

"She doesn't have the app on her phone, I called for her. She said she would pay me later," she started to cry again. "It wasn't long after we got there, maybe seven forty-five or so."

"Please, Tricia, go on. I'll need you to get your cell phone and give me the exact times you called for the Uber and the driver's name, OK? But we can do that later. I want you to go on now." Martinez didn't want her to lose her train of thought.

"Well, I stayed at the party and was talking to some kids and I got a call from the Uber asking where I was. I just figured she called her mom for a ride because it started to thunder and lightning, and she was afraid of lightning. She always told me that if she was playing golf and heard thunder, she would leave the course because a lot of golfers don't, and they can get hit by lightning."

"So, you didn't see her again and figured she called home for a ride?" Tricia looked at her mom and then back at Lydia and started to cry again.

"Did you think to text her or call her to see if she made it home after the Uber driver called you?"

"No, I don't know," she cried. I guess I was mad at her because all she was talking about was that stupid golf and I wanted to have some fun. Weeping again she cried, "I'm so sorry." Now her sobbing was heavy, and her mother finally put her arms around her and looking at Martinez said, "Can you stop for a while? Can't you see how upset she is?"

"Sure, but I want to see her cell phone. I need the exact times she called the Uber and the times he called back. I also need the Van Hooey boy's address and phone numbers. And

38

I'll need you to take her down to my office at district three headquarters on Beeline. If you can go later today or tomorrow that would be fine." She handed Mrs. Maddox her card and said, "Call me first before you go. If I'm not there I'll tell you who to ask for. Now could I see Tricia's cell?" Tricia retrieved her phone from her room and handed it over to Martinez, who recorded the information she needed.

Martinez left the Maddox residence and drove to a Starbucks on PGA Boulevard. She needed a coffee and would have loved one when Mrs. Maddox offered but the house stunk of cigarettes and looked like it hadn't been cleaned since Don Shula coached the Dolphins. Lydia called Lieutenant Cashin to bring him up to speed and told him what she had learned from the Dollbee family and Maddox interview. She asked her boss if he would have Telmany run a check on the Maddox's and interview the Uber driver. He might be a suspect if his alibi isn't rock solid. She figured that the mother was probably divorced (she was correct) and from her opening remarks someone in the household was not unfamiliar to the PBSO (correct again). Both Mrs. Maddox and her ex, Ron, had previous run-ins with the law—Ron for DUI and the lovely Mrs. Maddox for assault and battery on Ron. Thank God, I'm single and have no kids. It made her think of Dio. She really cared for him and was sorry their plans for the upcoming weekend did not work out. She was sorrier for Jasmin Dollbee and her grieving family.

She sat in Starbucks enjoying her coffee. If she suspected the barista was Latino, she would order in Spanish. She did this everywhere and it never failed to get her better service and a smile. Oftentimes the server would talk to her in Spanish and ask what it was like to be a cop. Her response was always positive, and she encouraged these kids to consider a career in law enforcement. Some guys would have their badge and gun on their hip and leave their jackets off when they went to get takeout. She was sure some servers or cooks spat in their orders. OK, what's next? she thought. Maybe the Van Hooey

39

kid. Did someone from his party do this? It would not be the first time a drunk or stoned teenager tried to get some from an unwilling girl and went too far. Then she thought that the brutality of the crime indicated a level or rage that a rejected teen might be incapable of. The autopsy would be more telling. But the Van Hooey kid is the next logical interview.

She would need to get the names and numbers of every kid at that party and interview each one. She hated dealing with teens; they're such smug assholes. That task would be given to Kiers and Telmany. Again, she thought, thank God I don't have any kids and it's too late for me and Dio to start a family. Wait, did I just imagine Dio and me long-term? She laughed out loud, finished her coffee, returned to her car, and headed back toward Jupiter Farms to see this Van Hooey kid. She tried his number on the way.

CHAPTER 11

As she suspected the call to Van Hooey went to voicemail. Why would a seventeen-year-old be up before 3:00 p.m. on a rainy Saturday in late February? She pulled into the driveway of the address Tricia had given her. She knew this neighborhood to be a bit more upscale and wondered if the Jupiter PD had closed the party Friday night, or did it just die a natural death? She parked her Crown Vic behind a late-model Chevy Camaro and made a note of the plate. As she walked up the path to the house, the front door opened and a sleepy-eyed brunette about seventeen came out.

"Are you the Uber driver I called? I'm sorry I'm late."

"No, I'm not. Where is Mark?"

"You're not his mom, are you?"

"No, I'm not," she said taking out her ID. "Let's try this one more time. Where's Mark?" The blonde looked at Lydia's badge and now noticed her nine millimeter Glock on her hip and pointed inside the house.

"OK, why don't you wait for your ride by the curb. Anybody else in there?" The girl just shrugged.

"Don't call Mark, OK." She just nodded and grabbed her cell phone. Martinez entered the house and heard a cell phone chime come from up the stairs. She took the steps two at a time and followed the ring tone to one of several bedrooms. She got to Mark's room just as he was grabbing for his phone. Martinez grabbed it out of his hand and saw the call was from Sandy.

"Thanks, Sandy," and she pressed home, ending the call.

"Hey, what's going on, and who the fuck are you?"

Her first thought was to smack him across the head with her Glock, but she knew that would not go over well. She pulled her jacket to the side and showed him her badge and he backed off right away. "Whoa, whoa, sorry lady," he said noticing her badge on her hip. "It was just a party. I mean if somebody got busted driving or whatever, it's not my fault. She told me she was eighteen, and we didn't do anything. Did she call you?" His tone was very defensive.

"Get up and put some pants on." She tossed a pair of jeans from the floor toward him. Looking at her he tried to put his pants on without her seeing his junk. Van Hooey complied and asked if he could pee and wash his face. "Sure, but I'm gonna be right behind you, got it?" He nodded.

"If this is about the party, I shut it down when the cops came last night."

"Where are your parents? I don't suppose that they gave you their blessing to have this little shindig here last night?"

"They went to a wedding in the Bahamas. They won't be back until tomorrow night. Look, Officer, I don't want any trouble, I'll cooperate with you. Just tell me why you are here." He finished peeing, washed his face, and asked if he could brush his teeth. Martinez noticed he was a well-built, nice-looking boy.

"Yeah, go ahead. Tell me, do you know a girl named Jasmin?"

"You mean the girl that came with Tricia? Yeah, I know her. She's on the school golf team. Good too she is. I wish I was that good, but she was only here for a short time."

"How do you know that?"

"We go to the same school."

"No, I mean how do you know she did not stay here long?"

"Oh, right. I saw her leave, then I saw her outside and asked her what she was doing. She said she was waiting for an Uber, because she had to be up early for The Florida Classic.

You know, she's a volunteer or something. Why? Did she say I did something to her? Because if she did, she's lying."

"Why would you think she would say you did something? Did you?"

"No, I swear." Martinez looked hard at Van Hooey and knew he was probably not telling the truth. She pressed him a little harder. He seemed not to know Jasmin was dead, but still he was holding back, and she knew it.

"Jasmin was found dead early this morning." Just like with Tricia Maddox, she watched his reaction looking for a sign, but his expression and reaction led her to believe he was not involved in poor Jasmin's demise.

"That's crazy. What happened? If you think I would do something, you're crazy."

"Well, then, you tell me why I'm crazy and why I should believe you." He told her that he did see her outside and tried to get a good night kiss. But when she blew him off, he let it go.

"I don't need to force myself on girls, plus I knew Sandy was staying over. I like her. The only reason I tried to kiss Jasmin was because I was a bit buzzed. I swear, Officer, I would never hurt anyone."

"OK, Mark, what else did you see outside?"

"Nothing, I swear I was out there getting an empty garbage pail from the garage. I had already put one full pail out there earlier before I saw her."

"Think, did you see any other vehicles? She was waiting for an Uber. Did you see anyone or anything on the street?"

Mark thought for a moment, "Well when I brought the first full pail out, Mike and Jen were outside smoking."

"They were outside smoking what?"

"I don't know, but that was the one rule I had—no smoking cigarettes in the house. The smell of weed would be gone but cigarette smoke is disgusting, and my mom would smell it."

"OK, let's get back to this Mike and Jen. What are their last names?"

"His is Pearce. I'm not sure of hers, but I know she's in the Air Force and was home on leave."

"OK, anything else?"

"No. After the cops came around midnight, I started cleaning up the house and yard and then Sandy ordered a pizza and we watched some TV until about 4:00 a.m."

She could see Van Hooey was trying hard to remember something, something that he saw but could not remember. Martinez had seen this look before, when a witness was trying to remember something, they felt was important. She did not want to prompt him and get false or wrong information as a witness or suspect will do to appease their interrogators. No, she would just let him keep thinking.

"There is one other thing, Officer, but I'm not sure it's important."

"Go on, Mark."

"Well when I brought the first pail out and was talking to Mike and Jen, I saw a car drive slowly by."

"Why do you feel that's unusual?"

"Well, it drove by again as I was going back in and then I saw it a third time when I was talking to Jasmin."

"You're sure it was the same car? What kind of car was it? Maybe it was Jasmin's Uber. Was there anything else that made you feel it was unusual?"

"Well yes, there was another person sitting behind the driver, and at first I thought it was an Uber, you know a driver and a passenger sitting in the back. And when I saw it a second time, the guy was still in the back seat."

"So maybe it was an Uber, and the driver could not find the house."

"Yes, but wouldn't the passenger know?" She was surprised by his sound reasoning.

"Very good, Mark, very good. Maybe you should think of becoming a cop." Mark smiled, pleased with himself.

"There's one more thing, Officer," but she cut him off.

"Mark, its Detective, I'm a detective. Maybe it was a taxicab but go on please."

"No, the car was an SUV, and most cabs have a light on top. No, I thought it might be the Uber, but that guy in the back—it was weird."

"Can you describe the driver or the guy in the back?"

"Not really, only the guy in the back had very blond hair, looked to be in his early thirties."

"How could you tell? It was dark and stormy."

"That's just it, when the lightning and thunder started, it lit up the back of the SUV and I could see the guy in the back as if a light went on."

"Do you think if you saw him again you could identify him?"

He thought for a second, "No I don't think so. All I remember is that he had very blond hair. Like I said, I had a few beers and maybe a little weed. You're not gonna tell my parents, are you? My dad will kill me."

"No, I'm not going to tell your folks."

"I'm sorry, Detective, I went back inside, and didn't much pay attention to anything else. That poor girl, what happened to her? Was she in an accident?"

Martinez did not want to go into details with him at this point. She figured he'd be calling Trisha Maddox as soon as she left.

"OK, Mark, you have been very helpful. I will need the names and numbers of all the kids that were here last night starting with Mike and Jen. Then I suggest you get this place cleaned up. Here is my card. I need you to come to district three homicide on Beeline and make a statement to myself or another detective. You can bring the names of all the kids at the party when you come in. And Mark, thank you. You have been very helpful."

Mark smiled, and Martinez thought that first impressions can be wrong sometimes. This was one of those times. She was not back in her car ten minutes when Van

45

Hooey called her and told her Mike Pearce just called him. And when he told him what happened, he said he and Jen were having brunch at Bearberry's at the Legacy Plaza Mall and would be happy to talk to her. Martinez asked Mark how much he told them, and Mark replied, "Only what they needed to know," and hung up. Yep, she liked this kid.

Mike and Jen were a bit older than the other kids at the party. They could not add much to what Lydia had learned from Mark, but they were outside not to smoke but to get away from the noise being made by the *young kids* inside. The only reason they were there was because Jen's kid sister was there, and they wanted to keep an eye on her. Yes, they saw a light-colored SUV pass by twice. Mike was a car guy and thought it was a late-model AMC Ranger, but no, they did not see another person in the car. Nor did they see anyone else outside. Making small talk, Lydia told Jen she was an army veteran and spent twenty years in the reserve. Jen replied that she was thinking of making a career of the Air Force and was currently stationed in San Antonio, Texas, studying to be a dentist. Once she received her doctor's license, she would be commissioned an officer and committed for another four years. Nice kids thought Martinez. She thanked them and gave them her card with the usual "If you can think of anything else, etc."

As she got up, the Pearce kid said, "Oh, shoot, wait a minute. There is something else."

"What's that, Mike?"

"The SUV had a marking on the side like a commercial vehicle, only this looked like it was stuck on and was slipping because of the rain."

"Do you remember what it said?"

"Yes, I do," he paused for effect, "it said Florida Classic Courtesy Car and had the logo from the tournament. I remember thinking, why would a courtesy car be out here in The Farms?"

Martinez shook her head, not knowing how critical this piece of information would be to her investigation. She thanked them both and got up and left. More nice kids, she thought.

CHAPTER 12

The rain that had started late Friday night continued as Martinez drove toward Legacy Place, a newer commercial and residential development off of PGA Boulevard, just east of Alternate A1A, when her cell phone rang. It was Doc Widman who told her that plans to do the autopsy would be pushed back. The ME said the other pathologist working at the ME's office was called away to Boston on a family emergency, and she had to do an autopsy on two victims of a fatal auto crash on I-95. And as long as her victim had been IDed, it could wait until Monday afternoon. She also told Martinez that she hoped to get it done between 3:00 and 5:00 p.m., as she had plans for dinner with some friends and did not want to cancel.

Unlike her, Doc Widman had a life. The morgue was operational 24/7 and, much like the Homicide Squad, cases were assigned in a rotating order. Each of the six pathologists working at the ME's office conducted on average fifteen to twenty autopsies per week. Violent, sudden, suspicious deaths or deaths where no doctor is in attendance are investigated by the ME's office.

Martinez decided that she would go into the office and catch up on her paperwork and make some calls from there. She could see what, if anything, Fat Eddy got from the Uber driver. She called the office from the Crown Vic and Detective Manganillo (everyone called him Mango and unlike Telmany he did not mind his nickname) told her it was quiet in the office. Telmany and Kiers were working her case, and he and his partner, Jack O'Sullivan, were going to grab dinner at Duffy's and watch college hoops. Martinez knew both guys were

48

big St. John's basketball fans. Lou Carnesecca, the former coach, was Mango's cousin. She told them she was expecting some witnesses to come in to make statements and to let the others know. Mango mentioned that Lieutenant Cashin was getting calls from the press about the body in The Preserve. Martinez knew Cashin would refer all calls from the media outlets to the Public Information Office.

"Any progress on your case?"

"Some, enjoy the game."

Martinez hung up and decided to head over to PGA. She wanted to follow the lead about the courtesy car Van Hooey and Pearce reported seeing last night. She thought Dio knew the head of security at PGA, but she could not recall his name—something else that made her think it may be time to retire. I never forget a contact name, she thought to herself. She called Dio and got him on the second ring.

"Hey, D, whatcha doing?"

"Hi, Lydia, I was just thinking about you."

"Good, I hope."

"Yeah, I just left church. They have a Saturday evening mass at this little church outside London. It's really strange hearing mass in English."

"You're in England, Dio, what did you expect?" She knew what he meant but loved to bust his balls.

"No, I mean the accent. I almost expect the priest to say that Jesus had a jolly good time changing water into wine, by Jove!"

"Yes, I can imagine. Hey, quick question. What's the name of your friend who runs security at PGA?"

"You mean Arnie Dansky? You think he's still there? He's gotta be close to eighty," he said with a chuckle.

Lydia wanted to say, like you're a spring chicken, but she knew how sensitive he was about their age difference, so she thought she would save the zinger for another time and she was nearing PGA Blvd.

She gave him a brief rundown of her case and told him she would have to cancel her plans to visit him next weekend. Dio was disappointed, but as a cop he understood how *the job* comes first.

"Does your case have something to do with PGA?"

"Just following a lead. Can't go into it right now. Could you send me his number? And when I get back to the office, I'll call you and fill you in on everything I got so far. OK?"

"Sure, I'll send it to you right away." He paused, "Er, Lyd, how do I do it?"

She wanted to say, pretty good, especially when you're lying on your back with me on top, but just smiled to herself admiring her quick wit. "Go to your contacts, pull up Arnie Dansky, and scroll down to share contact. It will prompt you to send it via email or message. Choose message and when the next screen comes up, enter my name and press send."

"OK. I'll pull over and send it now."

Lydia waited about ten minutes for her cell to ping indicating a message. There it was, Arnie Dansky's number. She figured Dio found some ten-year-old to help him, smiling to herself. She called the number and was surprised that Arnie answered on the first ring. Lydia identified herself and Arnie knew right away who she was.

"You're the detective who worked with Bosso on that double homicide in The Gardens last year, right?"

"Yeah, that's me."

"You're not calling me to tell me he's dead, are you?"

"No, he's fine. Listen, I need your help on a case I'm working. Are you at work today?"

"You're kidding. I'm here 24/7 during The Classic. We got rained out today, and we're trying to get this place in shape for tomorrow. How can I help you, Lydia?"

"I'm working a case, a homicide, and I need some information about your courtesy cars. Who has them? Where do they get them etc.?"

"Courtesy cars? Well they're all the same—late-model, gray AMC Rangers. We got some extras if you need a car."

"No Arnie, but thanks. Look, I'm close by. Can we meet and you can tell me all about the process?"

"Look, I'm pretty busy. But since you're a friend of Bosso's, I'll see what I can do. Where are you now?"

"I'm at PGA in front of the main clubhouse."

"Why didn't you say so?"

I just did, she thought, but she didn't want to crack wise.

"I'll come out. Stay in your car, and we can talk there. OK?"

"Sure, Arnie, that would be great."

PGA National was a large resort complex consisting of a hotel, five golf courses, and several hundred homes, condos, and cottages. There were various membership levels that owners could purchase. Several courses were open for public use. Because of The Classic, Martinez had to use her police ID to get access from PGA Blvd. About two minutes later, she saw Arnie pull up in a covered golf cart. The rain was a light drizzle as Arnie pulled up. She saw he was carrying two containers of coffee, so she reached over and opened the door for him.

"Hi, Lydia, nice to see you. Here, I brought you a coffee. It's regular. I hope that's OK."

Lydia learned from Dio and the other NYPD cops she met that regular coffee meant milk and sugar. Lydia took the coffee and Arnie asked how he could help. "Tell me about the courtesy cars. Who gets them? How many? What type? Everything about them."

"Well to start with, each golfer gets a general information booklet once they commit to playing the event and register upon arrival. In the booklet the golfer is given the instructions how to acquire a courtesy car and driver from the sponsor, AMC. This year they have the new Ranger SUV models with all the bells and whistles. A lot of the players live here in Palm Beach County, or close enough so they can drive to and from the course each day. Others stay with family or friends. So, on average maybe fifty to sixty golfers request cars."

"Jeez, Arnie, I'm not into golf, so excuse my naivete, but how many guys play in these things?"

"Well this year we have 152 golfers starting the tournament. After the second day, the field is cut to the top seventy players plus ties. I'm not sure of the exact number of golfers who made the cut, but I could find out."

"No, it's not important yet."

He went on. "Today's round three has been canceled because of the rain. Tomorrow they will try to get as many players out to finish by playing both front and back nines and making threesomes instead of twosomes." Arnie looked out the window up at the sky and saw the sun peeking through the clouds.

"The weather is supposed to improve, so we should get the third round in tomorrow for most of the golfers who made the cut, but it will definitely be a Monday finish. The information booklet also lists several hotels in the vicinity that offer discounts to the golfers, and the sponsor gives them lots of other shit like shirts, shoe bags, balls. Like these guys really need discounts. Are you shitting me? In order to keep your playing privileges, you have to earn at least a half-a-mil the previous year." Martinez just shrugged her shoulders. "Sorry, Lydia, I'm digressing here."

"It's OK, Arnie, I appreciate your help. How could I get a list of all the golfers who have courtesy cars?"

"Whoa, that's a tall order, Lydia. I'm not sure I can do that—way above my pay grade, if you know what I mean. Maybe if you tell me why you need that info, I can reach out and see what I can do."

"I also may need the hotel locations where the golfers who have courtesy cars are staying and maybe even need to be able to talk to them."

"Hold on, Lydia, that last request is definitely out of the question. These guys are prima donnas. Most of them are good people, but they're in the middle of their jobs, if you will."

Lydia spent the next ten minutes telling Arnie about the Dollbee homicide, including the fact the victim was a volunteer.

"Have you guys notified The Classic about this?"

"No, I think the family probably will make that call. You're the first person I spoke to on this, Arnie."

When she mentioned the press was starting to inquire about the body found earlier today, Arnie seemed concerned. Sure, he wanted to help, but he also knew that he had to protect The Classic from any bad publicity that might fall under his purview.

Arnie, like Dio, was a retired NYPD deputy inspector who moved to Florida after retirement. Unlike Dio, he did not go back to work right away. The job he had now came almost by accident. He was volunteering at The Florida Classic when it was at Marisol, another gated golf community. When it moved to PGA to accommodate its growth, George Goll asked Arnie to take over as the current security director was retiring. Arnie was businesslike, efficient, and a professional law enforcement/security manager. He was also an avid golfer and enjoyed the perks of free golf that came with the job.

"Listen, Lydia, I want to help you as much as I can, but there is only so much I can do. Your boss, Romain, is pretty tight with Mr. Goll, who runs the tournament. As a matter of fact, I saw him here yesterday in the VIP tent chatting with Mr. Goll. Maybe he can pull some strings and get you the information that you need."

Lydia was disappointed. The last thing she wanted to do was to have to kiss up to the higher-ups in the department to do her job. She also knew that she should not reach out to Romain without going through the proper chain of command, which would start with Lieutenant Cashin, then district commander, and so on up the ladder.

After Arnie got out of the Crown Vic, Lydia thought for a minute. "Fuck it," she said out loud and dialed a number she had on her cell phone. Lydia knew Major Colleen Adams who was the commanding officer of Sheriff Romain's staff. She and Adams met a few years back when they both attended the women-in-policing conferences. Lydia was one of several female officers from around the country who started the group. Adams was now the President. Lydia knew Adams worked Monday through Friday and was nervous about calling her cell on her day off.

"Hello," came a voice Lydia recognized as Adams.

"Major Adams, it's Lydia Martinez. Sorry to bother you on your day off, but I need a favor."

"Lydia, how are you, and why so formal?"

"Well, yeah OK, Colleen. Listen, I caught a homicide earlier today. A young female, you'll probably be getting calls from Public Information about it soon."

"Go on."

"Well, the victim, a sixteen-year-old girl named Jasmin Dollbee, was a volunteer at The Florida Classic golf tournament. And one of the leads I have, actually the only lead I have, has to do with The Classic. I need access to some information. I know your boss is friends with the powers that be at PGA, so I need you to reach out."

"The Classic, I was supposed to go there today, but it got rained out. I could go tomorrow, but Greg and I made plans to visit friends in Stuart. So, what do you need?"

Lydia explained to Adams everything she had so far, including the scrip of the guy in the back of the Ranger as reported by the Van Hooey kid.

"Well it's getting kinda of late, Lydia. I mean even if they were playing, they would soon be finished for the day. Sheriff Romain is attending a dinner and concert tonight. Let me see what I can do. I'll get back to you."

Lydia looked at her watch and noticed it was close to 6:00 p.m. Shit, where did the day go? I've got so much to do and it's too late to call Dio again, she thought to herself. He'll understand, he always understands. That's what I like about him. He never questions my work, only wants to help. As she thought this, she smiled to herself and for the first time she truly missed Dio. She knew she would have to tell Lieutenant Cashin about going over his head in reaching out to Adams, but sometimes you gotta do what you gotta do.

Lydia went back to the district homicide office and found several messages waiting for her as well as the calls from the Van Hooey kid and Tricia Maddox. Franks and Beans were there discussing The Florida Classic and who might be in a position to win. Would they be able to get two rounds in on Sunday etc.? Lydia liked both these guys and wished they worked her team. Mango and O'Sullivan were decent detectives as were Kiers and Telmany, but these two were probably the best homicide detectives in the county if not the state. Yep, she thought Jerry Nathans and Lee Bush were the best of the best.

The desk phone rang and broke her thoughts and startled her.

"Homicide, Martinez."

"Yeah, Detective, this is Sergeant Esposito on the desk downstairs. I got a kid named Van Hooey who showed me your card. Said you wanted to see him."

"Sure, Sarge, send him up. Thanks."

Mark Van Hooey walked into the squad room and gaped around like a kid in a candy store on Halloween.

"Over here, Mark," Martinez stood up and waved him over. He was dressed in chinos, a blue shirt, and tie. Oh shit, Martinez thought, not another one.

"Hello, Detective, I came like you told me too."

"Yes, thank you, Mark. Follow me." She took him to an interview room and told him to write down everything he told her Saturday morning, including the names and cell numbers of all the kids who were at the party. "You'll find a pad and pencils in that drawer. When you finish, sign and date the statement and initial each page."

As she started to leave the room he said, "Aren't you going to interview me again?" His voice sounded dejected.

"No, Mark, just write down in your own words what you told me and then you can go."

Not wanting to hurt his feelings, she said, "You look nice tonight, are you going somewhere special?" She gestured to the shirt and tie. He just put his head down and started to write. When she got back to her cubicle, her phone was ringing again. It was Sergeant Esposito.

"What, are you having a party up there? I got a young female named Maddox here to see you."

"Send her up." She placed Tricia Maddox in another cubicle and told her the same thing she told Van Hooey. "Write down everything you did since Jasmin arrived at your house. There is a pad and a pen in the drawer. You want a soda or something?"

"Yea, a Diet Coke." No please, no may I. Snot-nosed entitled teenager, Martinez thought. She went down to the vending machine on the main floor and bought two Diet Cokes. When she entered the room where Van Hooey was and gave him the Diet Coke, you thought he was given the keys to the city. Martinez could tell this kid had a teenage crush on her. She didn't bother to tell him Tricia Maddox was next door.

Lydia spent the next two hours writing up reports of the day's events. She knew that the paperwork part of the job was most important, not only on keeping your investigation going in the right direction but also in court if and when the perpetrators were arrested and prosecuted. Unlike the rest of the detectives in the squad, she was comfortable using a computer to complete her reports. The others had a hard time adjusting but once they got the hang of it, they all agreed it was a time saver.

After finishing her reports, she decided to call Dio. She knew he might be in bed, but she didn't care. She needed to talk. In a sleepy voice he answered.

56

"Dio Bosso, here."

"Don't you see my name on your home screen when I call? Do you have to be so goddamn formal?"

She was sorry for snapping at him that way.

"Home screen? No, I just answer the phone the way I always do, and I was sleeping." You havin' a bad day, Lyd?"

"No...yes. I am, and I'm sorry for snapping at you, D. I went over my boss's head on this case and I think it's gonna be a problem for me in the future."

"Well did it get you what you need?"

"Yes, it did. Or at least I hope it did."

"Then the hell with it. Once you solve the case, you'll be back in everyone's good graces. "How are you otherwise? Feeling OK?"

Lydia thought how sweet he was and replied, "Yeah, I'm good. It's just that (she hesitated a few seconds) I miss being with you. I miss your arms around me and making love to me the way we did last time we were together."

Dio was pleasantly surprised by this sudden show of affection. For a few seconds he didn't know how to respond. "Lydia, I told you several times how I feel about you. It makes me feel so good to think that you might feel the same way about me." Yes, he was fishing for an *I love you Dio*, but Lydia remained silent and changed the subject. They talked about the Dollbee homicide for the next hour or so.

"By the way, your friend Arnie was helpful, although I was hoping he could do more."

"Arnie, that old fucker, he's doing good?"

"Yep, got a nice gig, seems happy."

"Not as nice as mine. You know why?" He answered before she could say anything, "Because I got you."

"You're a sweet man, Dio Bosso."

"You're something else, Martinez."

This was becoming their usual sign off. Just as Lydia ended the call, the Van Hooey kid exited the interview room with the yellow pad in his hand.

"Detective, I'm finished. Do you want to check my statement?"

"No, Mark, leave it on my desk. I'm just on my way out."

"Where are you going?"

She shot him a look and could see the disappointment on his face. "Tricia Maddox is in that room there," she said pointing toward the other interview room. "Why don't you go see how she is doing, but don't compare statements. This isn't a history test."

"Oh, Ok, I hope I've been helpful."

"You have, Mark, you have. Thanks again." She left the office and headed down the stairs to her Crown Vic. It was past midnight before Lydia showered and went to bed. It was hard for her to fall asleep thinking about Jasmin Dollbee and the brutal way she was murdered. She was thinking about Dio and what their future together, if any, would be. Finally, she fell asleep.

CHAPTER 13

By early afternoon on Saturday, Tournament Director Goll, Head Golf Professional Fred Harkness, and Course Superintendent Don Taylor had decided the Champions Course was unplayable as the heavy rains continued. Play was suspended for the remainder of the day. They would play round three on Sunday, adjust tee times, and have threesomes rather than twosomes. It would be difficult to play thirty-six holes on Sunday, and a Monday final round was a probability more than a possibility. Monday finishes were the bane of professional golfers, as it would throw their schedules off. However, in this case it wasn't as bad as the next event on the tour would be in Miami at Trump Doral's Blue Monster.

Doral was only a two-and-a-half-hour drive from PGA National. Many of the pros lived in Palm Beach County, and half of the seventy-two players who made the cut found themselves hanging out in the homes of the local pros. Most others were staying at homes of relatives or friends of their sponsors. Only a handful were staying in hotels in the area.

Tournament officials were surprised to learn that Karl Messerschmitt withdrew from the tournament, citing pressing business issues in Germany. He had been scheduled to play Doral and the following week in Arnold Palmer's tournament in Bay Hill. He was leaving possibly six figures on the table at The Florida Classic. Plus, if he skipped Doral and Bay Hill, he might not get invited back next year. In addition, a victory or top-ten finish might earn him an automatic invite to The Masters, the most prestigious golf event in America. Goll and

PGA President Sean McCooey thought that to be a bit strange but had more pressing issues to deal with—the continuing rain.

CHAPTER 14

At 6:30 a.m. on Sunday morning, Lydia's cell phone rang. She picked it up without looking at the screen and assumed it was Dio. "Hi, handsome."

"Lydia, its Colleen. Thanks for the compliment but get a pen a paper."

"Oh, sorry Colleen, I thought it..."

Adams bluntly cut her off. "I spoke to the sheriff, and he in turn made some calls. He's not happy about the way you went about this, but I explained the situation the best I could." Before Lydia could say anything, Adams went on. "Be at PGA at 9:00 a.m. There is going to be a meeting in the main tournament HQ. Call your friend Dansky, and he will escort you to and from. There will be plenty of heavy weights there, so be prepared to state your case."

Lydia wanted to ask how Colleen knew about Dansky but figured she better not, as she could tell Colleen seemed put off. "OK, Colleen, thanks again."

"You can thank me when you see me. Romain wants me there also. Had to cancel my day off with Greg."

"Oh shit, Colleen, I'm sorry it's just..."

Colleen cut her off again, "OK, just be on time," and hung up.

When Martinez pulled into PGA National and showed her ID to the security officer on duty, she was told to pull to the side and wait.

"Chief Dansky is on his way here," the officer told her.

Chief, she thought, wait 'til I tell Dio. Just then Arnie pulled up in his golf cart and signaled Lydia to get in. He seemed at bit colder than yesterday and had no coffee to offer her. "You sure caused a lot of shit around here, Lydia. Mr. Goll does not like anything spoiling the ambiance of the tournament. Bad enough we got this shit weather. Now we got to deal with this idea of yours that somehow we're involved in your homicide."

"Gee, Arnie, I'm sure the victim's parents feel awful about their daughter's rape and murder interfering with your precious golf tournament. I'll be sure to tell them how upset your boss is," she said sarcastically.

Dansky just shot her a look and didn't say anything. She figured he got his ass reamed out. Just like everywhere else, shit flows downhill. Before they got to the main clubhouse, Arnie pulled the golf cart over, stopped, and gave Lydia a long look. "Listen, I have some info that might be helpful, but you didn't hear it from me, OK."

"Sure, Arnie, no problem."

"I know we talked about the courtesy cars. Friday night, one of the cars stopped at the main gate on Avenue of the Champions. The driver asked my security officer on duty for directions."

"What's so unusual about that, Arnie?"

"Well the security officer told the driver that the car had a GPS, but the driver said he didn't know how to use it, so he wrote out the directions to where he wanted to go. My security guy, whose name is Stan Kriegsman, noticed that there was a guy sitting in the back. Stan, upon noticing the rubber stick-on courtesy car plaque, asked the driver if he was a pro golfer. The driver said, 'No,' he is pointing over his shoulder, 'I'm just a lowly caddy.' He snickered but the guy in the back just lowered himself in his seat and muttered something in German to the driver, who just laughed and drove off."

"Did your security officer see the address?"

"He did, somewhere on Misty Lakes Blvd., but he didn't recall the house number."

Interesting Lydia thought. The Dollbees live on Misty Lakes Blvd. "So why did Stan think this was unusual?"

"According to Stan, the guy in the back looked scared and did not want to make eye contact with him. Stan said the guy looked like one of those guys who plays Nazi soldiers in the old WWII movies."

"Why would he say that?"

"We're Jews. Anybody who has blond hair and speaks German looks like a Nazi to us," Arnie said half-jokingly. "Well here's the kicker. After Stan told me this story, I checked to see if we had any German pros playing. And sure enough we had three—Martin Kaymer, Alex Cjeka, and Karl Messerschmitt. Only Kaymer and Messerschmitt made the cut, but Messerschmitt withdrew rather unexpectedly. I also went online to the PGA website and pulled up a picture of Messerschmitt, and Stan IDed him as the guy who was in the back of the courtesy car Friday night. Sounds a bit *fugazy* to me, don't ya think?" Fugazy, another NYPD word Lydia learned from Dio, meaning suspicious or unusual. Here in Florida, cops used the word *hinky*.

CHAPTER 15

Dansky escorted her to the main conference room, and she was surprised to see about ten people sitting around a large conference table. She recognized Sheriff Romain, Lieutenant Cashin, and Colleen Adams, all in uniform; the others she did not. Romain got up and extended his hand to Martinez. They had met on several occasions and he commented once again on the *Green Violinist* caper. He introduced her to the others in the room.

"This is George Goll, the Executive Director of The Florida Classic, and to his right is Mr. Sean McCooey, the President of the PGA of America. Next to Mr. McCooey is Ms. Ann Quick, the Volunteer Coordinator, and next to her is Mrs. Carol Blanshaft, Player Hospitality Coordinator." Lydia recognized that name but could not place it. "Also, to Mrs. Blanshaft's right is Mr. Eric Strumza, Executive VP of AMC Motors Corporation. Then you have Mrs. Kira El-Boury, head of our media relations team. Chief Dansky you know. The others are part of our staff." As almost an afterthought he added, "Of course you know Lt. Cashin, your commanding officer, who you should have notified before contacting Major Adams." Cashin just glared at Martinez with looks that could kill.

After Romain finished the intros, Goll took over. "Now Detective Martinez, tell us about the murder of our volunteer and what we can do to help you."

"Her name was Jasmin Dollbee, Mr. Goll."

"Yes, of course Detective, please go on."

Lydia was surprised at his conciliatory tone and began her narrative on what she had so far and what brought her to the conclusion that someone in a Florida Classic courtesy car was involved or at least a witness to the murder of Jasmin Dollbee. She left out the names of her witnesses or where she got the intel on the courtesy car and the info she got from Dansky.

"Jasmin was such a lovely and talented young lady," Ms. Quick said, "I can't believe she was so brutally murdered."

Mrs. Blanshaft added, "Detective Martinez, I believe you met my daughter, Deputy Kim Blanshaft, who assisted you on notifying the parents yesterday."

Martinez just nodded and, looking directly at Goll and McCooey, continued, "What can you tell me about a golfer named Karl Messerschmitt?" The room fell silent and both Goll and McCooey looked at one another.

It was McCooey who answered. "Why are you asking about Mr. Messerschmitt, Detective?"

"Well as I understand he suddenly withdrew from the tournament and returned to his home in Germany. As I stated before, I have witnesses and information that place one of your courtesy cars at the location where Miss Dollbee was last seen. I have information that Messerschmitt and his caddy were also in the same area around the same time."

Now it was Mr. Strumza's turn. "AMC Motors has a small sponsorship with Mr. Messerschmitt through our European partner Fiat. It was through that relationship that he got an invite to play in The Florida Classic."

McCooey continued, "I can't tell you much other than this is his first year playing on our tour. He has had a few victories on the European and Asia tours, but this is his first time playing in the States. He committed to at least three events and, depending on how he played, he could have qualified for The Masters." McCooey said this as if it were the most important thing in the world.

65

The mention of this seemed to have some significance to those in the room, but it was lost on Martinez. "So, what happened, he just kind of called in sick? How does that work with golfers?"

Again, McCooey answered, "Something like that. Each golfer playing in The Classic is given a welcome kit when they commit to play. Included in the kit are the local rules for the course, contact information, courtesy car requests, hotels, and other important information concerning the tournament. He or his caddy called the number on that sheet. All he said was he had pressing business back home in Germany."

"Did he say if he would be back for the other tournaments?"

"No, just what I told you."

"Who did he speak to? I'd like to speak to that person."

Ann Quick answered. "I believe it was one of my volunteers. I could find out who and make them available." Martinez just nodded a thank you.

McCooey handed Martinez a manila folder. "Here is a picture of Messerschmitt and his caddie, who I believe is named Dieter Spunkmeyer. They were staying at the Marriott in Palm Beach Gardens."

Now it was Cashin who spoke directly to Martinez. "I had Detective Manganillo contact the limo service the tournament listed in the handout Mr. McCooey mentioned. He interviewed the driver who told him that he drove two men fitting the description of Messerschmitt and Spunkmeyer to Palm Beach International, where they boarded a private jet that was waiting for them. He knew they were professional golfers as they were carrying golf travel bags. He knows a lot of golfers have their own planes. Although the driver did not recognize them, he told Mango that they spoke German and seemed to be arguing about something."

Martinez was looking at the photos and bios that McCooey handed her, while she was listening to Lieutenant Cashin giving his report. A brief silence came over the room, which Martinez broke. "Don't even private planes have to file a flight plan at the airport?"

It was Sheriff Romain who spoke next. "Lieutenant Cashin, could you have one of your detectives head over to Palm Beach International and check out where our two suspects were headed. I know Messerschmitt claimed to have *pressing business* back in Germany, but they could go anywhere correct?"

Cashin nodded.

Goll continued, "I think it would be best for all parties concerned if we kept this quiet about the possibility of one of our PGA members being involved." Looking at Martinez, he continued, "You can conduct your investigation, but I don't want any connection to The Florida Classic associated with this."

Martinez thought that Sheriff Romain would respond with something like, look George, you run your tournament, I'll run my police department, but instead he just nodded. In that moment, Martinez lost all respect for her boss.

"Is there anything else, Detective, that you might need from us?" asked Goll.

"Yes, Mr. Goll, there is. What I need from you folks are two things—a list of the names of all the players who requested courtesy cars and a list of where the players stayed. I know that might seem as an invasion of their privacy, and I can appreciate your concerns, but I will assure you that their privacy will not be intruded upon. Isn't that right, Lieutenant?" She looked at Cashin, who was still staring at her with venom in his eyes.

"OK," Goll continued, "Mrs. El-Boury and Mrs. Blanshaft will give the information you need and once again, Detective, I urge you to use the utmost discretion. Rick," he turned to Romain, "I want you to keep me personally informed on what your detective here learns, if anything, that may involve The Florida Classic."

Romain just nodded. He did not appreciate Goll dictating to him, especially in front of members of his department.

"Now ladies and gentlemen, let's get a move on. We got a tournament to finish here, and Mother Nature is not cooperating." He stood signaling the end of the meeting. As the room emptied out Romain told Martinez to wait, as he wanted to talk to her. El-Boury and Blanshaft could see that Martinez was going to get an ass-chewing, and Blanshaft said they would meet her in their office down the hall. As they walked out, they could see how upset Romain was.

"You ever pull a stunt like this again I'll have you back on road patrol so fast your head will spin." He wanted to say more, but he knew he could only go so far with a female officer. Any vulgarity, threats of sticking one's foot up one's ass, would not go over as well if Martinez were a male.

Cashin was next to give her some shit as he walked by. "You better make sure this don't backfire, or I'll be sure to see the sheriff's promise is carried out."

Next came Adams, and Lydia thought, OK here comes another punch in the gut.

Adams leaned over, put her hand on Lydia's shoulder, and whispered in Lydia's ear, "Good going, Lydia. Greg is going to meet me here, and we will watch the rest of the tourney drinking champagne and eating shrimp cocktail and avocado toast."

Lydia left the conference room, unshaken by the comments of Lieutenant Cashin and Sheriff Romain. She knew she had to do what she did to shake things up for the sake of Jasmin Dollbee and her grieving family.

As she entered the office shared by El-Boury and Blanshaft, both women stood up and offered their hands. "I'm Kira," said the attractive curly haired brunette. Lydia figured her for about early forties.

Carol Blanshaft, on the other hand, was older but also an attractive woman. "We both liked the way you handled yourself in there," said Blanshaft. "Sometimes Mr. Goll thinks that this tournament is the most important thing in the world. He does work very hard on it, and it does generate a lot of revenue for the community. But from what my daughter told me about this poor family, I just feel terrible and I want to help." Blanshaft continued, "Here is a list of all the golfers who requested courtesy cars. The list has the golfer's name, his driver's license information or his caddy's driver's information, and the plate number of the car he was assigned. I also checked the ones who did not make the cut, so those cars will either be picked up today and stored in the maintenance shed at the Palmer course or left at the hotel where the players stayed. Here is a list of hotels and the players who stayed at each. I also cross-referenced those who did not make the cut so it might be easier for you. You mentioned in the meeting that you have a witness who placed a courtesy car near the scene, correct?"

Lydia just nodded.

Kira spoke next, "I have gotten several calls from the local TV and radio stations requesting information on the possibility that the body of a young girl found out at Cypress Creek was connected to The Classic. I told them that I was in the dark as much as they were but would keep them appraised of any developments. But Mr. Goll wants this to stay out of the press until the tournament is over, which will most likely be tomorrow."

"I'm fine with that, Kira," replied Martinez, "I don't think the victim's family wants any publicity. The body is still at the morgue, and the ME will not be doing the autopsy until tomorrow."

"Well, Detective, Kira and I are both here to help you. So please let us know if you need anything else."

"Yes, I will, thank you both. You have been most helpful."

"If you give me your cell, I will call you as cars are returned and keep you up to speed on that," said Blanshaft. "As you can see by my list, only thirty of the seventy or so players who made the cut are staying in hotels, and the majority of them are at the Marriott in Palm Beach Gardens. Of those thirty one, twenty five have courtesy cars."

"I have a question. How are the cars identified as courtesy cars?" asked Martinez.

Once again Ann Blanshaft replied, "Each courtesy car is identified by a magnetized rubber plate that is attached to each door of the car identifying it as such. They are about two feet square and include our logo. I have one here I can show you."

"Yes, that would be helpful. Thank you both. I better get going as I have a lot of work to do, as I'm sure you ladies do too." As she left their office, Lydia wondered what kind of help she might get from a pissed off Lieutenant Cashin. She felt probably none, unless some pressure was put on him from Romain. But the chances of that were slim.

Arnie was waiting for her in his golf cart. "Come on, Lydia. I'll give you a lift back to your ride."

"Thanks, Arnie. Once again you have been very helpful. When Dio comes here next, you and your wife can join us for dinner on me."

Arnie had plenty of dough, but like most old timers would not pass up a free meal. "It's a deal. Let me know if you need anything else."

CHAPTER 16

Lydia spent the rest of Sunday going over her notes, writing reports, and reviewing the statements submitted by Trisha Maddox and the Van Hooey kid. It was quiet in the squad room and she was enjoying the solitude when the door burst open and Detectives Manganillo and O'Sullivan came rushing in.

"Hey, Lydia. We got Chinese. We're gonna watch the golf. Wanna join us? Plenty of food."

"No thanks, Mango, I'm just on my way out."

"Cashin had us check out the flight manifest for the private jet involved in your case. I sent you and email with my report. The plane is a converted DC-3 and is registered to the German conglomerate Krupp AG. The flight director at Signature Air told us the plane was headed to Frankfurt International Airport."

"Thanks, Mango."

He nodded and walked back toward the lunchroom. Don't those guys ever do anything but eat and watch sports? she thought to herself. Smiling, I guess they get it done or Cashin would be up their asses.

It was close to 9:00 p.m. by the time Martinez got back to her condo. She poured herself a glass of red wine, sat down at her desk, and started to write down everything she had so far on the Dollbee homicide. Some of the info she got from Kiers and some from Doc Widman's initial observations.

Martinez was exhausted now and wanted to get some sleep and changed into her usual bedclothes—a T-shirt, no bra, and a pair of cotton gym pants. She mused to herself that when she was with Dio, they both slept naked. "Oh shit," she said aloud, I forgot to call him. Well it's too late now. I'll call him first thing in the morning. She then decided to have another glass of wine and went over the written notes she had gotten from Frank Kiers. Unlike most of the other guys in the squad, Martinez did not golf or fish, which is why Ken Dollbee's comment about The Classic was originally lost on her. Thinking back to Dio for a moment she remembered his comments about golf. He tried it a few times, never got the hang of it, and never had the interest or time to pursue it. As for fishing he would say, "I joined the Air Force and went to and from Vietnam on a troop ship. I was seasick the whole time." On these topics they agreed.

She thought about her victim and pulled out the picture Mrs. Dollbee had given her. The color photo was obviously taken by a professional photographer, probably for a school yearbook. Martinez saw a very attractive blonde, blue-eyed girl, like so many others in Palm Beach County. She thought about her own high school graduation picture, which she hated. She had (and still has) thick, curly, dark—almost black—hair now with touches of gray starting to sprout in her roots. She would sometimes have her hair blown out if she was going somewhere fancy with Dio, but most times she just tied it back in a ponytail that hung halfway down her back. She lay down in bed and her thoughts ran between her current homicide and thoughts of Dio. Was she falling in love with this man? Would she solve this vicious homicide? Back and forth her mind raced until she finally fell asleep.

CHAPTER 17

Berlin Golf and Hunt Club (Berlin, Germany) was the site of the 1998 German Amateur Youth Golf Championship. While golf was not a very popular sport among young German boys in the late '90s, the wealthy upper class of this once-divided nation enjoyed the game. At that time there were no public golf courses but several hundred private clubs throughout the country of sixty three million. Most of the golf courses were in the western part of the country. In the East (formally Communist East Germany) there were only a handful of courses.

This year's championship would be played by sixty-four of the top male players over the age of sixteen. Heavily favored was Karl Messerschmitt—the grandson of Wilhelm Emil (Willy) Messerschmitt, the founder of the eponymous airplane-manufacturing firm. After the Second World War, Messerschmitt's company was prohibited from making airplanes, and he was sent to prison for using slave labor in his plants during the war. Upon his release in 1950, the company started to manufacture small automobiles—most notably the Messerschmitt Kabineroller—sewing machines, prefabricated buildings, and other products that brought Messerschmitt's enormous wealth.

Messerschmitt's only son, Frederich, did not follow in his father's footsteps but became a successful architect and frustrated semiprofessional golfer. In turn he wanted to ensure his only son Karl, born in 1984, would be given every

73

opportunity to become a professional golfer weather he wanted to or not. Karl did however like the game and took to it very well. He was small but muscular, and his father ensured he got the best instructions available and even arranged for him to have private lessons and play with Germany's most famous golfer, Bernard Langer.

Karl had easily won the amateur championship for the last three years and faced relatively little competition. This year would be different as more and more young German boys were getting away from fussball (soccer) and taking up golf. One such boy was a poor kid named Dieter Spunkmeyer. Spunkmeyer came from a working-class family from Magdeburg, in the state of Saxony, in the former East Germany. His father, Fritz, was a landscaper and was hired to help build the first private golf course in the Magdeburg area. His mother was an Albanian National and was an abusive alcoholic. She would often punish and humiliate Dieter for the slightest indiscretions. Fritz would take his son Dieter, his only child, with him to work as the course progressed, and the boy developed an interest in the game. Dieter was given an old seven iron by one of the designer's workers along with several dozen range balls. Without any lessons, young Dieter, also born in 1984, was teaching himself how to play golf.

When the golf course, Saxonwalt, that his dad worked on was completed, Dieter started to caddy. As in most golf courses, caddies could play on days the course was closed or after their loops were complete. The other caddies thought him to be strange and did not invite him to play. Therefore, he would play alone and use only the old seven iron. He did not use a driver, wedge, or putter until one day the club pro, Max Rhienhardt, asked, "Dieter, why are you only using that old seven iron?"

"It's all I have," was his reply. "I shot thirty-seven for the nine holes with it." The pro shook his head and told Dieter to meet him on the range in ten minutes. The pro returned with a full set of clubs and told Dieter to first hit some wedges then work his way up to driver. Dieter complied and when the pro returned an hour later, he was surprised to see how well the young boy was not only hitting each club but also shaping his shots left and right almost at will.

"You should not be caddying, Dieter. You should be playing competitive events. There is an amateur tournament next month in Berlin. I will speak to your father and see if he will permit me to enter you in the event. I will give you these clubs to use and buy you some decent clothes to wear. You can pay me back when you can. Is that OK?"

"I must work to help my family. I don't think my father will let me go to Berlin." Dieter was only fourteen but was big for his age and looked much older. He was exceptionally strong from the work he had done all his life. Dieter had inherited the hard looks of his maternal ancestors, but the pro saw in him the makings of a professional golfer; his looks were not important.

Rhienhardt convinced Dieter's father to let him take Dieter to Berlin for this tournament, promising him that the boy had talent way beyond anyone else he had seen. Mr. Spunkmeyer thought to himself, How many young golfers could Rhienhardt have seen? This is Germany, not Scotland or the US. However, knowing his only son was a bit of a loner, this might be a way for him to make some friends, especially friends of a higher class. He also wanted his son, who he loved, to be away from his abusive mother.

So two days before the tournament, Max picked up Dieter is his old Mercedes and off they went to Berlin. Dieter had never driven in anything other than his father's old, beat-up Opel Kadet. "Wow, Herr Rhienhardt, this sure is a nice car. What year is it?"

"It's vintage. I bought it from Herman Goring. He only used it to go to church on Sundays," he said with a laugh. Dieter had no idea what he was talking about, as East German youth were not taught about the Third Reich or the Holocaust. The history books of East Germany only covered the communists' glorious victory over Adolph Hitler and Nazism and the Italian Fascist.

Once in Berlin the first stop was the Berlin Golf and Hunt Club. Dieter had never seen something so beautiful. He wasn't allowed to play a practice round, but back in the hotel room, Rhienhardt told him how to play each hole. Dieter was entered in the fourteen-and-under group, so to his advantage he was pitted against boys who were his age or younger. The format was stroke play for the first two days then match play for the eight lowest scores. After eliminations the final two players would play a thirty-six-hole championship match. Players were seeded according to their first day scores.

Strangely enough Dieter was not nervous during play—not on the first tee nor trying to make a putt. He just was not made that way. After the first round, all the competitors and their families were invited to a buffet in the clubhouse dining room. Dieter saw that most of the boys had theirs parents and siblings along with them, and he could tell by how they dressed and behaved that they were from a different class than he was. One of the boys who he played with in a stroke play round saw Dieter sitting by himself (Max was off working the room) and came over to him. "Remember me, Markos? We were in the same foursome yesterday."

Markos was younger than Dieter and, like most of the boys there, was good looking, blond, and blue-eyed, unlike Dieter's dark curly hair and eyes. "I see you are alone. Would you like to join me and my family?" Markos pointed to a table to their right, where Dieter saw a man, woman, and a pretty blonde girl sitting and looking at them.

"Sure, I guess so," replied a somewhat dumbfounded Dieter. He was not used to people being nice or polite to him. He took his plate and followed Markos over to his table.

"Momma, Poppa, this is Dieter Spunkmeyer, the other golfer I was telling you about. And, oh yeah, this is my sister Maria." As Dieter offered his hand to Markos's family, he was surprised the boy knew his full name, not realizing that all the names had been posted on the leaderboard.

"Please join us, Dieter," said Markos's father, pointing to an extra chair next to Maria. "Are your parents not here?"

"No, I'm here with the pro from the golf course where I caddy, Herr Rhienhardt." Dieter looked around and saw Max talking with a few other men. He felt very uncomfortable sitting with these people who kept asking him questions about where he lived and his family. Maria didn't say a word to him and seemed quite disinterested in the whole conversation. She seemed to be about eighteen or nineteen and had long blonde hair and the same light blue eyes as her brother and father. As a matter of fact, almost everyone there had blond hair and blue eyes. Although not taught about the Second World War in school, Dieter knew enough that these people are what other Germans called Aryans, while he was considered a Saxon. But sometimes he heard people refer to him as *Segoiner*, a German slang for Gypsy—a derogatory remark. After about an hour, Max returned from his conversation and found Dieter. Introductions were made all around, and Dieter and Markos excused themselves from the table.

"Wait, I will go too," said Maria. The three teens went outside where Maria took out a pack of cigarettes, gave one to her brother, and offered the pack to Dieter. Dieter had tried smoking cigarettes once, but it made him dizzy, so he never tried again.

"No, thank you."

"What, a peasant boy from Saxony is a nonsmoker?" said Maria with a laugh. As if on cue Markos said, "I must go to the toilette. Dieter, stay here and keep Maria company. She does not like to smoke alone." He was gone before Dieter could say a word.

"Here, take a drag," as she offered him the cigarette.

"They're Marlboros from America. I get them from some GIs in Berlin," Dieter did not know what she meant.

"No, thank you, I don't smoke."

"Well then you can't kiss me. You do want to kiss me, don't you?" Dieter was confused but murmured, "Yes." She held the butt out to him, and he took it as she moved her body into his. He looked around and saw they were alone. She put her hand around his neck and started to grind her body next to his. He could feel himself get hard and was sure she could too. He went to kiss her, and she pushed him away.

"Do you think I would kiss a peasant boy?" she asked mockingly. "I would never stoop so low. I only kiss handsome American GIs who give me cigarettes and records from America." Now she was laughing as she danced away from him. Dieter didn't know how to feel—angry, hurt, or embarrassed. He abruptly turned on his heels and went back into the dining room just as Markos was coming out.

"Hey, Dieter, where are you going? What happened? Did my sister tease you, get your cock hard, and run away? She does it all the time to me. She's a real bitch, isn't she?" He was saying this as a matter of fact. Dieter felt a rage in him he had never known before. He found Max Rhienhardt and said he wanted to go back to the hotel. He felt ill and wanted to rest before the next day's matches.

Dieter was seeded number four but lost his first match and was eliminated from the final round. The tournament was won by the favorite, Karl Messerschmitt.

"Well, Dieter we could go home but as long as we have our room until Sunday, I am going to drive into the city (Berlin) and visit an old friend. You can stay here and work on your game. You did not play well today." Dieter did not reply. He was still upset about the way Maria first encouraged him, teased him, and then blew him off.

"Can I take a ride with you to Berlin? I've never been in a city before. You can drop me off, and I will take a train back here."

"Sure, why not, let's go."

It was about a half-hour drive to the city. Dieter told Max that he would walk around then take the train back to the hotel. Max gave him some cash and said, "OK, but don't be late. Be careful here in the city." Dieter walked around the city and was awestruck at how large many of the buildings seemed.

Max had dropped him by the main Bahnhof (train station) so he would know where to get a train back to the hotel in the suburbs. He wandered around and found himself on the Reeperbahn, a street where there seemed to be bars and dance clubs every other building. He also noticed several women scantily dressed on each street. He was a country boy but not naive enough to know they were hookers. He was approached by a few, but he was too frightened to say anything to them and just kept his hands in his pockets and his head down. He was ready to start back to the train station and decided he was hungry and stopped for a bratwurst and cola at a corner stand. While he sat on a stool eating, he could not stop thinking about Maria and how she humiliated him. Just then he heard a voice that shook him from his daydream.

"Are you alone?"

He looked up and was shocked to see a young woman who looked a lot like Maria only a bit older, maybe twenty-one or twenty-two, but with the same blonde hair and light blue eyes. She even had the same hairstyle. "Cigarette?" she offered. Dieter saw it was a Marlboro and he took one. "My name is Dagmar. What's yours?"

"Markos," Dieter lied.

"How old are you, Markos?" asked Dagmar.

Again he lied, "Seventeen, soon to be eighteen."

He knew this woman was a hooker. Why else would she approach him? "Do you want a date?" Dieter did not know what she meant, and she could tell, so she made a gesture making a circle of her left thumb and forefinger and using her right forefinger made an in-and-out motion. "Do you want sex—you know, fuckie fuckie?"

"Er, yes," said Dieter.

Dagmar waited, "So do you want to know how much? And do you want it here on the stool?"

"Er, no, I mean yes. I would but..."

Dagmar cut him off, "First time, I can tell. How much money do you have?"

Dieter reached into his pocket and took out what he had, about twenty D-Marks. "OK, finish your beer and follow me." Dieter obeyed. They walked together for about half a block and entered a building. Dagmar made small talk about how handsome he was and how she knew this was his first time and how gentle she would be. She used a key to open the door and walked up two flights to a small apartment. She used another key to open the door. Dieter did not know what to expect, but as soon as he gave her the twenty D-Marks, she told him to undress and get on the bed that she pointed to. Besides a dresser, it was the only furniture in the room. Dagmar went into the bathroom and Dieter lay on the bed wearing only his underpants. She came out wearing fishnet stockings, black panties, and a black bra. She knelt on the bed and grabbed Dieter's cock, which was hard. She started to stroke it and Dieter exploded in no more than ten seconds. He was embarrassed that he came so fast but tried to kiss Dagmar, but she pulled away.

"No kissing, and we are done here. You got your rocks off, so put your clothes back on. I will do the same." Dieter felt enraged—the same way he felt about Maria just less than twenty hours before. He tried to talk but his mouth was dry and tasted of bile. Dagmar lit up a cigarette, but this time did not offer one to Dieter.

"Come on, hurry up. Let's go. Chop, chop. I don't have all night." What happened to the sweet caring woman I met at the bratwurst stand no more than thirty minutes ago? he thought. Now the rage was growing inside of him. He started to get dressed but stopped when he heard her peeing in the small bathroom. He got up, now fully dressed. He walked into the bathroom, and she saw him in the mirror. She could see the rage in his eyes and became frightened. As she turned around, he grabbed her throat and started to squeeze. She tried to scream and attempted to kick at him, but he was too strong. He adjusted his grip on her neck so only one hand applied pressure on her throat. With his other hand, he punched her hard in her stomach. Her body tried to double over but he held her up by the throat, still applying pressure. He saw her eyes start to bulge and the pleading look on her face. He could feel his cock get hard, much harder than it had been just a few minutes ago. Much harder than it had ever been. He could feel she was losing consciousness but keep applying pressure to her neck.

"I am strong for a boy," he said, "and you, Maria, will never cocktease me again." Yes, in his enraged mind, Dagmar became Maria, Markos's sister. Finally, he could feel the life ooze out of Dagmar/Maria. He released his grip and she slumped to the bathroom floor.

His body was covered with sweat, but his cock was still hard. He was panting hard and realized that he never got to see her naked. All he got for his twenty D-Marks was a hand job that took ten seconds. He dragged the lifeless body to the bed, undressed her, and stared at her naked dead body. He wanted to masturbate, but thought, No, I have a better idea. He turned her over on her belly. Looking around he saw some K-Y jelly on the shelf over the bed along with some candles. He removed his trousers and smeared the jelly on his still hard penis, and he entered her. He pumped away for about four or five minutes until he felt himself starting to ejaculate. The sensation was something he had never experienced before—not in the several years he had been masturbating in his bedroom back in Magdeburg. He had to suppress himself from screaming; the sensation was so great. Finally, he exploded into her lifeless vagina. He withdrew and sat on the edge of the bed completely spent and breathing very hard.

Finally, after about ten minutes, reality started to come back to him. He stood up and was thinking about the consequences of what he had done. He must cover his tracks. First he looked in her purse and found his twenty D-Marks, plus another fifty D-Marks and some coins. He also saw her driver's license. Her name was not Dagmar but Edletraud Gimke. What a name? he thought. Really old German. He put the license in his pocket. He searched the apartment for anything else of value and found some additional cash in the one small dresser. He looked in the bathroom and found nothing of value— tampons, condoms, douche, and alcohol. He also found a bottle of Jägermeister, a potent German cordial. He took a swig from the bottle, and the liquor burned his throat and stomach but tasted good nonetheless.

As he started to dress, he looked once more at the corpse of Dagmar/Edletraud/Maria laying on the bed and felt and erection coming on. He sat the body up and placed his cock into her dead mouth and, using his hand on the back of her lifeless head, gave himself…he didn't know what to call it— a blow job from a dead woman had no name that he could think of. He was hard as a rock and was trying hard to come. But as hard as he pushed her head, he could not. He then pushed her back on the bed, turned her over on her belly, and using the K-Y jelly he lathered his cock and her butt. He then entered her anus and pumped away for about ten minutes. He was sweating profusely but could not stop until he came again. Once again he came into her lifeless body. This time the orgasm was even more intense than the last one. He could not believe how wonderful this felt. He was fully spent and removed his flaccid cock from Dagmar/Edletraud/Maria's anus.

Dieter knew it was time to go. He knew enough that he had left his fingerprints all over the small apartment. What to do? he thought. He then thought of the alcohol and Jägermeister. He poured both on the body and splashed some on the bed linens. He wiped down the dresser and bathroom door and after dressing, he placed all of Dagmar/Edletraud/Maria's purse contents on the bed. He lit the clothes and bed sheets. He was surprised how quickly it started to burn. He went to the apartment door and after looking around, he slowly exited the small apartment.

He walked briskly down the stairs hoping no one would see him. No one did. He went back toward the train station but stopped and stood in the doorway of a darkened building watching as the flames burned in Dagmar/Edletrudes/Maria's apartment. He didn't care if the whole building went up in smoke. After a few minutes he heard the fire engines blaring their alarms as they neared the fire, now engulfing the entire building. He noticed several people rushing out of the four-story building, some carrying pets and some carrying other important belongings. He started to walk toward the train station, smiling.

CHAPTER 18

He made his way back to the Bahnhof, caught a train, and was back in the hotel room in thirty minutes. He showered and went to bed. He did not hear Herr Rhienhardt return. The next morning, they went back to the golf course to watch the final thirty-six-hole match between Karl Messerschmitt and another Aryan named Martin Schmidt. Messerschmitt easily defeated Schmidt six and five. Rhienhardt was telling Dieter that this kid was the best young golfer not only in Germany but probably all of Europe.

"But you, Dieter, are not far behind. If you keep practicing, you can be as good as he is and better." Dieter was not listening. All he could think about was last night, how good it had felt, and how good he felt thinking about it. His mind was not on golf. It was on Dagmar/Edletraud/Maria and how he wanted to fuck her again. But how her body is nothing more than charred bones, he hoped.

On the ride back to Magdeburg, Dieter was silent. Rhienhardt did all the talking, telling him how he believed that Dieter could be a great golfer and he would speak to some club members and raise enough money to have him trained by coaches even better than himself. Dieter was lost in his own thoughts, vacillating from how awful it was what he had done, but how wonderful and powerful the killing had made him feel.

Over the next several months Dieter and Herr Rhienhardt traveled all over Germany with Dieter playing in tournaments and getting closer to wining. It was during these months that Dieter met and befriended Karl Messerschmitt. The two boys, separated only by months in age, became friends and, when not playing golf, were always in the company of either Rhienhardt or Karl's father or his personal couch Herr Van Boven. The boys' conversation was pretty much about golf and how he, Karl, hoped to play on the PGA Tour first in Europe and then in the US.

Dieter on the other hand had very little knowledge of the professional golf world but was learning about it through the dreams of his new friend. As the summer approached, both coaches—Rhienhardt and Van Boven—spoke of taking the boys to tournaments abroad in England and Scotland. When told about that, Karl was greatly excited. Dieter on the other hand was fearful, as he had never traveled father than Berlin.

CHAPTER 19

Lydia awoke at about 7:00 a.m. to her cell phone ringing. She picked it up and saw it was Dio.

"Good morning, Dio. Or should I say, good afternoon?"

"Hey Lyd, I was starting to think you'd forgotten about me." Although they were lovers, they had not reached the point of calling each other *honey*, *sweetheart*, or other terms of endearment, at least not on the phone. Lydia would call him "D," but that was as far as cutesy names went. It was just not her way.

"Sorry, D, I caught a bad one and I had to go over my boss's head. I'm sure it will come back to bite me on the ass."

He refrained from telling her that she had already mentioned the Dollbee homicide to him. "Jesus, you got any leads you want to talk about it?"

"Not now, I have a shit load of things to do, and I'm working alone. Chris is out with back surgery."

"Well you like doing things your own way. Doesn't your new boss...what's his name?"

"Cashin."

"Doesn't he have other *dicks* (cop talk for detective) to help?"

"Yeah I got a couple of guys. Kiers and Telmany are doing interviews. They're both pretty good."

"But more importantly I won't be able to get over to London next weekend, like we planned." She waited for an answer. "Dio, you there?"

"Yeah, I'm just thinking maybe I should fly over and maybe I could help out, you know...."

Lydia cut him off, "No, Dio, that's not a good idea. Listen, I got to get in the shower and get going. I got a lot to do. The ME is planning on the autopsy today and I've got to get in touch with the crime lab. I'll call you later and give you all the details." She knew her abruptness would bother him. She knew how insecure he was about their relationship, the age factor, the distance, and her work first, you second attitude. That part he understood from his own marriage. He missed Celia at these times. He cared a great deal for Lydia and had told her he loved her on more than one occasion. He never got an "I love you too" in return.

CHAPTER 20

Dio was in his office reviewing reports and making calls to clients and staff. His thoughts were of Lydia and their long-distance relationship. He thought of the first time they made love and how nervous he was. It had been some time since he had last made love to Celia, and he had not dated after her death. He thought their age difference might come into play. Would he be able to please her? On and on went his thoughts, but on that first night in his London apartment after a great dinner and two bottles of wine, Lydia climbed into bed next to him, kissed him good night, rolled over, and went to sleep. It was as if they were an old married couple. He laid there for what seemed to be an eternity looking at her, realizing that her body clock was five hours ahead and just smiled and went to sleep. In the morning they made love, and to his surprise he responded to her as if they had been together for years. They spent all day and the next just lounging in his apartment, making love, and ordering in. It was like a honeymoon that ended all too quickly. The following morning when he awoke, Lydia was dressed and packed.

"Well, I'm on my way to the airport. I'll call you when I get home."

"That's it? That's all you've got to say?"

"No, actually it's not," she said with that snarky look she would give him when she was going to throw a zinger at him.

"Yeah, what?"

"Well, Dio, I'm quite surprised you did not wear a tie with your pajamas." She reached over and gave him a kiss. "You're a sweet man, Dio Bosso, and I really enjoyed this weekend. You made me feel wonderful. I will admit I was nervous. It had been a while since I slept with someone."

Dio shot one back at her. "Ah, nervous, so that's why you went to sleep." They both laughed, and she gave him a hug. He drew her in, "You're something else, Martinez. Have a safe trip. I hope to see you soon."

With that, she left. He never thought to offer a ride. He looked out the window and saw a cab waiting outside. Within a few seconds, she appeared and got into the cab. Over the next several months, they visited each other at least once a month. Dio would fly to Miami and then drive a rental to West Palm. They would talk about whatever case she was working on.

Homicides were down in district three, so she was only *catching* about one or two cases a month, and the majority were domestic, or gang related. They talked about the Stabins homicide and how unfair the system was to certain victims. Domestics were easy to solve as the perp was usually the spouse or a spurned lover. Gang shootings were generally drive-bys. They got solved for the most part, and there was no urgency in clearing these because nobody outside the family really cared. Martinez would often muse about how sad it was that so many young black men under thirty died each year as victims of a homicide. Her colleagues would argue that they made a choice by joining a gang, dealing and using drugs, and carrying a gun. Really, what choice did they have? They were surrounded by violence, and in most cases being raised by their grandmothers. It seemed to be a vicious cycle to her. But then she would think, I'm a cop, I got to clean up the mess society makes. Let the social workers worry with the family issues.

Dio would listen and sympathize with her. He was not as cynical as other cops she knew. Maybe it was because he was a ranking executive. But he always seemed to see the bigger picture not only in police work but in the world in general.

CHAPTER 21

Martinez placed a call to the lab to see who was assigned to her case. She had a good working relationship with most of the techs. She was pleased when she learned Senior Lab Technician Stacey Stack would be the lead tech to examine and analyze the evidence from the crime scene. She called Stacey's work number. "Hey, Stacey, it's Lydia."

"Hey, Lydia, what's going on?"

"You working that teenage girl rape and homicide?" Lydia wanted to tell her she had it backward, but what would be the point?

"Well Doc Widman over at the ME is doing the autopsy sometime today, and I want to have our labs and her labs ready at the same time. If my gut feeling is correct, I have a short window to work with."

"Doc Widman, eh. Every time I talk to her, she is either eating or going to lunch. How does she keep so thin? Strange lady she is."

"They're all strange, Stacy. That's why they're pathologists."

"Yeah, I guess you're right. OK, I'll start with the evidence Crime Scene submitted. If you have additional evidence, get it over to me and I'll log it in. I'll do as much as I can, but I got a date tonight with this stud I met last week, and I don't want to blow him...," she paused for effect, "off. Ha ha, you get that?"

"Yeah, Stacey, real funny. I got to use it sometime."

"So, Lydia, are you seeing anybody new? I hear you're pretty tight with that old guy you worked that big case with last year?"

"He's not *that* old, Stacey." Stacey was about forty-two and liked to date guys in their twenties and thirties. Although she was not offended by Stacey's comment about Dio, she took a shot and threw a dig back at Stacey. "So, this date you have tonight, is he out of high school yet? Do you have to get him home before his curfew?"

"Ha ha ha, very funny." Stacey was divorced but had no kids. Lydia had gone out with her for drinks a few times but found her to be always on the prowl. She was a very attractive blonde with a cute figure and each time Lydia saw her, she had a different hairstyle. Some of the other techs Lydia knew referred to her as "the crime lab cougar." Lydia thought they were not wrong.

CHAPTER 22

On her way over to the morgue, Lydia decided to call Dio.

"Hello, Dio Bosso, here."

"Hi, D, it's me." Why is he so fuckin' formal? she thought, but maybe that's why she liked him—so different, so old school. "How are you doing?"

"I'm fine, Lydia. How is your homicide coming along? Care to share?"

"I'm making progress, following leads, gathering evidence. I saw your old buddy Arnie Dansky a few times. He was very helpful." She spent the next fifteen minutes telling Dio what she had so far and how she though that the *doer* may have something to do with The Florida Classic. She would know more later today when Doc Widman performed the autopsy. They made small talk for a while. She said she had paperwork to do, and he was going to get dressed and go out to dinner with some people from work. She could not resist the opportunity to shoot him a zinger. "Wear that nice blue-green-striped tie you wore on our last date in London. It looks great on you."

He didn't get it. "Oh, OK, yeah I like that tie too."

"So, the people from work, are there any single females in the dinner party tonight?"

"They're all single woman in the dinner party tonight (touché). Do I detect a bit of jealousy, Martinez?"

She sighed, "You're damn right. You're the handsomest bachelor in London." They both laughed.

"Well, D, I gotta go now. You enjoy your dinner, and I'll talk to you soon."

"OK, Lydia," he hesitated.

"Dio, you there?"

"Yeah, I'm here. It's just that I miss you. I wish you were here, that's all."

"OK, bye now." She hung up. Holding the phone away from her face and looking at it as if she could see him, she smiled. On the other side of the line, two thousand miles away, he did the same thing.

Just as she hung up, her cell phone rang and this time it was Ann Quick, the volunteer coordinator from The Florida Classic. "Hello, Detective Martinez." Martinez could tell by her voice she was a bit upset. "I was doing some checking after our conference yesterday, and I realized that I assigned Jasmin as a standard bearer for the pro-am and rounds one and two to the group in which Karl Messerschmitt was playing. I feel so terrible. If I had not assigned her, she might still be alive." Quick started to cry and Martinez tried to assure her that was not the case (although it was).

"Listen, Ms. Quick, we're not sure that there is a direct connection," she lied. "In any case you could not have known the outcome of your random assignment."

"Normally I would not have assigned a first-time volunteer to be a standard bearer. But in this case, I know Jasmin's mom, Pat, and her golf coach, Beth Donovan. I know the kid is on her way to becoming a great college golfer." Not anymore thought Martinez, but she kept that thought to herself.

"I appreciate your call, Ms. Quick."

"There's something else," she paused.

"Yes, go on."

"One of my volunteers told me that after the second round, Messerschmitt's caddy asked for Jasmin Dollbee's home address."

"Is that not unusual? Did she give it to him?"

"Well, er, yes, but only after he told her that he wanted to send her a gift from Germany. Something about a figurine she wanted to start collecting. The volunteer feels terrible."

"I'm going to need to talk to her. What's her name and address?"

"Wendy Berry. I'll get you her address and phone number."

CHAPTER 23

Back in London, Dio was hard at work in his office. His job consisted of reviewing security protocols for the hundreds of properties his clients owned throughout Great Britain and Europe. He traveled extensively but traveling by private jet with a chauffeured Bentley, Mercedes Benz, or BMW at each airport was hardly work as far as he was concerned. He did not actually do the security reviews but just read the reports prepared by his agents in the various client cities.

Lloyd's also insured most of the major golf courses in Europe, so he was always being invited to play. His response was that he was too busy as a young detective to take the game up and now too old. Another part of his job was meeting client executives and joining them for lunch or dinner in Europe's best restaurants. Fortunately, he worked out each day and kept his weight at 185 pounds, which suited his six-foot-one frame very well.

Most retired cops would kill for this job and he knew it, but he still missed *chasing the bad guys*. He still missed the comradery of the NYPD. And he still missed Lydia Martinez.

CHAPTER 24

It was early afternoon on Monday when Martinez arrived at the ME's office hoping she would not have to wait too long for Doc Widman to begin the autopsy. She was sitting in her office, working on her computer, and eating a sandwich when Lydia tapped on the open door. She looked up at Martinez and said with a mouthful of food, "Bacon, egg, and cheese. I got another if you want."

"No thanks, Doc, I had something at home," she lied.

Martinez watched as Doc Widman performed the autopsy. Her assistant, a ghoulish-looking guy named Peter Rogers, took each organ the pathologist handed him, weighed it, and placed it in a tray. Using a syphon, he removed several ounces of water from the victim's lungs. The water would be analyzed, but the fact that the lungs contained water indicated that the victim was alive when she was placed in the pond.

Doc Widman verbally recorded every step of the postmortem exam. She stated that although the victim sustained several severe blows to the back of the head, the cause of death was drowning. This was evident by the amount of water in the lungs and the fact that the hyoid bone in her throat was not fractured, even though some strangulation did occur as evidenced by the bruising around the neck.

Doc Widman continued and noted that there was no evidence of defensive wounds on the victim's hands. She did however remove for analysis slivers of black material from under several fingers on each hand. There was bruising around the victim's neck, windpipe, and esophagus, indicating strangulation but, again, not the cause of death.

Doc Widman continued with the autopsy and stated that the victim was sexually assaulted anally, but there was no DNA in the anus and no vital reaction, which indicates that the sexual assault occurred after the victim was dead. There was also evidence of latex in the anal area, indicating that the perp used a condom.

Martinez was thinking to herself, So this sick motherfucker places something over her head, whacks her on the back of the neck, strangles Jasmin unconscious, carries her to the pond, and as he gets ready to dump her in, he realizes she is still alive, drowns her, then decides to anally rape her? She again looked at the photo of Messerschmitt and said aloud, "My god, what kind of sick bastard am I dealing with?"

Once the autopsy was complete, Doc Widman turned off the overhead mic, removed her protective face shield, and told her assistant to get the organs and fluids to the lab for a full toxicology panel.

"You can close her up, Pete. I'll complete the paperwork to get her released to the funeral parlor."

Rogers just nodded and shuffled off, pushing the remains of Jasmin Dollbee back into the cooler. He made Martinez think of Igor, from the Frankenstein movies, only without the hump in his back.

Martinez followed Doc Widman to her office. "I need a coffee. How about you, Lydia, you want a coffee? I have some Krispy Kremes in my desk."

"No thanks, Doc, I gotta run."

"Sure, no problem."

Lydia pulled up the newest number in her cell phone and dialed Carol Blanshaft, the hospitality coordinator for The Florida Classic. She started with small talk. "Hi, Carol, I must tell you how professional your daughter was the other day. It's a dreadful assignment when a cop has to make a notification like that." Lydia played up Kim's role, but nonetheless it's a horrible part of police work.

"Thanks, Detective, I appreciate you saying so. My late husband, Don, was a thirty-year veteran of the NYPD, and my son, Steve, is a Sergeant in Naples, so police work is in our DNA. How can I help you?" Blanshaft was savvy enough to know that Martinez didn't call just to compliment her daughter.

"A golfer named Messerschmitt suddenly withdrew from the tournament. Do you know if he returned his courtesy car?"

"Funny you should ask. Kira just got a call from the Marriott on Donald Ross Road. It seems a courtesy car was parked in the handicap spot, and the hotel desk clerk thought that by now the car and player would be on the course. I checked the plate number of the car and it was the one assigned to the golfer you mentioned, Karl Messerschmitt."

Martinez could feel the rush of excitement, as she now was sure this Messerschmitt guy was somehow involved in the Dollbee homicide. Normally she would have enough to bring him in for questioning, but he was in the wind, so to speak. "Carol, do me a favor. Call the hotel and tell the clerk not to touch the car. I will be there shortly. Oh, and by the way, do you have duplicate keys for the car?"

"That won't be necessary. The clerk said the keys were left at the desk."

"Great, also tell the clerk not to have the room cleaned."

"OK, I'll call him right away."

"Thanks, Carol."

CHAPTER 25

Martinez arrived at the Marriott hotel and was met in the parking lot by the irate desk clerk and a uniformed security officer. "These damn golfers think they can park anywhere they want. I only have three handicap spots in my lot, and this asshole took up one and just left."

"Which asshole are you referring to?"

"The Kraut golfer. What's his name? Messer-something or other. I have to check the list. About fifteen golfers and caddies stayed here. It's been hectic and this jerk leaves his car in the handicap spot."

"Well, let me have the keys, and I'll move it after I take a look. By the way did your housekeeping clean the room that Mr. Messerschmitt was staying in?"

"No, I only learned that he checked out this morning. The room was booked until tomorrow."

"OK, leave it as is. I want to have a look after I check the car out and I may want my crime scene team to check the room."

The clerk was now inquisitive. "Did he do something wrong? Why do you want to check his room?"

"Did you have any contact with Mr. Messerschmitt? What's your name, by the way?"

"Dowler, Lou Dowler, I'm the manager of the hotel. Been working for Marriott about ten years now."

"Thanks, Mr. Dowler. Now if you gentlemen will excuse me, I'd like to look at the car."

Dowler handed the keys over to Martinez, and he and the guard left her by the vehicle. The first thing Martinez did was check the tires. All four had small pebbles or gravel in the treads. Taking several plastic baggies from her attaché case, she then used the Swiss Army knife Dio gave her to pry loose several pieces of gravel from each tire. Marking each baggie, she placed them inside the attaché case. Putting on rubber gloves, Martinez opened the front door of the Ranger and immediately noticed small clumps of dried mud on the floorboard. Once again, she carefully placed this material in a baggie, this time using a pair of tweezers from the attaché case. Each time she used these objects—glove, baggies, tweezers and Swiss Army knife—she thought of Dio and how meticulous he was about gathering possible evidence. Breaking her reverie, she proceeded to carefully inspect the rest of the interior of the SUV and found similar pieces of dried mud in the driver's side back seat. In the front passenger's seat, no mud was found, but she did find and bag several slivers of a black material.

Martinez placed a call to Crime Scene and got a hold of Tommy Chisholm. She explained what she wanted and where she was. She wanted the car and Messerschmitt's room dusted and checked for any signs of a struggle, thinking if this guy is involved, did he take his victim to his room or did she meet him there? Chisholm told her that he and Whalen would be there within the hour. Although she wanted to get this new evidence to the lab, she decided to take a quick look at the room Messerschmitt stayed in.

Martinez got the room key from Mr. Dowler, who was still griping about the car parked in the handicap spot. When she entered the room, she immediately noticed that both king-sized beds were used. She figured that Messerschmitt and his caddy both stayed there. Other than the unmade beds, the room appeared to be as normal as any hotel room that had not been cleaned after checkout. There was no visible evidence of blood or a struggle, the used towels in the bathroom were piled on the floor, and the closets were emptied.

Martinez was ready to leave the room when she noticed a small white plastic bag with the hotel logo inside the bathroom trash pail. It appeared as if something was inside, so she took a look. Inside she found a black nylon bag that had The Florida Classic logo on its front. Not being a golfer, it took her a few seconds to realize that it was a shoe bag. However, it appeared that the middle section that would separate the shoes was cut out. As she examined the bag, she noticed horizontal marks on the outer shell that appeared to be scratch marks. The material appeared to be the same material as the black flakes she found in the courtesy car—further proof linking Messerschmitt to the Dollbee girl.

If the lab could connect the shoe bag to those flakes both in the car and under Jasmin's fingers, and if the victim's DNA is on the bag, she would have more solid evidence connecting Messerschmitt to this gruesome crime. She thought about motive but knew that a homicide like this—vicious, brutal, and with sexual overtones—does not need a motive when it's the work of a sexual sadist or, worse yet, a serial killer. She wondered to herself whether this was his first such murder.

She took the shoe bag with her and left the room. She wanted to get this new piece of evidence vouchered and logged into the crime lab. She called Stacey Stack and told her that she would be dropping off additional evidence for examination and asked her to have Doc Widman send her a DNA sample from the victim.

After leaving the hotel, she drove to the crime lab and logged in the new evidence. She then drove out to the Cypress Creek Natural Area. The yellow crime scene tape was gone, and there were several cars in the parking area. Martinez walked down to the pond where the body was found. It seemed so peaceful and serene. She searched the area again not really knowing why. She sat on a bench and tried to visualize the brutal rape and murder that occurred in that very spot just three days ago. After a few minutes, she got back into the Crown Vic, stopped at Publix, and picked up a sandwich.

CHAPTER 26

At The Florida Classic, play resumed. Half of the golfers that made the cut were able to finish their final round on Sunday, and nobody had a low enough score to possibly win, unless several of the players who would finish today had horrendous rounds. The lowest score going into Monday was over eleven under. Rory McIlroy and Sergio Garcia were at the top at fifteen under, and seven others were eleven under, so in all likelihood the winner would be one of the twenty or so golfers finishing Monday.

The rain had stopped, and cooler dry air made the course more receptive to play. A relative newcomer to the tour, Keith Mitchell, shot a seven under round to finish at eighteen under and nose out both McIlroy and Garcia. In spite of the Monday finish, the tournament was declared a success. Record attendance coupled with record sales of golf apparel would translate into record contributions to the local charities. The *Palm Beach Post* sports section had several pages dedicated to The Florida Classic, with bold print columns about the relative unknown golfer who defeated two of the best golfers in the world and what this victory meant to his rookie season and career. There were stories of failures of the big names like Tiger Woods and Phil Mickelson. Page after page of golf stories. Even the local section ran articles on the charities that would benefit from this year's Classic. There was no mention of Karl Messerschmitt or his withdrawal. On the last page of the local section, there was a single-column item that read, "Body of Local Girl Found in the Cypress Creek North Preserve, Foul Play Suspected."

CHAPTER 27

On Tuesday morning Martinez met with Lieutenant Cashin in his office and once again was read the riot act on her behavior. After the ass-chewing, she was told that he wanted her to continue the investigation, keeping Messerschmitt as a person-of-interest, but to reinterview everyone she had spoken to over the past few days. He also told her that he would be working alone. "I just lost Manganillo and O'Sullivan to a new human-trafficking task force started by the state's attorney. The others were all working their own cases."

She didn't think she would gain any additional information from the reinterviews, especially since she believed Messerschmitt, or his caddy were most probably the doers. She knew this would be a waste of time, but she would comply. At least the Van Hooey kid would be happy to see her again, she chuckled to herself. She scheduled reinterviews with the Van Hooey kid, Tricia Maddox, Mike Pearce and his girlfriend Jen, and Mary Thomas. She also wanted to get a statement from Wendy Berry, the volunteer who gave Jasmin's address to Spunkmeyer. Now she would show them a picture of Karl Messerschmitt she printed from the official PGA website. She also needed to reinterview the hotel manager Dowler, the Uber driver, Arnie Dansky, and his security officer, Stan Kriegsman. In addition, Cashin wanted to have both the ME's and the PBSO's labs retested to be sure the results were consistent. He wanted all this done and on his desk by weeks end.

Martinez hadn't talked to Dio since Sunday and wanted to wait until she had time to talk to him without having to cut the conversation short. Finally, on Wednesday morning she put in a call to his office.

"Well hello, stranger. How is my favorite Florida detective doing?" She was surprised he didn't answer in his usual formal "Dio Bosso, here," but she assumed that his secretary told him who was calling.

"Hi, Dio, I wanted to wait until I had enough time to talk to you in length. I've been so busy here, and my cell is running low on power, which is why I called your office."

"Not a problem, I figured as much. So how you doing? How is your homicide coming along?"

"Well I think I have identified a person-of-interest, and I may need your help." Dio sat up in his chair. The thought of helping her made his juices flow, but he would hear her out before saying anything. "To start with, my boss here is having me do all unnecessary reinterviews of the witnesses I spoke to last week. Apparently, I stepped on some toes here, and the shit is flowing down." She continued on telling him the timeline of what she had and what she was planning to do. As she did this, they both made notes. For her it helped to get a fresh look at what steps she had taken and logically showed why she thought Messerschmitt was a person-of-interest. For Dio it gave him a starting point as to how he could help the woman he loved solve this horrible crime.

Dio did not interrupt her as to not break the flow of information but made notes that he would go back to and question her on, just as he would during his NYPD days with conducting an interview or interrogation. When Lydia finished, he had a fairly good idea of what had occurred and why she believed that Messerschmitt was involved. "I don't understand why your superiors don't see the facts of this case pointing to this Messerschmitt guy."

"Well, Dio, he's a professional golfer and both The Florida Classic and the PGA don't want to tarnish their image."

"Yes, but what about the poor victim and her family?"

"My thoughts exactly. However, I think now that the tournament is over, things might loosen up a bit for me here. I think Cashin is giving me this busy work on word from higher ups. Even if they believe my theory that Messerschmitt is involved, they know he's out of the country and can't harm anyone else here."

"Good point. So how can I help?"

"Well I know from our past conversations that Lloyd's insures a lot of the major golf courses in Europe. I was wondering if you have any contacts in the golf world in Europe, especially in Germany or the European PGA. There's a golfer named Karl Messerschmitt that I need you to check out for me. If you can, get me a complete profile."

Dio sounded excited, "Sure Lyd, let me see what I can do. I know some people over here and I've met with the heads of several police agencies both here in England and on the continent. You'd be surprised how much juice Lloyd's has here in Europe. I'll be happy to help."

"That's great, Dio. I really appreciate you doing this for me."

"Well you can show me how much you appreciate it next time you see me," he said sheepishly.

"Why, Dio Bosso, are you suggesting I repay your help with sexual favors?"

"Yes ma'am, I am."

"Well I'll be happy to oblige."

This exchange was the most they had ever discussed sex in any form, and it made them both feel excited and silly at the same time.

"I miss you, Lydia."

"I miss you too, D."

He wanted to say he loved her, but he knew he would not get the reply he wanted, so he let it go. "Ok then, let me get started and see what I can do, and I'll call you in a day or so."

"Good, I've got stuff to do, and I want to attend the funeral for my victim."

They broke the connection and Lydia checked her cell to see if she had missed any calls. There was one from the Van Hooey kid. What does he want now? she thought. She decided not to return the call just yet.

CHAPTER 28

Dio checked his calendar and was pleased he had no travel plans for the next several business days. He had several meetings here in London with his boss, General Council Jerimiah Clifford, and CEO John Powers. Other than he had very little to do. He reached into his contacts on his rolodex and pulled out the card of Kurt Gropp, who is the secretary general of Interpol, the International Police Organization with headquarters in Lyon, France. Interpol was established in 1923 as an organization that facilitates worldwide police cooperation.

Dio had met Gropp at an Interpol convention when he first arrived in London last year. Gropp was the former deputy head of Germany's Federal Criminal Police Office. He and Dio had hit it off quite well as both were former police executives in their home countries. Contrary to frequent portrayals in popular culture, Interpol is not a law enforcement agency, and its agents do not have the powers of arrest. Instead it functions as a network of law enforcement agencies throughout the world. It provides member countries, of which there are close to two hundred, with intelligence on a variety of criminal topics. It also acts as a liaison between member country's law enforcement agencies.

When Dio reached Gropp and explained what he needed, he was only too happy to assist. He told Dio that he knew who Karl Messerschmitt was, as he was a golfer and golf fan.

"We should play some time, Dio. You do golf, don't you?" Gropp had only the slightest hint of a German accent.

"Not my game, Kurt. Tried it once or twice but never had the time to play enough."

"Too bad, you have access to some of the best courses in Europe in your firm's portfolio. I'm jealous."

Dio did not pick up on the fact that Gropp may have been fishing for an invite, but he was quick to get back on point about Messerschmitt. Gropp said he would run a complete background check on Karl Messerschmitt, make some calls to his contacts in the German federal police, and get back to him in a day or two.

CHAPTER 29

On Wednesday morning Lydia attended the funeral mass for Jasmin Dollbee in St. Paul's Roman Catholic Church in Palm Beach Gardens. The church was packed with family, friends, and schoolmates of Jasmin. Martinez noticed that besides Ann Quick, no one from the tournament was in attendance. Martinez did not make the trip to the cemetery, but she did however get the opportunity to pull Ken Dollbee aside. She told him that she had made progress but at the same time she implied that the family should not be fearful to speak out and be an advocate for Jasmin, especially if the police are not successful in the investigation.

"Are you suggesting that we should speak to the press, Detective? I would think you would want us to keep out of your way and let you and your people conduct your investigation. My wife and I are confident that you will do your best. Are you not?"

"Yes, I am confident in myself and the sheriff's office. What I'm trying to say here..." Martinez looked around to see who was in earshot, "there may come a time in this investigation that my hands and the hands of my department may be tied. If that should happen, then you need to speak up on behalf of your daughter."

"I don't understand, Detective. What are you trying to say?"

"Mr. Dollbee trust me. You'll know when."

She again offered her condolences to Dollbee and his family and made her way back to the homicide office. She stopped at Publix and bought a chicken wrap. Publix was becoming her favorite lunch spot. She was back in her cubicle just finishing lunch when her cell rang. "Homicide, Martinez."

"Hey, Lydia, it's Stacey. I got some prelims for you and it's pretty interesting, so I thought you would want to know."

Looking at her watch she saw it was past 5:00 p.m. and thought if Stacey is still working, she must have something good.

"Great, Stacey, whaddya got?"

"Well I examined the evidence you brought in. The pebbles you collected from the tires are typical of the gravel and Sure/Pac one would find on any off-road unpaved surface. I would guess if you check your tires and the police vehicles at the scene, you would find the same materiel. As the ground was wet, these pebbles easily get picked up in the tire treads."

Stacey's voice seemed to grow louder with excitement as she went on, "The crumbly mud from the driver's side interior of the courtesy car, as you labeled it, is dried clay and is found adjacent to ponds and canals here in Palm Beach County. According to your report, the same substance was found in the back seat behind the driver but not in the front seat passenger's side. Is that correct?" Without waiting for Martinez to respond she continued, "There was no mud on the victim's shoes and clothing, which makes me think that she was carried from the road to the pond."

Martinez cut in, "Let me do the detective work, Stacey. Just give me the labs, OK."

"Yeah sure, it's just when things fall into place, I get a bit jacked-up."

Lydia thought to herself, OK fine, why is she so excited? Maybe the new boyfriend.

"Aren't you going to ask me anything else, Detective?"

"OK I'll bite. Anything else Stacey?"

"You bet there is, and it's the best part." Stacey was now overly excited. "I got a sample of the water taken from your victim's lungs from the stuff the ME sent over here and guess what?" Stacey waited for effect.

"OK, Stacey, I give up. What?"

"Well there are two things actually," she paused, "The slivers removed from under the victim's fingernails are the same material as the black flakes you submitted from the courtesy car. They also match the golfer's shoe bag you dropped off earlier. It may be a stretch, but I think some of the slivers from under the victim's nails match the scratch marks on the bag. Plus, the victim's DNA was all over the inside of the shoe bag."

"That's great, Stacey." Lydia could sense there was something else and knew she had to ask. "Anything else, Stacey?"

"You bet there is, and it's huge!" Now Lydia was getting excited too. Stacey's exuberance was contagious. "Well do you know what diatoms are, Lydia?"

"No, Stacey, I don't. I'm a cop. You're the scientist."

Stacey chuckled. "Well diatoms are microscopic organisms that live in ponds. Some are protozoa, some cluster, sort of like algae but much smaller. They can't be seen with the naked eye. Some can be found on decaying leaves, and some live on other decaying matter. In many instances some of the organisms are found only in a specific body of water. There can be as many as several thousand in a single drop of water. That's how small they are. By placing a few small pieces of the clay residue on a slide and putting it under my microscope, I was able to make that determination."

"Stacey, please, enough with the biology lesson. Where is this going?"

"Hang on girl, here is the good part. The same type of microorganisms or diatoms, the same exact type, were found in the water inside your victim's lungs."

"Holy shit, Stacey, you're telling me that the person or persons who were driving or in that car are the ones who murdered or at least placed the victim in the pond? Stacey, this is wonderful news, great job." Even Lydia was excited now. "Did you tell this to Doc Widman?"

"I called but she was at lunch. I left that doofus assistant of hers, what's his name Rogers, a message. Dudes always asking me out."

"OK, Stacey, this is great news. Thanks so much and I will be sure that the powers that be know what a great job you did here. I gotta go now."

"How about a drink some time? I know a great new place where you can meet guys, you now, like your own age."

"Yeah sure, Stacey, but right now I gotta go. Good job, Stacey."

"Oh, and Lydia, one more thing. I'd like to check the water in the pond to confirm what I found in the lungs and mud. Oftentimes diatoms can be different from one pond to another. Also check your tires and see if you can dig out some gravel from the treads. And lastly contact the uniforms who were at the scene. Have them do the same and get those samples to me so I can make a comparison with the gravel."

"Stacey, one question. How did you get the water sample from the ME's office so quickly?"

"Oh, I told Rogers I would have lunch with him if he got me the samples I needed. Dude was here in twenty minutes."

"Oh, so how was lunch?"

"Well, when he got here, I had another tech signed for the evidence who told him I got called to a meeting."

CHAPTER 30

On Thursday morning Dio received a call from Kurt Gropp from Interpol and was told by him that Karl Messerschmitt was in fact back at his father's estate outside of Frankfurt and had temporarily withdrawn from the next several PGA and European events with no explanation given. Through his contact in the German federal police, he was able to arrange surveillance on the Messerschmitt estate. The German surveillance team reported that Karl and his father had several meetings with the law firm of MacLeod and Mone, one of Europe's most prestigious law firms. Both Malcolm MacLeod and Mathias Mone were present at these meetings, leading Gropp to believe something big was going on. Rarely, if ever, do both senior partners of this law firm attend a meeting unless the client is very important and in serious trouble.

Dio asked Gropp if he knew of the extradition agreement between Germany and the United States, and Gropp told him that Germany, like most other countries in the EU, will not extradite to countries where capital punishment is a possible sentence. He would however look further into the meeting between the Messerschmitt's and the lawyers. Dio felt this inquiry may be somewhat premature, but he trusted Lydia's instincts. And she was telling him that this guy Messerschmitt is involved, and if she wanted to pursue this avenue of investigation, she would be well served by knowing what the chances were of getting Messerschmitt back in Florida for a possible trial.

Dio put in a call to Lydia and gave her the information he received from Gropp. The subject turned to personal topics and Dio once again told Lydia how he missed her.

"You may see me sooner than you think, Dio."

"Why, you think the sheriff's office will send you over here on this?"

Not sure what direction this is heading, but the state's attorney has assigned an ASA to the case, and the sponsors are doing a Pontius Pilot now that their big event is over."

"So, what's your next move?"

She hesitated then continued. "Well I've already ruffled some feathers here. Both my CO and the sheriff reamed me out for going over their heads to get the people at The Florida Classic to talk to me. The autopsy reports from the ME's office and our crime lab have been completed. The results clearly indicate this Messerschmitt guy and his caddy are most likely our doers. If this was some local perp, the guy would be in cuffs already based on all the evidence we have. The fact that he's a German national currently in Germany makes this more difficult for the state's attorney. They may have to go to the feds on this one. I'm not sure but I've done all I can do on my end."

"That doesn't sound like you, Lyd, if you don't mind me saying so."

"I know, D. It's..." she paused, "it's just that, I don't know what, but I'm tired. Tired of seeing all of this shit I deal with and not getting the support I need."

Dio knew she was venting and was happy it was with him that she felt comfortable enough to talk to about her feelings. So, he just listened and let her go on.

"Maybe I should retire, do something else." She waited for a response, but Dio just listened until she said, "D, do you think I should retire?"

"I think you are just feeling a bit shitty because of all you have been through with this case. If you want my opinion, then I will tell you to give it a while and see how you feel, see how thinks shake out. Remember this case is not closed if you believe this Messerschmitt guy is the doer. By the way, my contact at Interpol gave me some additional info that may be important."

He waited for Lydia to say, "So go on."

"It seems this golfer, Messerschmitt, is a big deal in Germany. His grandfather built planes for the Nazis. And his father is a well-known architect. Ever hear of a plane called a Messerschmitt?"

"Can't say that I have but go on."

"Well it appears Messerschmitt canceled all his upcoming golf tournaments, claiming an injury. Now I know you told me he withdrew from the tournament there due to pressing business in Germany. So, right there we have conflicting statements. Also Kurt told me that his family has met with the 'M&Ms.' You know the high-level law firm I told you about. I know for a fact we have used them on occasion as an outside council. Apparently both senior partners met with the Messerschmitt's at their estate outside of Frankfurt."

They continued their conversation for another twenty minutes before Lydia ended the conversation. "I guess you're right, D. I need to take a step back and evaluate what I should do. It's just that I don't want to see justice not being served for this young girl."

"Well, you know I'm here for you and I will continue to do what I can to help. I'll talk to you soon."

She in turn decided to play by the rules and spoke to Lieutenant Cashin and filled him in on what she had. He seemed more concerned with the follow-up interviews, which she had spent the last two days conducting and learning nothing new, except that the Van Hooey kid professed to be smitten with her and actually asked her on a date.

Cashin seemed to believe, and so did his superiors right up to Sheriff Romain, that they had no choice but to continue the investigation here in Florida. "Forget about this Messerschmitt guy for now Martinez. Continue your investigation and look for other possible perpetrators that we can actually prosecute."

In a loud voice she replied, "Are you suggesting I try to frame someone else for this, Lieutenant? Because if you are, I'm not going there."

Now his voice was raised, "I'm not suggesting any such thing, but what do we do? Tell everyone we think this pro golfer brutally murdered our victim and we can't do a thing about it? How do you think that will sit with the public?"

"Fuck the public, what about the victim herself and her family?" Her voice was so loud that the other detectives in the squad room stopped what they were doing and listened in.

"Looks like Martinez and the lieutenant are going at it pretty good," said Kiers.

"Between you and me, that guy's a desk jockey," said Telmany. "Martinez got more street savvy then Cashin and Romain put together and probably more balls."

With that Martinez came storming out of Cashin's office and returned to her cubicle, got her things, and left the squad room without saying a word. Kiers and Telmany just looked at one another and went back to typing their reports.

CHAPTER 31

Lydia was furious. She could not believe the department would just drop the ball on this case. Could she go to the press? Tell the family? No, she knew that would be career suicide. She decided to go home and call Dio. She didn't care what time it was.

When she got Dio on the phone, she was so upset that she actually started to cry. Dio had never heard her so emotional. His heart went out to her. They talked for a while and after she calmed down a bit, he repeated what he learned from Gropp, trying to ameliorate her feelings. Then he made the following suggestion: "Lydia, if you're sure this guy Messerschmitt is your perp, why not take a vacation and come over here, and we will work the case together, just like the *Green Violinist.* If we get enough facts, maybe we can get the Germans to extradite. Of course, you would have to have the backing of your state's attorney and the promise not to seek the death penalty."

"I don't know, Dio. I do have enough time on the books to take a vacation. Even though I'm steamed right now, I don't know what I want other than justice for Jasmin Dollbee and her family. Let me sleep on it. By tomorrow, Cashin will have calmed down and maybe he and I can reach some agreement as to how to proceed."

Their conversation ended with the usual goodbye and I miss you.

CHAPTER 32

The next morning Lydia went into the office and noticed a note on her phone to call Major Adams at the sheriff's command office.

"Good morning, Colleen, it's Lydia, retuning your call."

"Hey Lydia, how are you doing?" Without waiting for an answer, Adams continued, "Listen, your boss just left. He met with the sheriff and the chief of detective and the ASA assigned to this case. You may know her, Nancy Heichemer."

"Only by name, never had her on a case. Go on."

"Well your boss, Lieutenant Cashin, convinced us that in all probability your suspect in this case, pro golfer Karl Messerschmitt, is involved in this crime based on all the evidence that you, the CSU, the ME's office, and the lab have put together."

Lydia wanted to say, why was I not there? I'm the case detective but decided to wait.

Adams went on. "You will be getting a call from Heichemer, and she will want to set up a meeting. In the meantime, she will be talking to her boss Ed McDonald about how to proceed. They even discussed the possibility of sending you over to Germany to do the interview but as of now that is all speculation. I will say that Cashin went to bat for you big time. He professed his trust in your investigation and your instincts. You're not sleeping with him, are you? Just kidding. But truth be told, I've known him a while and never seen him so aggressive in his defense of an unpopular position. He actually had the sheriff and chief nodding in agreement."

"That's great news, Colleen. But what about the ASA? What's her name? Heichemer, what's her story?"

"Strictly law and order and was visibly shaken by the report from the ME of the brutality of this vicious crime. I think you should start packing your bags and brush up on your German. Maybe you can get your boyfriend over in London to help with his contacts."

Lydia did not want to mention she already had and did not disclose the meeting between the Messerschmitt's and the high-end lawyers they met with.

CHAPTER 33

Lydia no sooner hung up the phone when her cell rang. "Martinez, homicide."

"Good morning, Detective. This is Nancy Heichemer, Senior Executive State's Attorney." Without waiting for a response, she continued, "How soon can you be in my office? I want to discuss your ongoing investigation in the Dollbee homicide."

Lydia did not want to let on that she spoke to Colleen, so she played dumb. "Are there any new developments I'm not aware of Ms. Heichemer?"

"It's Nancy. No, but if you can be here, let's say by 1:00 p.m., we can discuss all that. Does that work for you, Detective?"

"Yes, it does. I'll see you at 1:00 p.m."

"Good, we will meet in the conference room on the fifth floor. See you then." She hung up without saying goodbye or waiting for one.

The Palm Beach County State Attorney's Office is located on Dixie Highway in West Palm Beach. The six-story building was home to the county judicial system that included the criminal and civil courts, the state attorney's office, and other ancillary divisions of the criminal justice system for the county.

Martinez arrived at the fifth-floor meeting room at about twelve forty-five, and after presenting her credentials was asked to wait in the conference room marked number one. At exactly 1:00 p.m., a petite attractive woman with short brown hair entered the room followed by a man in his thirties and another young woman.

120

Extending her hand to Martinez, she said, "Detective Martinez, I'm Nancy Heichemer. This is ASA Dan Deyoe and my secretary, Amy Abel." They exchanged business cards. Lydia noticed the spelling of Mr. Deyoe's name. It was pronounced the same as Dio's but was obviously a surname. The all took seats.

A young female staffer entered carrying a tray of coffee. "Would you like some coffee or tea?"

"No thanks, I'm good."

Without a word the young woman served the petite brunette tea from a ceramic teapot and coffee for the other two.

"So, Detective, let's begin."

Deyoe and Abel started to write on the identical yellow pads.

"I have reviewed all the reports and documents related to the homicide in question. And it appears to me that you have conducted a very thorough investigation, and we concur with your finding, or at least that the German citizens Karl Messerschmitt and Dieter Spunkmeyer are persons-of-interest in this case. Spunkmeyer also holds an Albanian passport." This did not seem important, so Martinez just nodded.

"As stated, both men are German nationals and as such we can't conduct a routine investigation, nor can we plan to extradite for the sole purpose of said interrogation. However, we can still indict them if the evidence is submitted to a grand jury." She continued as if she were reading from a script, "Since it became aware to us that your investigation and suspicions led to foreign nationals, our office contacted both the German embassy in New York and the council general's office in Miami. Both are adamant that we do not pursue extradition until their citizens can be interviewed by their authorities. They claim that they will have law enforcement in Germany arrange an interview with Mr. Messerschmitt. Soon after that conversation, we were contacted by the International Law Firm of MacLeod and Mone. Ever heard of them, Detective?"

Lydia did not want to disclose what Dio had told her, so she played dumb. "No, can't say that I have."

"MacLeod and Mone are one of the largest law firms in Europe. They have over five hundred lawyers based in every country in Europe and specialize in all aspects of international law. The firm's criminal law division has defended many defendants accused of war crimes, most notably Radovan Karadzic and Ratko Mladic, both convicted of genocide in Srebrenica and crimes against humanity during the war in the former Yugoslavia in the early '90s. In addition, the firm has defended several high-profile European drug dealers, members of human trafficking gangs, and even a terrorist. The firm is referred to by its clients as the M&Ms, after the initials of the founding partners Malcolm MacLeod and Mathias Mone. The firm does not have a presence in the United States, but they did contact us through a local criminal law firm Corcoran, Denihan, and O'Shea. You've probably heard their sales jingles on TV and the radio. The firm handles all forms of criminal cases from homicide to traffic infractions."

"So what did they say?"

"They want us to cease and desist any further investigation on their client Karl Messerschmitt until such time as the German authorities conclude their interview with Messerschmitt."

"Did they say when that would be?"

"No, but don't count on it being done any time soon."

"What about the other guy, Spunkmeyer? Did they mention anything about him?"

"No, they only told me he has dual citizenship. His mom is Albanian. I didn't see how that was relevant, but I didn't push it."

Lydia didn't understand what she meant by that, but as long as some progress is being made, she decided to hold back and let Nancy handle her side of the street. "So where does that leave us and the Dollbee family, who only want justice for their slain daughter?"

"You can cut the soap opera dramatics, Detective. We are all on the same page here."

Lydia just nodded knowing she was being overly dramatic. "The state attorney's office is interested in seeing justice in this case just as you are, but there are extenuating circumstances involved here, all of which I just outlined. Just as a point of information, I spoke to George Goll from The Florida Classic to confirm that Messerschmitt did withdraw from the competition, further implicating him in this crime."

"And?"

"He said that his organization, the PGA of America, and the AMC Corporation all concur that we should proceed with our investigation. He didn't have to say now that the tournament is over, but I sensed that's how he felt."

CHAPTER 34

It took about a week, but it was finally decided between the state attorney's office (Nancy Heichemer), the PBSO (Rick Romain and Lieutenant Cashin), and the department of state that the case would remain open and under continued investigation. Martinez was told that she would turn over the case to the newly formed Cold Case Squad (CCS). This further pissed off Martinez, as the case was less than a month old, which was unusual for a case to be deemed cold. This is what she expected when she told Ken Dollbee that he may have to get vocal during the funeral services. As she suspected, nobody wanted to put pressure on the German authorities to interview Messerschmitt—nobody but her, and she was determined to do so.

She put in a call to Colleen Adams. "Colleen, can you tell me what happened?"

"One minute you're telling me to pack my bags. Next thing I know the case goes cold. What the fuck happened?"

"Not sure, but Heichemer, my boss, and your boss were all on board to have you continue the investigation and fly over to Germany. Once the state department got involved, then things went sideways. I'm not sure what happened or who said what—way above my pay grade."

"That sucks, Colleen."

"Yeah, I know, but like I said they (whoever they are) tied our hands."

"Maybe, but I'm not letting it go."

"What does that mean Lydia? Let's not lose sight of your career here. And I strongly suggest you don't do something stupid like go to the media. You know department policy of that."

"No, don't worry. I'm aware of department policy."

Colleen could detect the sarcasm in her voice. After a pause Colleen continued, "So what are you gonna do?"

"I don't know. I got plenty of time on the books, plus vacation. Maybe I'll take off and go visit Dio in London."

"That's a great idea." Colleen knew the best thing for Lydia, and for her, was for Lydia to get away and let this case proceed without her.

CHAPTER 35

When Lydia walked into the homicide office, it was like a scene from an old TV western. Everyone stopped what they were doing and looked at her. Frank Kiers and Ed Telmany were both at their cubicles working. Franks and Beans were standing by the coffee machine discussing why they think everyone should chip in to buy a Keurig coffee dispenser and the cost involved.

"Hi, fellas. Do I have a wardrobe malfunction here? Why are you all starting at me?"

"Oh hi, Martinez," replied Kiers, "No, we were just surprised to see you, right Ed?"

He turned to Fat Eddy, "Yeah we're all happy to see you, that's all."

"Boy, if bullshit was dollars, you guys would be rich."

They all chuckled and went back to what they were doing. Jerry "Franks" Nathans, who was probably the closest of all the other guys to Martinez, came over to her and in his fatherly way said to her, "We all agree that they shafted you on this case. But you know as well as we all do that politics plays a big part in what we do."

"Not in homicide, Jerry, that's not what I believe. I'm as sure as shit that this Messerschmitt guy is involved in this homicide and is probably the doer. Every bit of evidence I gathered points to him and his caddy. Whatever the reason, the department pulling the plug on me is pure bullshit. You know it, he knows it (pointing to Lieutenant Cashin's office), and the whole fucking department knows it."

Nathans just shook his head and walked back to his partner and continued on with their conversation. Beans went on, "So if all of us pony up twenty dollars each, we can buy one of those Keurig coffee makers and have fresh coffee any time we want. I'm getting tired of drinking this stale shit. What do you guys think?" he asked the other detectives.

Fat Eddy replied, "So who's gonna go buy the coffee when those pods run out? Do we start another *whose-up-next list* like we do with cases?" Kiers laughed at that and said, "Maybe the department will buy us a new coffee pot. I'm mean we're the best detectives in the whole damn state of Florida."

Lieutenant Cashin came out of his office. "Don't you guys have more important things to do than discuss the coffee situation here? Martinez, in my office." She got up from her cubicle. All eyes followed her into Cashin's office. "Don't take this the wrong way, Martinez, but you got screwed on the Dollbee case. I'm not sure what happened, but the word came from higher than the department. Sounds real hinky to me."

"That's OK, Lou. Listen I'm thinking of taking some time off. Now that the Dollbee case has been handed over to the CCS."

"That's a good idea, Martinez. Just be sure you hand over everything you got on Dollbee and get it over to Detective..." Cashin looked at a paper on his desk, "Detective Fran Budrow at CCS. You know her?" Martinez shook her head no. "She'll be handling it from here on in. You may want to give her a verbal in addition to your paperwork."

"Will do, Lieutenant. I'll call her as soon as I send over all my reports." Unbeknownst to Cashin, Martinez sent copies of all her reports to her personal computer, and from there she routed them to Dio in London.

"So how much time are you thinking of taking off?"

"Well I've got a month's vacation, plus another ten or twelve days of comp time. So let's say five to six weeks. But if things heat up I will come back sooner."

127

"That should be OK. I got a call from Chris Clarkson, and he's been cleared to return to work on light duty. Plus, he told me his wife and kids are driving him crazy, so he's anxious to get back. We'll be fine here."

"OK, so I'll finish up and be on my way. You have my cell if you need me." She could sense Cashin's relief when she told him she would be gone for a while.

CHAPTER 36

Lydia returned to her apartment and her first call was to Dio. He answered in his usual professional manner, "Dio Bosso."

"Hi, D, how are you doing?"

"Great, Lyd, I've got some additional info on our boy Messerschmitt. I was just gonna call you."

"Hold that thought. I just booked a flight to London. I'm leaving Miami the day after tomorrow. I have a 2:00 p.m. flight on Delta and should arrive at Heathrow at 9:00 p.m. your time. Can you arrange to pick me up or should I get a cab?"

Dio was so excited he didn't know what to say. "No, I mean, that's great. No, don't get a cab. I'll pick you up. How long you gonna be here? I mean, you can stay as long as you like."

"D, please calm down."

"Sorry, just didn't expect this, but it's wonderful that you're coming. By the way, I got the reports you forwarded to me, but I haven't had time to go over them. Are you coming on official business?"

"No, they sent my case to the Cold Case Squad, which reminds me, I've got to contact the detective assigned and brief her on it. I will text you all my flight info and, Dio, I am really looking forward to being with you."

"Me too, Lyd, I've missed you terribly."

"OK, I got a ton of shit to do, so goodbye for now. I call you before I leave for London."

"Bye." Dio sat back in his office chair and just smiled. He was so happy that Lydia was finally coming to see him again. It had been over a month since he saw her in Florida, now she would be here in two days. He knew why she was coming. She was determined to get to the bottom of the Dollbee case and learn if and how Karl Messerschmitt murdered Jasmin Dollbee. But he was also pleased that she would be staying with him and they would work this case unofficially and hopefully see that justice was done.

CHAPTER 37

Once Lydia made up her mind about taking the vacation and accepted the fact that the Dollbee homicide was shit-canned to Cold Case, she knew she had a lot to do in the next day and a half. First, she called Detective Budrow to set up a meeting to hand over the case. She also put in a call to Ken Dollbee and asked if she could stop by at a convenient time to discuss the progress (or lack thereof) on his daughter's murder. He suggested that they meet for lunch at Johnathan's Landing (JL) Golf Club where he had just recently joined, "They have a nice outside patio dining area, and I'd like to buy you lunch to show our appreciation of how you handled this whole terrible time for my family."

Martinez thought that he might not feel the same way when she told him the case had been reassigned to CCS, but she believed she owed him that. Plus she wanted him to know her plans and for him to start putting pressure on the department and the state's attorney to keep the case active.

She met with Detective Budrow at the Cold Case Squad, which was located on the fourth floor of the headquarters building on Gun Club Road. At first she was surprised how tiny Detective Budrow was—no more than five-foot-two and probably 100–105 pounds. Martinez figured she was about thirty-five to forty years old and wondered how she ever carried all of that equipment on her tiny waist when she was a patrol deputy.

"Hi, Detective, I'm Lydia Martinez. We spoke on the phone."

"Fran Budrow, nice to meet you, Lydia. I've heard a lot about you."

"Good I hope." After they explained pleasantries, Lydia got down to business. She told Budrow all of what she had done, all of which was in the file.

Budrow just nodded and after Martinez finished said, "I read all the reports and I must say you did a very thorough job here. I can't imagine why they sent this case to me. The crime only took place less than two weeks ago. Usually they don't send us cases until three, four, five months out. Anything I should know here off the record?"

"Well as you can see, all my leads led to this German golfer Karl Messerschmitt and his caddy Dieter Spunkmeyer. I think for some reason someone wants to stonewall the investigation. That's why it got dumped on you."

Detective Budrow just nodded.

"Are you on someone's shit list or do you guys just catch cases on a rotating basis?"

Budrow didn't answer. She detected the sarcasm in Martinez' comment. "So you think anything I will do with this case is a waste of time? Is that what you're telling me?"

"No, that's not what I'm saying. You may find something I missed, but I will tell you this. Anything new you find will still point to Messerschmitt and Spunkmeyer. That much I'm certain of."

Budrow stood up to signal the meeting was over. Extending her hand, "Thanks, Lydia, I have your contact information here should I need to reach out to you." Lydia could see that although Budrow was small, it was quite evident she worked out. Her thin arms showed definition that indicated she was a lifter, and Martinez noticed that there was not an ounce of fat on her petite body. Martinez did not bother to tell her she would be out of town for the next five to six weeks—not that it mattered.

On her way out, she paused and turned to Detective Budrow, "Fran, one word of caution." Budrow looked up.

"When you interview the Van Hooey kid, be sure to wear a wedding ring. He's got a thing for older lady detectives." She smiled to herself and walked out.

CHAPTER 38

When she met with Ken Dollbee, she was surprised to see that he seemed more reconciled to the fact that his daughter was gone. The pain she saw in his face that first time at the morgue and the funereal seemed to be gone. He stood up when she was shown to his table and she could tell by his clothes that he had probably played golf prior to their meeting.

"Thanks for seeing me here, Detective. I'm finding it harder and harder to be around Pat and the girls. I keep telling them we have to move on, but it's harder for them I guess than it is for me."

Martinez just nodded. A waitress came over and handed Lydia a menu. She had an accent that Lydia could not discern right away, but her nametag stated the name Edrei and that she was from South Africa.

Ken noticed her looking at the nametag and said, "A lot of the clubs hire international workers during the season. They come here on a work visa. They are great workers and know how to wait tables and treat people."

Lydia looked at the menu and when Edrei returned she ordered a small Asian salad. Ken said he would have the same and another Coors Light. Lydia order an iced tea.

Ken was making small talk about why he decided to leave PGA National and join JL. She assumed that JL meant Jonathans Landing, but she wasn't really paying attention. She had a lot of packing to do and was thinking that she would probably stop at The Home Depot, pick up a box or two, and ship her clothes to Dio's apartment. The thought of lugging two suitcases through security and passport control did not appeal to her in the least. Finally, Ken stopped talking about golf and asked her if there were any new developments.

"Have you ever heard of a golfer named Karl Messerschmitt, from Germany?"

"Yes, but only because Jasmin was the standard bearer for his group during the pro-am and the two rounds before." He paused as a sadness returned to his face. "Do you think he has something to do with her…" he paused not wanting to say the word, "murder?"

"Let's just say that the evidence indicates that he is a person-of-interest. And the fact he withdrew from The Classic and returned to Germany makes me more suspicious."

"Well can't you go after him. I mean, Germany is an ally, right?"

"It's not that easy Ken, er, I mean Mr. Dollbee."

"Ken is fine. Please go on."

"You told me Jasmin always wore the gold anklet with the charm. Did you or your wife happen to find it in her room? It wasn't on her…" she paused thinking of how she wanted to say "leg when we found her. I had the surrounding area searched, and it was not found."

"No, we haven't gone through her things yet, but she wore that bracelet all the time, I can tell you that."

Changing the subject Lydia continued, "Remember at Jasmin's funeral I mentioned that at some point you may have to become her advocate with the sheriff's office and the state's attorney?" He just nodded. "Well, the case has been moved to the Cold Case Squad. I have given all of the evidence I have gleaned from my investigation and interviews to a detective named Fran Budrow. She will be handling the case from here on. You'll probably be getting a call from her soon."

"What?" His voice grew louder, "You're telling me you are giving up? I thought you said you have evidence pointed to this Messerschmitt. I don't understand."

"It's complicated. That's why I need you to start making noise."

He gave her a quizzical look. "What do you mean?"

"Has anyone from the media tried to contact you?"

"Yes, but we just said, "no comment" as you suggested early on.

"Do you have a family lawyer, or a friend who might be a lawyer?"

"You think we need a lawyer, Detective?"

"Well it might be better if a family lawyer starts to ask questions as to why the case has been reassigned to the Cold Case Squad after only a short time since the murder."

"What about you, Detective? Can't you speak out?"

"I already did and look where it got me. Listen, Mr. Dollbee, Ken, I'm not saying the department or the state's attorney are dropping the ball here. I think that because this crime may involve a foreign national, who is back in his home country, that they are exploring ways to interview Messerschmitt in Germany, but I'm not sure how that works."

Martinez did not reveal that she was planning to travel to Europe *unofficially* and see what she could do there. "I believe that if you, through an attorney, question the wisdom of the case going cold, some pressure could be applied to both the sheriff and the state's attorney."

"I see, but what about you?"

"Well, first of all, we never had this conversation. I will continue to assist CCS on this as best I can. The next move is yours, Ken. You have to make some noise, and now is the time."

Ken just shook his head. Edrei brought their lunch and they made small talk, mostly Ken talking about golf.

CHAPTER 39

Martinez left Ken Dollbee at Jonathan's Landing and returned to the homicide office to finish up some paperwork and put in a call to Dio to bring him up to date. After she explained all that transpired, he told her what he had learned from Kurt Gropp at Interpol concerning Karl Messerschmitt. "How long do you think you will be staying, Lyd?"

"Are you worried I might overstay my welcome, D?"

"Not at all, Lydia. I'm thrilled you're coming, and you can stay as long as you like. The reason I ask is I want to be sure to schedule my work so that I can assist you in your case. Am I correct in assuming you plan on pursuing this unofficially while you're here and not just coming to see me?"

"Why Dio Bosso, you give yourself so little credit," she said mockingly. "Of course you are right, but I could not think of a better way to work this case unofficially than with such a handsome, sexy, and talented investigator like you." Without waiting for a response, she continued, "I will send you my flight info once it's finalized. I still may get some *official* support from my department and the state's attorney, but I'm not counting on it. Oh, and one last thing, Dio."

"Sure Lyd, what's that?"

"I'll be shipping a box or two of clothes over. You know, raincoat, sweaters, and the like. Things we don't usually need here in sunny south Florida."

"Not a problem, I have plenty of closet space in the spare bedrooms, so ship whatever you want."

"You're making me stay in the spare bedroom?" she said coyly.

"Well we'll see. If you pack some sexy nightclothes, maybe I'll let you sleep in my bed." They both enjoyed this back and forth sexual banter. They chatted a bit more and finally Dio said, "I can't wait to see you Lydia. I've missed you and will so enjoy you being here."

"I miss you too, Dio."

After she hung up, Lieutenant Cashin called her on her desk phone and asked her to step into his office. "What's up, Lieutenant?"

"Looks like your vic's father has hired a lawyer, who in turn is speaking to the TV people about his daughter's murder being reassigned to Cold Case. You wouldn't know anything about that would you, Martinez?"

"Me? No, Lou, but I'm not surprised. I guess they want justice for their daughter, unlike this department and the state's attorney office."

"Hold on, Martinez, that kind of talk will do none of us any good. You know the situation we are in here. With your suspect being a foreign national and out of the country, there is not much we can do, is there?"

"You're asking me, Lieutenant? Yes, there is something we can do. Go public with Karl Messerschmitt being a person of interest. Demand the German authorities make him available for questioning. He can come here and play golf as a professional, earn a ton of money, and not be held accountable or at least explain his actions? Yes, that's what we could and should do."

Cashin just gave her a look and sighed. "But instead you shit-can it to Cold Case and tell me to go on vacation, and now you want me to explain why the family is questioning our actions." Martinez purposely said our actions as opposed to your actions. No point pissing him off more than he already was.

Cashin changed the subject. "So I signed your vacation request. When are you leaving?"

"As soon as I book my flight and pack."

"Going anywhere special?"

"Yes, Europe. I'll be staying in London but traveling to Germany." She left without waiting for Cashin's response.

CHAPTER 40

Martinez's flight from Miami International to London's Heathrow Airport was uneventful. Dio arranged to use some of his points to upgrade her to first class, which made the nine-hour flight more relaxing. Although she slept most of the way, she did spend time thinking about how she would get to interview Karl Messerschmitt. She was not going to be in Europe in an official capacity, and she was aware of the fact that Messerschmitt's family and attorney had gone into a full defensive mode. Even the local authorities were having a difficult time trying to question Messerschmitt.

She was also somewhat apprehensive about seeing Dio. After all, it had been over a month and she wasn't sure how she would respond. Sure, their phone conversations were enjoyable and relaxed, but she was a bit apprehensive about spending an open-ended amount of time with him. Closing her eyes, she just tried to clear her mind. To herself she thought, I'm on vacation, just enjoy it. If Dio can help me get to Messerschmitt—great; if not, so what? They sent my homicide to Cold Case. Let them worry about it. As fast as those thoughts entered her mind, they were that quick to leave. She knew why she was coming here. Sure, Dio is a wonderful man and I may even be falling in love with him. But who said I can't mix pleasure with business? These were her last thoughts as she drifted off to sleep in the roomy, fully reclined first-class seat.

Dio was sitting in his office going over all the things he wanted to share with Lydia—the information her learned from Kurt Gropp concerning Karl Messerschmitt. He was excited about them working together and perhaps solving another homicide. He also shared the same apprehension as Lydia concerning their relationship. It's been a while, he thought to himself. Her flight was due to arrive around 8:00 p.m. London time, and Dio knew that Lydia's body clock would be five hours ahead. So instead of making a reservation at one of London's finer restaurants, he decided to go home first, change into something casual, and then drive to the airport. Through his contacts at the metro police, he was able to gain access to the customs and passport control area so he would be able to greet her and expedite the process. He had also received the boxes of clothing she shipped via FedEx and placed them in one of the other bedrooms of his condo.

Lydia was able to freshen up in the first-class lounge before deplaning. As she walked into the customs and passport control area, she spotted Dio right away. He was carrying a bouquet of fresh flowers. Both their faces lit up in big smiles as they walked toward each other and embraced.

"It's so good to see you, Martinez."

"Nice to be seen, D. How are you?" She looked over his dress shirt and slacks but did not want to comment on his dressing down. She figured she would have plenty of time to bust his shoes over the next several weeks.

They parted. "We'd better get you over to customs. You have anything to declare?"

"Nope, just clothing and cosmetics. I sent the sexy undies in the box, along with my gun," she said with that sheepish grin Dio loved.

"Ok, let's go right to passport control. They have your name and you can hand in that customs form there. A colleague of mine was able to get me access to this area so I could get you out lickety-split." Within forty minutes of landing in London, Lydia and Dio were in his Bentley heading back to Mayfair.

"Nice ride, D."

"Oh it's a company car. I don't drive it too often. I mean, well they gave me a driver, so I mostly sit back there (he

141

motioned with his thumb) and work." He was uncomfortable talking about his new lifestyle to her but didn't know why. He was the same guy she met over a year ago. His reluctance to talk about his life of ease was natural for someone brought up the way he was.

They made small talk the rest of the drive to Dio's condo in Mayfair. They both seemed a little apprehensive. Dio told her that he figured she ate well on the plane and decided not to plan a dinner, not wanting to upset her body clock.

"That's fine, D. Why don't we just go back to the apartment and get to know one another again."

He caught that sheepish grin in her eye as she reached over and placed her hand on his thigh. He could feel himself getting aroused, something he had not felt since they last were together. He just smiled and continued the drive.

CHAPTER 41

Their lovemaking that night started almost as soon as they got into the apartment. Lydia was the aggressor this time, kissing him hard and full as soon as she took her coat off.

"Do you want a drink or something, Lyd?"

"No, I just want you to fuck me."

This was the first time he heard Lydia use this term, and it increased his arousal. He carried her into the bedroom, both clumsily trying to undress each other while maintain the kiss. For the next thirty or so minutes, they made love. The passion that poured out of Martinez seemed to come from deep within her body, as if some suppressed emotional volcano had erupted. Although he was caught by surprise by the ferocity of her lovemaking, he responded with equal vigor. When they finally climaxed, both moaning and covered in sweat, Lydia was on top. She rolled over to her side breathing heavily and laughing slightly said, "Oh my god, Dio, that was so good. I needed that so bad, D. You can't imagine how I needed for you to make love to me."

Dio was pleased with himself but more than just an ego boost, he truly felt passion and pleasure unlike what he had experienced with Celia. Why do I have to compare everything she does to Celia? Can't I let it go? he thought to himself.

"D, you OK?"

"Sure, Lyd, I'm great." He learned over and kissed her, and she turned her back to him and got into a spoon position, which is how they slept. She snuggled her bare butt next to his crotch, just in the right position where his now flaccid dick snuggled between her cheeks. This is great, he thought.

"You've had a long day, Lyd. Why don't you try to sleep and tomorrow we can go over all of the stuff I learned." Before he could finish, he felt Lydia's breathing become more rhythmic. He looked over at her and saw she was asleep, a smile on her face. He kissed her on her forehead and softly said, "I'm so happy you're here, Martinez. You're really something else."

CHAPTER 42

Lydia awoke to the smell of fresh brewed coffee and the distinct aroma of bacon. Getting out of bed she reached for the terry cloth robe Dio placed at the foot of the bed. What service, she thought to herself. After washing her face, brushing her teeth, and combing her hair, she followed the scent of breakfast into the kitchen. Dio's apartment was spectacular, with views overlooking Hyde Park on the west and the Thames on the east. Dio was already dressed in gray slacks and a blue dress shirt opened at the collar. He was busy tending the bacon when Lydia walked over and gave him a hug from behind and a kiss on the back of his neck. "You keep that up young lady and we'll never get started today. How do you want your eggs? Do you still like them over easy?"

"It hasn't been that long, D," she said with a smile. Dio finished the eggs as Lydia poured herself a cup of coffee. She always liked it black, but since dating Dio, she started to add a little honey and fresh milk just as he did.

"I've arranged my schedule so I can spend as much time with you as you can take, Martinez. I assumed that you want to continue with your unofficial investigation of The Florida Classic homicide?"

"Your damn right I do. I'm still a bit pissed about the way the case was shit-canned to the Cold Case Squad. I don't know the detectives assigned to Cold Case, but I spoke to one. Her name is Fran Budrow, and I get a sense she knows what she's doing. But I don't think she will find anything different than my investigation did." Lydia continued talking about the case as they ate the bacon and eggs Dio prepared. She talked about all the evidence she had on Messerschmitt: the victim's DNA on the shoe bag she found in his hotel room, the mud and gravel from the interior of the car, and the slivers of shoe bag material. She went into detail repeating what Stacey had told her about the diatoms. Dio just listened and did not comment. He just nodded as he took in the information. There was so much evidence implicating Messerschmitt and his caddy. When breakfast was done, Lydia got up to clear the table and Dio went into the living room.

"When you finish, grab a fresh coffee and join me in the living room. There is something I want you to see."

"Let me hop in the shower and put some clothes on first, D." When she returned to the living room, Dio had the TV on and had a tape cued up on the screen.

"I gave a lot of thought to the information you gave me about The Florida Classic homicide, and I want you to know that I don't disagree with your assumptions and conclusions. But during my career in the NYPD, I always liked having a fresh set of eyes look at evidence, especially when that fresh set of eyes was mine. Now I want you to understand that what I'm about to show you does not dispute your findings, but I think you'll find my analysis interesting."

"Dio, please, stop being so formal. I'm not offended by anything you may think. I know you're doing this for me, and I appreciate it. So stop apologizing for something you may not need to apologize for."

"Good enough. So during your investigation, you never mentioned that you looked at any video of the actual golf tournament to see if your victim and suspect had any interaction other than the fact that she was a standard bearer for Messerschmitt's group during the pro-am and the first two rounds of the event. I made some calls and learned that the TV coverage of the entire tournament was provided by either the Golf Channel or CBS Sports. Unfortunately, any footage of the Messerschmitt group was deleted as nobody in that group, other than Messerschmitt, played golf worthy of airtime. I did

146

however, through my contact at Interpol, learn that Sky TV, which is a British-owned, subscription sports network did have a camera crew following Messerschmitt during the pro-am and the first two rounds. They even commented on his abrupt withdrawal." Dio could see Lydia was getting impatient, but this was his methodical way of introducing evidence that may shed some light on the murder. "OK, so what we are going to view now is Messerschmitt playing in the pro-am and the first two rounds of golf." He used the remote to bring the video up on the seventy-two inch Samsung TV. He let the tape play through the introductions and the three players' first tee shots.

"Now I'm going to fast-forward and show you a few things I think you'll find important." He pressed the fast-forward button on the remote and stopped at one point. "See this, Lydia. This is just after Messerschmitt's second shot on the first hole. In the top of the screen you can see your victim carrying the standard. Look at Messerschmitt's caddie looking at her. He is walking directly behind her."

He froze the frame and enlarged the picture. You could see the caddy walking closer to Jasmin Dollbee than his golfer Messerschmitt. Dio then fast-forwarded the tape several more times and froze the picture several times. Each time you could see Messerschmitt's caddie either talking to or staring at Jasmin. Messerschmitt on the other hand was pretty much ignoring not only her but the other golfers in the pro-am as well as his two playing partners during the first two rounds. Lydia just sat there looking at the frozen picture of Jasmin Dollbee. Once again, she was saddened seeing the young pretty blonde so alive and full of life. It was troubling knowing Jasmin would be brutally murdered and raped within a day or two.

"That's amazing, Dio."

"Wait, Lyd, I want to show you something else." He pressed the fast-forward again to the start of the second round. On the first tee you could see Messerschmitt almost admonishing his caddy and pointing toward Jasmin. The caddy just smirked and nodded, and they went about playing the round.

"I played the entire tape and did not find anything like I did earlier, as far as the caddy *ogling* Jasmin, so I assume that Messerschmitt gave him an ass-chewing before the round. I did find one more thing interesting that I want you to see." He fast-forwarded to the last hole and zoomed in on the caddy giving Jasmin a signed golf glove. In the zoom mode you could see two things: the caddy's deformed right hand and the frightened look on Jasmin Dollbee's face.

"D roll back the tape a bit. I want you to stop just before the caddy gave Jasmin the glove. Good, stop. Now can you zoom in on Jasmin's right leg?"

"Yeah, sure." As he did so, Lydia pointed out to him the gold anklet on the right leg. Jasmin was wearing no-show socks and the anklet was clearly visible.

"See that, D, the ankle bracelet?"

"Yep."

"Well when I arrived on the scene, the right leg was sticking out of the water." She opened her phone and showed Dio the photos of the body. "You see, the ankle bracelet is missing. Her dad told me she always wore it."

Playing devil's advocate, Dio responded, "Maybe it fell off in the struggle or fell into the pond."

"Not likely. I had crime scene double-check the area, and our divers found nothing in the pond."

"Maybe your doer took it as a souvenir. Good observation, Detective."

Moving on Lydia asked, "Were you able to find out about the caddy, Dio?"

"Yes, again my contacts at both Interpol and the German police were very helpful. Messerschmitt's caddy is named Dieter Spunkmeyer. He was a top-ranked amateur and played with Messerschmitt for several years in the '90s on the German national youth team. He was at one time as good as golfer as Messerschmitt, but he had some sort of accident or incident that led to the deformed right hand. He has been Messerschmitt's caddy ever since. Unlike Messerschmitt, whose family is very wealthy, Spunkmeyer came from the former East Germany from a lower-class working family."

Lydia just shook her head. "Wow, Dio, this Spunkmeyer fits the script of the guy driving the AMC Ranger the night of the murder, so I know he was involved but I thought as an accomplice not the actual doer. Do you have anything else?"

"Not at the moment, but my Interpol contact, by the way his name is Kurt Gropp, is going to meet with us in Lyon, France, tomorrow, that is, if you want."

"If I want? Fuck yeah, I want. Can we get more info on this Spunkmeyer guy?"

"Well like I said. He's been Messerschmitt's caddy for about fifteen years or so. By the way, Lyd, does the name Messerschmitt mean anything to you?"

"You mean outside the investigation? No, should it?"

"No, you're too young to remember, but Messerschmitt's grandfather manufactured airplanes for the Germany Luftwaffe during the Second World War. Spent some time in prison afterward. But still made a fortune in the postwar West German economy."

"Interesting. Do we know if either Messerschmitt or Spunkmeyer have records?" she stopped herself realizing it was a dumb question. Dio however did not think so.

"It's different here than in the states as far as public access to criminal records, especially youthful offenders and doubly different if you're from the upper class like Karl Messerschmitt."

"What about the other guy? She laughed, "I can't say his name without it seeming funny, Spunkmeyer. He must have gotten his balls broken in school."

Dio did not pick up the connection or pretended not to. "You know, Lyd, the class system still exists here in Europe, or at least in the western part. It seems that people accept that and work within that system. Sure, I imagine some kids from the lower classes who are bright are able to rise up to a certain station in life, but for the most part not. I think it is more prevalent here in England than in mainland Europe. But we shall see."

"Sort of like Blacks and Latinos in the states," she said sarcastically. They spent the rest of the morning reviewing the reports that Lydia had copied and sent to Dio on her private home computer. After lunch they made love again. They were both beginning to feel more comfortable with each other's bodies.

Before they went out for dinner, Lydia called Detective Budrow at the Cold Case Squad. Budrow was not there but she got her partner on the phone. "Cold Case, Detective Stitzel," answered a female voice.

"Hi, Detective, this is Detective Martinez from district three homicide, is Detective Budrow there?"

"No, I'm sorry but she's not. I'm her partner. Are you calling about the Dollbee case?"

"Yes, I am. Has any progress been made?"

Without answering her directly, Stitzel said, "I thought you were on vacation and off this case." Lydia was taken aback by her abruptness.

"Well yes to both those questions, but I have some additional information that I thought Detective Budrow might find interesting."

"Just tell me and I will pass it along. We are working the case together you know."

Martinez did not only dislike her abruptness, now she didn't like her tone. "Tell Fran I called. She has my cell," Lydia just hung up without waiting for a response.

CHAPTER 43

They dined that evening at The Ledbury in Notting Hill. Lydia was in a playful mood and right away got on Dio about being the only guy in the restaurant wearing a tie. Their conversation went from casual small talk about each other's careers to the current case they were about to jointly embark on.

"I hope we have as much success as we did with the *Green Violinist*. I wonder how that weasel DeAngelis is doing."

"I'm surprised you're not pen pals, since you let him walk on my homicide."

"Do I detect a note of sarcasm, Detective Martinez? Don't forget we did learn who the perps were, and they were prosecuted in New York. Once they get out of prison in twenty-five years or so, then Florida will have its shot. If they are still alive. And, I might add, DeAngelis had nothing to do with the actual homicides."

"Yeah, I know. But he was still responsible for getting those two local knuckleheads, Barth and Penny, involved in the burglary, which led to their murders."

Wanting to change the subject he picked up the menu just as the sommelier brought over the bottle of Opus One that Dio had ordered.

"Nice."

"Shall we order?"

After dinner they went back to the apartment, and after a nightcap of brandy, they went to bed and made love. For each of them it was the most sex they had in so short a period. As they lay on their backs, Lydia touched the scar on Dio's right shoulder. She knew that this was scar from a bullet wound. She figured the raised scars on his back were shrapnel wounds. "Dio, you never spoke to me about your time in the service."

"And you never told me about your time in the service," he replied. "Funny we both served our country in different wars. These scars are all I have. I mean I never had nightmares or PTSD like so many other guys from Nam. I guess it's because up until those last few weeks, I had it pretty good. Being assigned to the embassy in Saigon was considered a tit job. Oops sorry, Lyd, didn't mean to be so crass," as he fondled her nipple. "I bet you saw more shit than I did in your tours in Iraq and Afghanistan."

She didn't reply, just snuggled up close to him and ran her hand down his chest and let it rest on his now semi hard dick. "Yeah but at least we were thanked for our service when we came home. I worked with a couple of guys when I was a rookie who were in Vietnam. They told me all the shit they got when they came home. You know the baby-killer taunts."

"Yep. I got some taunts when I got back to the states. But the war was over and I was only home two weeks before I went into the police academy. I believed then and still do now that most of those protesters were a bunch of draft-dodging cowards. Imagine going to Canada to avoid serving your country. I knew two guys who were Quakers—opposed to war but served in noncombat roles."

As she drifted off to sleep, Dio's thoughts raced back to his last days in Vietnam.

CHAPTER 44

US EMBASSY, SAIGON—APRIL 1975

The security detail for the US Embassy in Saigon was tasked to the US Marines and US Air Force military police. Twenty-year-old Staff Sergeant Dio Bosso was in charge of a squad of Air Force military police that provided perimeter security for the embassy compound and conducted patrols of Saigon. The marines were responsible for the interior of several buildings in the compound and also served as protection for visiting dignitaries and sometimes as drivers. There were also several *civilian* security personnel that Dio assumed were either state department or CIA (Central Intelligence Agency).

Everyone at the embassy knew the war was lost, and since the Tet Offensive in 1968, the tide had turned in favor of the Vietcong (VC) and the North Vietnamese Army (NVA). In attempts to obtain "peace with honor," President Nixon halted the bombing of North Vietnam. Secretary of State Henry Kissinger was in Paris at the peace talks.

During the last week of April, the entire military staff at the embassy was placed on twenty-four-hour alert. Nonessential personnel were evacuated, and a sense of doom permeated throughout the compound. Most Vietnamese civilians who worked for the Americans were trying desperately to seek asylum inside the embassy or make their way out of the country. On the morning of April 28, Dio could hear the thunderous sounds of cannons and howitzers being fired on the villages surrounding Saigon.

Dio ordered his men to dig in. The men worked hard placing sandbags around the perimeter of the compound and digging foxholes to prepare for an attack. To Dio it seemed surreal, as locals were seen leaving town carrying as much of their belongings as they could fit in the vehicles or horse-drawn carts. Smoke was billowing from Tan Son Nhat International Airport just miles from the embassy. Boeing CH-47 Chinook helicopters were flying in and out taking personnel to the super carrier USS *Kitty Hawk* (CV-63) in the South China Sea. Dio had been in country for eleven months.

Most of his duties involved setting schedules for his squad and patrolling the streets of downtown Saigon breaking up fights between drunk servicemen on *R and R* or fights between servicemen and locals. Orders were to not interfere with the local authorities. If a service member got into a scape with a local or refused to pay a hooker, it was his problem. But Dio had a good working relationship with the local police commander, Colonel Tron. The monthly bottle of Johnnie Walker Black that Dio gave the commander went a long way. Most disputes with locals were settled with a payoff by the offending GI.

Prostitution was also rampant, but the military had a hands-off policy as long as violence wasn't an issue. STDs were rampant among the soldiers stationed in Saigon, mostly cases of the clap or crabs, which could be treated by the medics assigned to the detachment. Yep, Dio thought to himself, I had a pretty good run here compared to what other guys went through. This would be the first time he would face danger from the enemy as opposed to some drunk GI, who wanted to fight the cops. In every one of those instances, Dio and his colleagues would just convince the offender that this was not the way to go. Dio was good at using his baton to get a drunk's attention. In most cases a whack on the knees was enough. The military had a *drunk tank*, where they would let GIs sleep it off. Only in the most severe cases would charges be filed. The policy was especially lenient toward soldiers who had spent time in the field and needed to let off some steam.

On April 29, the NVA had reached the outskirts of Saigon. At the embassy, almost everyone who needed to go was gone. Ambassador Graham Martin was the last civilian to leave. Inside the embassy pandemonium reigned as marines and airmen kept busy shredding documents and destroying computers and telecommunications equipment. Hundreds of Vietnamese civilians were crushing at the gates hoping to get in and be airlifted out. Dio had several marines and air police on the gate trying to hold back the throngs of screaming civilians. Dio knew, as did they, that once the city fell, they would be executed for working for the American government. Dio had sympathy for them but there was nothing he could do.

He now had to ensure the safety of his own men. The first shell that landed in the compound killed the two officers who outranked him. Dio knew that he was now in a position to make decisions that his life and the lives of his men depended on. To say the scene was chaotic is an understatement. People were running in every direction. One Chinook was hit with an RPG (rocket-propelled grenade) but managed to stay aloft and made it out of the range of fire.

Dio didn't know if he and the remaining GIs would get out. From his position inside the compound, Dio could see a company of Army of the Republic of Vietnam (ARVN) troops arrive in a deuce-and-a-half truck. They mostly were pushing the people around the gate trying to gain access to the compound. Dio like most GIs had very little respect for the ARVN. Their officers were incompetent to a man and were corrupt as well. The soldiers themselves were poorly trained and most were now becoming sympathetic to the VC and NVA. Using his PRC-25 radio, Dio contacted the *Kitty Hawk* and gave a situation report (Sit-Rep). He was ordered to ensure no Americans civilians remained in the compound. They were to hold off the enemy until another Huey (Bell UH-1 Iroquois) could be deployed to extract the remaining soldiers.

155

Armed with only a .45-caliber pistol, Dio made his way around the compound. He reported casualties and wounded to the carrier and requested a medevac ASAP. As Dio made his way toward the front of the compound, he could see that most of the civilians trying to gain entry had run away. Smoke filled the compound and Dio noticed a civilian who worked in the commissary, a local they all called "Dinky Dow" coming from behind the main building carrying a backpack. Dio knew in an instant that he was about to toss the satchel full of explosives at one of the foxholes Dio's men were in. Without hesitation he fired several shots at Dinky. The backpack exploded and Dinky was blown to bits. The soldiers in the foxhole turned to see just as Dio yelled, "Get down, sapper."

Dio wondered how many more *friendlies* would turn against his men. His ears were ringing from the explosion, but Dio made his way to the foxhole and ordered the men to follow him. They would make their way to the back of the compound and await evacuation. He tried to survey the area to ensure any wounded and dead were not left behind. The two officers who were killed with the first blast were carried by four medics on two stretchers.

Dio then radioed the carrier for air support. "Get some fire power outside the embassy. Get us the hell out of here. We will be in the rear of the compound by the auxiliary chopper pad. Don't know how much longer we can hold them off."

Dio was surprised at how calm he was. Here he was a twenty-year-old, who just killed for the first time and was attempting to save the lives of the remaining airmen in his squad. He could see several black pajama-clad VC scaling the main gate. Dio's buddy, Sergeant Tony Frongillo, opened fire on them killing several before an explosion from an RPG tore into the compound. It played in slow motion as Dio saw his friend fly into the air and land about ten feet from where he last stood. Without hesitation Dio ran toward his stricken comrade—dodging left and right to avoid enemy fire. When he got to Frongillo, he could see his friend laying in his own blood with his left leg gone and his intestines oozing out of his torn fatigue shirt. For a brief second, Tony looked up at Dio with a wry smile on his face. Dio took his hand. "Hang on Tony, I'll get you out of here. Hang on," he shouted.

Dio picked up Tony's M-16 as two VC ran toward him. He fired a burst of the 7.62-mm rounds and both insurgents fell but not before he felt the hot sting of a round pierce his left shoulder and upper arm. Shit is all he said. Overhead he could hear that thump, thump, thump of helicopters. Two Huey choppers were laying down suppressing fire as two medevacs and one Huey flew into the compound. Dio picked up Tony's body and carried it to the rear of the compound.

The other airmen and marines provided cover as the VC were now coming over the gate and walls at will. One of the Hueys flew over, riddling the VC with .50-caliber rounds from the door gunner. To Dio it seemed surreal. The chopper was blasting music—The Doors' "Riders on the Storm." Dio could see the gunner's face, grinning as he mowed down VC, his Grateful Dead ball cap turned backward. This gave Dio time to get Tony back to the rear of the compound just as the medevac was landing. Bleeding badly in two places, a medic who Dio knew as Doc Brown bandaged both of his wounds. Dio had not realized that he had been hit with shrapnel from an RPG.

"You're a lucky motherfucker, Sarge. No vital organs damaged, but your shoulder may need some surgery. Can't say the same for your buddy here though. He's a goner." Tony still had that wry smile on his face. That smile would stay with Dio the rest of his life.

Dio spent the next several weeks in an army hospital in Osaka, Japan. Once his wounds started to heal, he was given some physical therapy to restore the power to his damaged arm. Each day he thought about his friend Tony and the others who died as the embassy was overrun. Tony was from Framingham, Massachusetts, and Dio made a promise he would go and visit Tony's family and his grave, but he never did.

His concern was that his injury would keep him from his life-long dream of becoming a New York City police officer. Dio had taken and passed the written portion of the test and was placed on a military list of applicants but would have to pass the rigorous physical exam before being appointed. He worked extra hard getting his arm and shoulder back into shape. One day while returning from therapy he was told to report to the main muster room on the first floor. When he walked into the large day room, he was surprised to see several other soldiers in pajamas sitting either in wheelchairs or on crutches.

Vice Admiral Robert Cullen, CO of the US Naval Medical Hospital in Osaka, addressed the assembled group. There were several other ranking officers from all the other services. "Men, I am here today to award medals to those of you who have displayed courage and gallantry in the face of a hostile enemy." As he called out each man's name, he would walk over and pin a Purple Heart on the pajama top and shake the soldier's hand. "You men have served your country and shed your blood for all free people in the world."

Dio didn't pay much mind to that and was shocked when the admiral said, "To USAF Staff Sergeant Diomede Bosso, I am hereby awarding a Bronze Star with 'V' device for actions taken on 29–30 April, 1975, at the US Embassy in the city of Saigon, Republic of Vietnam. Sergeant Bosso, please stand up and be recognized."

Dio was taken aback by this as he stood in front of the admiral who pinned the Bronze Star on his fatigue jacket. Next he pinned on the Purple Heart and read the narrative of Dio's exploits that day. Dio knew he would be getting a Purple Heart, but the Bronze Star came as a surprise. Not knowing what to do, Dio just shook the admiral's hand and went back to his place. Several of his buddies started to clap, and Dio's face reddened.

The Admiral continued with posthumous awards, and Dio was pleased that in addition to a Purple Heart, Tony Frongillo was also awarded a Bronze Star with "V" device. Dio was unaware of the actions Tony had taken at the front gate as the VC started to overtake the compound, but when the narrative was read, Dio knew that his friend died a hero.

After the admiral and his entourage left, coffee and donuts were served by USO volunteers. These *donut dollies*, as they were referred to by GIs, were young, attractive, friendly, and eager to chat up soldiers with the usual questions, "Where's your home, handsome?" or shit like that. Dio appreciated their effort. It took courage on their part to volunteer and support the troops in this very unpopular war. An Air Force major whose nametag read H. Finn came over to Dio and congratulated him again for his bravery. Dio could see by his insignia that he was a medical doctor. Dio asked him if he thought he would have any permanent damage to his arm. He told Major Finn of his plans to be a police officer.

"Any police department in the country should be proud to have you as a member, Sergeant. For a man of your age, you showed great courage and leadership under the most difficult of circumstances."

Dio just shook his head. "Major, how or who, I should say, reported my actions at the embassy?" pointing to the Bronze Star pinned on his fatigue jacket.

"Like most of the awards today, other than the Purple Hearts, your fellow GIs made the recommendation." Dio said nothing and looked down at the bronze medal with the red and blue banner. The major handed him two cases, one for each medal. Inside each case was a copy of the special order awarding the medals and a bar for his dress uniform. "I'm sure you will want to wear them on your way home."

Dio looked at him with surprise. "What, I'm going home?"

"Yes, you're well enough to travel and your enlistment is up in two months. Here are your travel orders to Wrightstown Air Base in New Jersey. As you can see you're out of here in forty-eight hours. So if I were you, I would go back to your ward and start packing."

Dio had mixed emotions. Sure he wanted to go home. Sure he missed his family and friends. But what about the other guys here?

Major Finn looked him square in the eye and said, "The war is over son, Nixon negotiated to get our POWs back. We lost fifty thousand lives for really nothing. Vietnam is now a communist country. You go home and heal, get married, have a family, raise kids, whatever. But don't forget what you did here. It may take a long time, but some day people in America will thank you for your service." In the fifty years since Vietnam, no one ever thanked Dio for his service.

CHAPTER 45

The sun had not yet risen when Dio's phone rang. Before grabbing the phone, he looked over at Lydia who was still sound asleep. The alarm clock read 6:15 a.m. "Hello," Dio's voice was a bit raspy.

"Good morning, Dio. Sorry to call so early but I wanted to get to you before you left for Lyon." It was Kurt Gropp. "Looks like Karl Messerschmitt has agreed to be interviewed by the Bundespolizei (BPOL). That's the German federal criminal police office. I got a call last night that he's agreed to speak to the German cops. From what I gathered, the prosecutor in Florida spoke with his lawyers and some arrangement was made. I don't know what that arrangement is, but both parties agreed to allow you and the Florida detective to be present. However, they made it clear that she will be an observer. They do not want her to conduct the interview or ask any questions. I know that might be a problem for your friend, but at least she will hear what he has to say."

"I agree, but it's not going to be easy to keep her silent."

Lydia—now awake—said, "Keep me silent about what?"

He held up his hand, "Hold on, Lyd."

"OK, Kurt, so when and where is this interview to be conducted?"

"Wednesday morning at the Frankfurt law office of MacLeod and Mone. You know who they are, right?"

"Yes, the M&M's as they are called. I know them, and we use them sometimes here at Lloyd's. Very white-shoe European and very expensive."

"OK. So my contact in the BPOL is Polizeidirektor Walter Boser—excellent investigator. Worked for me when I was in charge of investigations in Berlin."

"Dio, can you and the detective from Florida, by the way what's her name again?"

"Martinez, Lydia Martinez."

"So if you and Martinez could meet me in Frankfurt on Wednesday morning, I will send you the address and we can meet there. The meeting is scheduled for 1300 hours."

"Not a problem. We will see you Wednesday. Pick a place we can meet before the interview so Lydia can go over the details of her investigation. If you can get Boser to join us, that would be helpful."

"OK, Dio, I will see what I can do."

Lydia was impatient to hear about Dio's conversation but knew enough to wait until he was finished speaking with Gropp.

"Well it seems like the state's attorney in Palm Beach County and Messerschmitt's attorney have spoken to one another. Messerschmitt has agreed to be interviewed by the German authorities. We can be present but only as observers. The meeting will take place at Messerschmitt's solicitor's office in Frankfurt, and I arranged to meet with Gropp and the German cop who will be accompanying us. I'm hoping we can meet them prior to the interview so that you can brief the German cop on your case."

"Interesting, I think I'll call my department and see if this new information loosens up some of their thought processes." Picking up her cell, she started to call her office number.

"Hold on, Lyd, it's only 1:00 a.m. in Florida. You sure you want to call now?"

Giving him a snarky look, she pressed the cancel button on her phone. "Let's get some breakfast. All this lovemaking is giving me an appetite."

"Sounds good to me. I've got to make a few calls."

Lydia showered and put on a pair of jeans and a pullover. She also unpacked the box of clothes she shipped and put on a pair of socks and sneakers. Looking out to the street below, she knew she would need her raincoat and was glad she packed it. The rain in London was different than in Florida—chillier and constant as opposed to the thunderstorms that were a daily occurrence in the sunshine state.

After breakfast Dio and Lydia spent the rest of the morning in the apartment. Dio busied himself with Lloyd's work, and Lydia waited until 3:00 p.m. to call Detective Budrow. "Hello, Fran, its Lydia Martinez. Any progress on the Dollbee case?"

"I only got the case file last week, so no, nothing to report." Lydia sensed a bit of annoyance in her voice but let it ride. Rather than tell her about the upcoming interview with Messerschmitt, she decided to hold off on that and just tell her that she had seen some video of Messerschmitt and Jasmin Dollbee that was taken by Sky Sports. She suggested that Budrow check with the Golf Channel or CBS to see if they had any coverage of the tournament.

Budrow said that she and her partner were going to reinterview both Mark Van Hooey and Tricia Maddox as well as the other teens at the party. They were also going to speak to the security staff at PGA and anyone else mentioned in Martinez's reports. Budrow also said she reviewed the reports submitted by Crime Scene, the crime lab, and the ME's office. She was impressed with the diatom findings that Stacey Stack had discovered. She never heard of that before and went on about how much science and technology was making their jobs as investigators so much easier. Martinez was starting to regret having called her when she should have called Nancy Heichemer, the ASA assigned to this case.

When Budrow finished talking, Lydia asked about her partner, "What's the deal with your partner, Detective Stitzel? When I called the other day, she acted as if I was some rookie rather than the lead detective on this case."

163

"Yeah well Eileen can be a little testy sometimes. She's just getting back to full duty from a knee-replacement surgery. Way too soon, if you ask me. Plus her husband has some medical issues to boot. She's really a nice person and a good investigator. This is our first cold case together, so I'll give her the benefit of the doubt."

Martinez thought to herself, Well better you than me.

"OK, Fran, I gotta go now. OK if I check back with you in a few days? I still have a vested interest in this case."

"Sure, Lydia, anytime. I know this case was taken away from you a bit premature, but that was not my call. Keep in touch, OK."

"Will do. Thanks, Fran." Why did I bother calling Cold Case? she said aloud to herself. She then selected the stored number she had for ASA Heichemer.

After a few rings she answered, "ASA Heichemer."

"Ms. Heichemer, it's Detective Martinez. How are you?"

"It's Nancy, Detective, and I'm fine. Is this a social call? I thought you were in London."

"Yes, I am. I want to bring you up to speed on what is happening over here on the Dollbee case. Have you got a minute?"

"I'm listening. Go on."

"Well you know I have a friend here in London, who has a friend in Interpol, and he in turn has contacts in the BPOL, which is the German federal criminal police."

"So you're not on vacation?"

"Well," she paused, "yes and no. Listen, Nancy, I've only had this case a short period of time and I developed several leads that led me to believe that this Messerschmitt guy is involved in this crime. Once the PGA and The Florida Classic got involved, the handcuffs were placed on me rather than him."

"So did you call me from London to vent? Or do you have something else you want to tell me?"

164

"Sorry I guess I digressed a bit there. Well the reason I'm calling is to let you know that Karl Messerschmitt had agreed to be interviewed by the German police. My friend, who as you know has a lot of contacts in Europe, was able to have us be present for the interview. But we will not be able to ask any questions."

"Interesting. By the way, your friend, does he have a name?" Heichemer not only knew his name, but she also knew about the upcoming interview as it was arranged through her office and Messerschmitt's attorney in Florida.

"Dio Bosso."

"He's the retired NYPD cop that you worked with on the *Green Violinist* double homicide, is he not?"

"Yes, that would be him. He is now head of worldwide security for Lloyd's of London, and one of his contacts is the head of Interpol. He got us the invite to the interview through his contacts at BPOL."

"OK, so now that you impressed me with your contacts, how do I or this office fit in to this?"

"Well, if my suspicions are correct, Messerschmitt is only going to make a statement and not answer too many questions. His family has hired one of Europe's top law firms, MacLeod and Mone—ever heard of them?"

"Of course I have. They have handled some of the largest international mergers and acquisitions, and their criminal defense team has defended everything from terrorist to war criminals. Furthermore, they hired a local firm— Corcoran, Denihan, and O'Shea—as their reps here in Florida. My boss, Ed McDonald, spoke to them on several occasions."

"I know that firm. Corcoran got me all rattled on a cross-examination when I was a rookie. Fortunately, the jury was savvier than I was and voted to convict."

"I'll tell you this much, Lydia, these guys are top-shelf. They have a reputation of going after their opponents in a most despicable way. They seem to stretch the boundaries of decency and ethics to the *n*th degree. Never going too far and breaking the law, but close."

"What about you, Martinez? Any suggestions?"

"Right now, no. But like I said, if Messerschmitt does make some sort of confession, then I think we ought to pursue extradition. I don't know jack shit about how we go about that, but I figure you do or at least can find out, should that become necessary." She did not want to tell Nancy about the video Dio showed her. She now suspected the caddy was more involved than she originally believed, but figured if she tells Nancy this, it might prompt her to back off the Messerschmitt interview.

"OK, I'll do some research. Truth be told I never handled a case where domestic extradition came into play let alone international."

"Well, I know for a fact Germany and most European Union countries will not extradite capital cases. Anyway, I'm glad we spoke. I will call you again after I get back from Germany. Let's see where this goes."

"OK, Lydia, thanks for filling me in. Oh, by the way, your victim's dad has been talking to the press about the lack of development in his daughter's murder—questioning why the case was reassigned to Cold Case."

"Really?" is all Lydia said, smiling to herself.

They exchanged goodbyes and ended the call.

CHAPTER 46

Dio spent the next day in his office, and Lydia did a walking tour of London. Dio offered his car and driver, but Lydia said she wanted to walk the city to get a feel for London, ride the Tube, and maybe stop in a pub for some of that "good English home cooking" she heard so much about. Lydia did stop in a pub called The Pig & Whistle and had a pint of local beer (too warm) and an order of fish and chips, which was quite tasty. She figured all the walking made her hungry. After returning home she waited for Dio and after they made love again, they spent the night talking and watching reruns of *Monty Python* on the BBC.

CHAPTER 47

Early the next morning Dio's driver, Charlie Neligan, was waiting as they left the apartment at 7:00 a.m. Neligan was a retired metro London constable, knew his way around London, and only spoke when spoken to. The drive to Heathrow lasted almost an hour due to traffic, but once at the airport Charlie drove them to the private jet terminal where Lloyd's Gulfstream G550 was waiting to take them to Frankfurt. The 660-kilometer flight would take less than two hours.

Lydia had never flown on a private jet before and was expecting something similar to the first-class trips she had taken to London (thanks to Dio). This plane was something else and Lydia, who is not impressed easily, was awed by the luxurious cabin. There were several other Lloyd's execs on the flight. Lydia and Dio sat in the first cabin, which had two facing seats on each side of the spacious aisle. The middle cabin was more or less a lounge, and the back cabin was equipped for in-flight meetings and could be turned into a sleep area if necessary. She was not surprised that the restroom was just a bit smaller than the one in her condo. Lydia was the only female on board. All of the other Lloyd's employees were dressed in business attire as was Dio (of course). She felt somewhat underdressed in her jeans, black wool turtleneck, and scarf. Dio didn't seem to mind. The other execs kept to themselves and just nodded at Dio as they walked past.

Frankfurt International Airport, one of the busiest in Europe, accommodates private jets about five kilometers from the main runways. As they taxied Lydia looked out the window and saw several vehicles waiting to take the various passengers to meetings. She knew that the black Mercedes Benz SUV with the flashing lights in the grill would be their ride. Outside the car she saw two men in suits accompanied by a uniformed female officer. She figured the two to be Boser and Gropp, whom Dio spoke to her about. She heard the familiar sound of Dio's cell phone (the USAF theme song) and turned and saw Dio answer. At the same time, she saw the taller of the two German cops on his cell. Yep, she thought, those are our guys. They waited until the other passengers exited the jet, each nodding or offering a good day to Dio and Lydia as they hurried off.

Dio made the introductions and Lydia was not surprised that Kurt Gropp spoke almost flawless English. Polizeidirektor Boser on the other hand had a thick German accent. They did not include the uniformed officer in the intros.

"I've arranged an early lunch at a restaurant nearby," said Gropp. We have about two hours before the scheduled meeting with Messerschmitt and his lawyers."

Boser spoke next. "This will give you the opportunity to tell us all about your case in America, Detective Martinez." Lydia didn't bother with the usual *Lydia, please.*

They made small talk on the way to the restaurant, talking about their various backgrounds in law enforcement. It seemed to Lydia that no matter how high up you might be in your department or agency; everyone wants to talk about what it's like being a cop in New York City.

Lydia never saw this proud side of Dio as he explained how he rose from a patrol cop to detective and then through the civil service ranks to a borough commander of detectives. Neither Gropp nor Boser, who rose to higher ranks in their respective organizations, had as many working detectives as Dio had in his last NYPD assignment. Dio, being modest, left out the details of how he got his Gold Shield. He also did not go into details about how he was forced to retire when two detectives under his command were murdered while transporting a prisoner to court. There was malfeasance on the part of the murdered cops, but Dio took the hit to save their families the pain of knowing their loved ones were partially responsible for their own deaths and more importantly to save their pensions for their families. The conversation continued until they reached the restaurant.

"Well, Detective Martinez, have you ever had real German food? This place has been serving homestyle German cooking since the '60's. Food is great." Boser just nodded as they got out of the Mercedes. Lydia smiled at the uniformed female holding the door for her.

Extending her hand Lydia said, "Hi, I'm Lydia. What's your name? Are you joining us?" Lydia could sense confusion in the officer's face.

"Polizeikommissar Shokes will remain with the vehicle," an annoyed Boser said looking at Martinez. Dio gave her a look and whispered, "Gee, Lyd, what are you doing? These guys are trying to help us, and you seem to want to hashtag them for being chauvinist."

"Well, I was just trying to be friendly," she lied. Once they were seated, she apologized to Boser.

"That's OK, Detective. Polizeikommissar Shokes is my niece, and she is very happy to have the assignment she has."

That comment got a chuckle out of Gropp. He picked up the conversation. "So, Detective, my friend here Dio has told me a lot about you and your case involving Karl Messerschmitt. Why don't you tell us everything you know including the evidence, forensics, and current status of your investigation?"

For the next twenty minutes, Lydia related everything she had so far on the Dollbee homicide. She did not mention that the case had been reassigned to Cold Case and hoped Dio would not mention that. He didn't. In fact, he didn't say much except to order his lunch. Gropp and Boser listened intently with Boser taking notes as she spoke. She noticed that he was writing his notes in German. They seemed impressed the way

170

she laid out her case, detailing the information she gleaned from the lab, ME, and crime scene.

The only question Boser asked was about DNA.

"We found the victim's DNA on the golf shoe bag that we believe was placed over her head prior to being rendered unconscious." She was using dialogue that she would use as if testifying in court.

When lunch was delivered, Lydia and Dio both ordered sauerbraten with red cabbage and dumplings. Gropp and Boser had something that looked like a rolled piece of beef also with red cabbage and dumplings. Gropp ordered a bottle of Gewürztraminer, a dry sweet wine, which Lydia had never had but quite enjoyed. Dio asked for the check and used his Lloyd's-issued Amex card to pay the tab. The drive from the restaurant to the Messerschmitt residence took less than fifteen minutes.

"I thought we were meeting at his lawyers'?" Lydia asked.

"It's been changed," said Boser.

CHAPTER 48

The road leading to the Messerschmitt's home was about a mile down a tree-lined road. Red oak and elm formed a canopy that all but shut out any sunlight. Lydia was a bit surprised when she saw that the Messerschmitt's lived in Kronberg Castle. Built in the mid-thirteenth century, the castle was purchased by Karl Messerschmitt's grandfather. After his death Karl's father, Frederich, a successful architect, renovated parts of the complex to house his wife and son. Portions of the castle are used for private functions such as weddings, corporate events, and the like. Additionally, a three-hole golf course was constructed on the property along with a practice facility so young Karl could work on his golfing skills. Both Gropp and Boser made comments about the castle. Lydia was thinking more about how she would get herself involved in the afternoon's proceedings. Did they think she was just going to sit by and take notes?

They were met at the door by a tall, thin, stern-looking man in a gray three-piece suit. No introductions were made. In German, he invited them in and told them to follow. They were led down a large hall decorated with what Lydia assumed were expensive paintings. Dio recognized some as old masters and stopped to look at a Titian. The gray suit now said, in English, "They're waiting for you to start." Dio just nodded, gave Lydia a side look, and walked on.

They were led into a large board room/library. Both Lydia and Dio were surprised to see that Karl Messerschmitt was not in the room. There was a large table filled with what appeared to be a buffet of cold cuts, salads, and baked goods.

The first person to speak was a rather distinguished well-dressed, middle-aged man with a full head of gray hair. Lydia could not detect his accent but would learn it was that of a Scotsman who lived a long time in London.

"Good afternoon, madam, gentlemen. I hope you had a pleasant journey here. My name is Malcolm MacLeod, and I am here as the solicitor for the Messerschmitt family." Gropp and Boser knew who he was, but each person introduced themselves and shook hands. Looking directly at Lydia, he continued, "Well, Detective Martinez, you have come a long way."

She saw this as her opportunity to talk and before MacLeod could continue, she responded, "Yes, I have. But I believe Mr. Messerschmitt can be a great help in solving a very heinous crime that occurred in my jurisdiction."

"And where is that again, Detective?"

She knew he knew but played along. "Palm Beach County, Florida."

He continued, "We know the reason why all of you are here. You think Karl is involved in this murder of yours. But in a few minutes, Karl will be here, and he will give a statement. This will not be an interrogation of my client."

It was now Boser who spoke. "With all due respect, sir, your client is a witness to or may be involved in a murder in a country that has been our ally for the last seventy years. Cooperation between our law enforcement agencies and those in the US, both on a federal level and local level, have led to numerous leads to help stem terrorism here. Also Herr Gropp from Interpol assured me that we are perfectly within our rights to assist Detective Martinez."

"Is Detective Martinez here in an official capacity?" The room went silent. "I thought not. And what about Mr. Bosso? Does Lloyd's have an interest here?" Dio knew MacLeod was blowing smoke. They had met several times for business and Dio always enjoyed his company. Dio first met him at the last open championship at St. Andrews. Dio also knew that

173

MacLeod fancied himself a lady's man. And he could see by the way he addressed Lydia that he was turning on the charm.

Lydia picked up on it too. She thought to herself, yep this guy is charming, but I already got an old geezer boyfriend. She looked over at Dio and placed her hand on his thigh as MacLeod went on about the format for the interview.

"By the way, Malcolm, where is young Herr Messerschmitt?" This was Gropp speaking for the first time, looking down at his wristwatch.

"He'll be here shortly. He was out on the range working on his game. You know all this business has cost him quite a bit of income." He was looking at Lydia when he said that, but the twinkle in his eye was gone. Lydia wanted to scream out and comment on such a thoughtless remark. Dio could feel her tense up and just squeezed her hand. Just then the door opened behind them. The gray suit reappeared this time, accompanied by Karl and another man whom Lydia guessed was the elder Messerschmitt. Lydia had seen the official PGA headshot of Karl Messerschmitt, so she recognized him straight away. What surprised her was how small he was, five-foot-five maybe five-foot-six, but he had the body of someone who spends time in the gym.

The elder Messerschmitt introduced himself and shook the hand of each person in the room. They sat across the large mahogany desk from the four visitors. MacLeod once again started the dialogue. "My client, Karl Messerschmitt, has been made aware that he is…as you say in American…a person-of-interest in a murder investigation. He is going to make a statement. Please do not interrupt the statement and as a precaution, Herr Inge," he pointed to the gray suit, "scanned each of you to be sure you are not carrying a recording device." Lydia looked over toward Gropp and Boser who just shrugged their shoulders.

Lydia immediately disliked Karl Messerschmitt. He made no eye contact with anyone other than MacLeod and spoke to him in German. Lydia heard the word *golf* and Karl made a golf-swing gesture as he took a seat between MacLeod and the senior Messerschmitt.

Lydia was not used to being in a position where she was not conducting the interview. Heck, she thought, this isn't an interview. It's gonna be a dog-and-pony show.

Still looking down, holding several sheets of typewritten paper, Karl began in English. There was only a hint of a German accent. Karl was taught *proper* English. "My name is Karl Messerschmitt. I am a professional golfer on both the PGA Tour in Europe and as of 2016, a member of the PGA Tour in the US. I am thirty-three years old and I live here at my family home here in Frankfurt."

OK, let's move on, thought Lydia, already wanting to reach over the desk and force his head up to meet her eyes.

"I am making this statement in the presence of my solicitor to help clarify a matter of which I may know about but was no way responsible for."

Now we're getting somewhere, she thought, looking at Dio.

"This all started on the Monday before The Florida Classic. We, my caddy Dieter Spunkmeyer and I, arrived in Miami. I played a round of golf at Trump Doral in Miami. Dieter said he wasn't feeling well, so I gave him off and I hired a club caddy. That night I ate dinner alone in South Beach, and the next day we took a limo to West Palm Beach. We checked in with the players' tournament hospitality, received our gift bags and courtesy car, and then went to the hotel. I wanted to go back to PGA and try to play some holes, but again Dieter was not feeling well, but he came with me. We had to wait an hour to get on the golf course, so I went to the range and worked on my swing. Dieter usually accompanies me during these sessions. He can analyze my swing better than most of the coaches I've had over the years." Looking up at Gropp and Boser for the first time he said, "Do you play?"

Gropp said he did and was smart enough not to go into details about his game. He wanted to keep Karl on point. Boser just nodded that he did not play. He did not look toward Lydia's or Dio's side of the table.

He continued, "I've known Dieter Spunkmeyer since we were competing as teens. Most boys our age are into football (soccer). I guess golf was not for everyone back then," he said looking around his opulent setting. "I mean it was only available to a certain, you know, class of boys." He looked up at Martinez with a smirk on his face.

She thought to herself, I'd like to punch this douchebag in his smug face.

Focusing back on the papers in his hand, Messerschmitt continued, "Dieter was an excellent golfer and we always competed or played as partners. We won all of the events we played here in Germany and most of the junior events in Great Britain. Unfortunately, Dieter had an accident that left his right hand deformed, and he could no longer hold a golf club properly. At that time, we decided that he would caddy for me and help me make it on tour, both here in Europe and the US. He knows my game better than any instructor I've had."

Lydia and Dio both had questions they wanted to ask after each sentence, but they knew they were not permitted. Dio wondered if Gropp and Boser felt the same way.

Reading from the prepared script he continued, "Well after a few years of playing around the world—you know, Asia, South America, some mini tours here in Europe—I finally got my PGA Tour card. It was then that Dieter started to change. He did not seem bitter about not playing. He seemed to enjoy being my caddy and did not appear to be jealous of my success. After all, my father," he nodded toward the elder Messerschmitt, "gave him a very lucrative contract. He just seemed angry at other people. He is not much at conversation and, well you know how it is, I meet a lot of woman on the tour."

He glanced over at Martinez when he said women and actually smiled at her. Now she really wanted to smack him upside the head.

176

"Dieter did some strange things. I tried to warn him that he would get us in trouble." He paused, "Well as you can see, I had to leave the states and withdraw from two tournaments because of him, so I don't feel guilty for his actions. I have done nothing wrong. I have never broken the laws of this or any other country that I have traveled to for my profession. Thank you."

MacLeod broke the momentary silence as questions danced in Lydia's head. "Thank you, Karl. Why don't you leave us here to finish up our business?" Making a golf swing he said, "You can always work on your short game, eh."

"Wait, that's it? That's all he's gonna say?" Lydia drew all eyes toward hers with the exception of Dio who was looking at Karl.

MacLeod raised his voice an octave, "Detective, let me remind you of our previous conversation. You are not here on official business, and I have arranged this meeting so my client could offer you some assistance in your investigation."

"How can he possibly help me if I can't question him? At least follow-up questions." The pleading tone of her voice made an impression on MacLeod.

He nodded in agreement. "I'm sure these gentlemen here," pointing toward Gropp and Boser, "can direct you to the proper channels. If and when I learn of that, and only then, will I permit you to speak to anyone in the Messerschmitt household." He stood up, signaling an end to the meeting.

Lydia extended her hand and gave a nod of acknowledgement. "Thank you, Mr. MacLeod. Hopefully we will meet again after I obtain whatever documents I need to be able to question your client. He knows more about my case than he is letting on." Now she had the floor. "Here is something else, Mr. MacLeod. I've been doing this a long time. And in my experience, a crime as brutal as the murder of Jasmin Dollbee, was not the first such deed committed by those responsible. I have sufficient evidence indicating your client and his caddy are involved. If we were in the United States, they would both be in handcuffs."

MacLeod was not fazed by her comments. "Well we are not in the United States, are we Detective? And I will once again remind you of your unofficial status in this matter."

Martinez did not respond, just looked at MacLeod. She knew he was right, at least for now.

"Well then," he said, "thank you all for coming. Herr Inge will show you out." Handing Lydia a card, he smiled and the eye twinkle returned. "Detective Martinez, this card has all my contact information. I believe you gentlemen know how to reach me," he said to the others.

After handshakes and danke schoens, Lydia saw MacLeod draw Gropp and Boser into a tight circle and say something in German. Turning to Dio, Lydia said, "What's that about, D?"

"Damned if I know. I'll ask Kurt later."

CHAPTER 49

Gropp and Boser said their goodbyes to Lydia and Dio at the airport. Gropp said he had some business meetings in Frankfurt and would probably spend the night and fly back to Lyon in the morning. On the trip back to London, Dio and Lydia went to work. First they attempted to reconstruct Karl Messerschmitt's statement on separate yellow legal pads. By the time they landed, they pretty much had verbatim what the German golfer had said. They both thought someone should have inquired about the whereabouts of the caddy, Spunkmeyer.

They arrived back in Mayfair around 4:00 p.m., picking up the hour they lost on the trip to Frankfurt. What a day, Lydia thought. They both showered and changed into what Dio referred to as *soft clothes*. For Lydia that meant sweatpants and a cotton turtleneck. For Dio, well he took off his suit and put on slacks and an opened-neck dress shirt. They decided on Chinese and Dio called in an order.

"Twenty minutes. They're always right on time. Do you want a drink or a glass of wine?"

"Sure, how about a nice white for a change?"

"Sounds good, Lyd. I have a Joseph Phelps Sauvignon Blanc I'll open, then we can get to work."

CHAPTER 50

They sat comfortably at Dio's kitchen table, eating Chinese out of the boxes, family style, washed down with the Joseph Phelps. It was a no-brainer to see that Karl was lying or at least holding back vital information. Both knew they could get the truth out of him if given the chance to interrogate. But how? Dio suggested that the first step should be to notify her squad commander just to let him know about the meeting with Messerschmitt.

"No point not to, Lyd. He is your CO, and you should let him know about your conversations with the state's attorney."

"You're thinking like a boss, D. But you may be right. After all, Cashin did go to bat for me after the meeting with The Florida Classic people."

The conversation turned to the extradition process, should it come to that. Lydia admitted she did not fully understand the process of extradition, but Dio did. He explained, as only Dio could, that extradition is an agreement or treaty between two countries whereby one country will request through their courts to extradite any person convicted of an "extraditable crime" in both jurisdictions. The United States and many other countries will not extradite its citizens for any reason, and some countries will not extradite so-called political prisoners or to jurisdictions where the person extradited may face the death penalty.

"This will not be a formality like getting a search warrant for a perp's crib, Lyd."

"Yeah, I guess so. But I remember us getting bad guys extradited from Mexico for drug murders, and I don't recall it being such a big deal."

"Probably because the Mexicans didn't want them either. Anyway, you should think about calling the ASA you mentioned and fill her in."

"I plan to first thing in the morning. Now how about we call it a day?" She gave him that look that he was starting to realize was the signal for sex. They wasted no time. Lydia liked scented candles and by the time Dio came out of the bathroom, Lydia was under the sheets beckoning him in the glow of the flickering candlelight. Their lovemaking was becoming more and more intense each time.

Dio entered Lydia from the top and after several minutes of slow rhythmic thrusts, she stopped him. "Hold on," she whispered and turned herself over on her belly. Dio withdrew and sat back on his knees. Lydia presented her butt to him, and he reentered her now sopping wet pussy. They didn't last long and only after a minute or two of in-and-out thrusts, they came together. Dio collapsed on top of Lydia's sweat-soaked back and remained there breathing heavily into her hair. Rolling over, she smiled. "This is getting better and better. I may never want to leave."

"You don't have to, you know."

She didn't answer. Rolling over so they were now face-to-face she said, "You're a sweet man, Dio Bosso, and one hell of a fuck," she chuckled.

"Thanks, you're not so bad yourself." Dio was now running his hand over her butt and never before appreciated how round and firm it was. He liked that. "You know, Lydia, I always fancied myself a breast man, but not anymore," he said as he continued to run his hand over her butt.

Sleep came easy for the lovers. The next morning it was Dio who was awakened by the smell of fresh coffee and the unmistakable scent of bacon frying in the skillet.

CHAPTER 51

After breakfast Dio called for his driver to pick him up. He wanted to get into his office and catch up on some reports he had to review and comment on. Lydia was waiting not so patiently to call ASA Heichemer. From what she gathered from Messerschmitt's statement, she was sure Heichemer would start the paperwork to extradite both Karl Messerschmitt and Dieter Spunkmeyer back to Florida to stand trial for the murder of Jasmin Dollbee. She was now convinced more than ever that these two were responsible for Jasmin's death.

"How many others?" she asked to the empty room. Lydia waited until a little past 2:00 p.m. London time to call ASA Heichemer.

"Good morning, Detective Martinez, enjoying your vacation?" The tone was friendly, but Lydia detected some sarcasm in Nancy's voice.

"I am, Nancy. But the reason I'm calling is to let you know that I was present at Karl Messerschmitt's home yesterday in Frankfurt, where he gave a statement implicating his caddy, Dieter Spunkmeyer, in the Dollbee homicide."

"My god, he did?"

"Yes, at least that's how we interpreted it."

"We?"

"Yes. I was accompanied by the heads of Interpol and the German federal police. Messerschmitt's attorney, or solicitor as they're called over here..." she paused to look at his card, "Malcolm MacLeod, presided over the meeting and would not permit any questioning of Herr Messerschmitt." She used a mocking German accent when saying his name. She

182

immediately regretted that as she realized Heichemer could be a German name and Nancy might take offense. She thought to apologize but Nancy seemed not to pick up on the remark.

"I've never done an international extradition before. I will have to get some help here. Maybe the US attorney. But before I do that, send me a report of what you just told me. And by the way, how did you manage to get Interpol and the local cops involved? Wouldn't have anything to do with your gentleman friend over there, would it?"

Lydia paused for a second and thought to herself, well at least she didn't say that old guy you're dating.

"Well yes, as I mentioned previously, in his position at Lloyd's, Dio has made contacts with the upper-echelons of most of the major city and state law enforcement agencies. Plus as you well know, Nancy, a good reputation is always a door-opener."

"OK, good. So now we have to work on getting you back on this case officially. I'll have to call the PBSO and see how we do that. I also want you to be able to conduct a proper interrogation of Messerschmitt. But again, I will have to reach out and see how we can get this done. By the way I am aware of the M&M law firm and the law firm they use here. They will be a formidable adversary once we commence extradition." Changing the subject Heichemer continued, "What about this Spunkmeyer guy, the caddy? Where is he?"

"Good question. From what I learned, he lives on the estate, or castle, or whatever you want to call the place Messerschmitt lives. Did you know his grandfather built planes for the Nazis?"

"I know the name, but I did not make the connection."

"Well anyway, Spunkmeyer's name was brought up by Messerschmitt. As I was not permitted to ask questions, the entire interview was a farce as far as I am concerned. And Nancy, one other thing you should know. We viewed video of the pro-am and first rounds of the tournament. Probably the last photos taken of Jasmin Dollbee. Anyway, in these videos, you can see the caddy Spunkmeyer ogling Jasmin, and on more than one occasion actually talking to her instead of paying attention to Messerschmitt."

"OK, Lydia, let me get going here. I got a lot to do. The (Palm Beach) Post has been running an ongoing story about what they are now calling 'Murder at The Florida Classic.' The local TV stations are also getting involved. I'll get back to you as soon as I have something."

Lydia smiled to herself knowing it was she who put the bug in Ken Dollbee's ear that got the press to pay attention. She wondered how George Goll and the other mucky-mucks on PGA Blvd. would be handling this unwanted attention to their precious tournament.

CHAPTER 52

Just as Lydia ended the call with Heichemer, her cell phone rang. It was Dio. "Hey, Lyd, whatcha doing?"

"I've been in contact with the ASA handling the Dollbee case, and guess what?"

"They want you back?"

"No, but they are going to start the extradition proceedings and try to set up an interview, a real interview, with me and Messerschmitt. How they hope to accomplish that, with his high-price lawyer in the three-thousand-dollar suit, is beyond me. But at this point I'll take what I can get."

"Euros."

"What?"

"Three-thousand-euro suit. They use euros here. Of course if he bought it in England, it would be pounds."

Lydia just shook her head.

"Euros, pounds, dollars, whatever. Do you have anything we could use, D, or did you just call to school me on the European monetary system?"

"Well, I may have some good news. Remember when we agreed that based on the brutality of Jasmin's murder that it appeared to be an act of rage. That the way the body was abused indicated a lack of compassion or morality on the part of the perp or perps."

"Yeah, I remember we discussed that, and we also thought that Jasmin might be the victim of a sexual sadist or serial killer?"

"Correct. After our meeting yesterday, I ran something by Kurt and Boser. I asked them if there was a way to cross-check any unsolved/open homicides of a similar nature to coincide with golf tournaments that Messerschmitt and Spunkmeyer played in."

"That seems like quite a task, Dio."

"Not really. Since the European Union came into existence, all of the law enforcement agencies of the union centralized their criminal records with the help of Interpol. Gropp as president of Interpol oversaw the transformation of records into a system similar to the FBI's NCIS (National Crime Information System). This allows member nations to search and harvest data from one central computer system. Its ability to access police records from all member countries is a routine matter. With help from the European Amateur Golf Association, we should be able to find out if these two were playing in a tournament when someone went missing and turned up dead."

CHAPTER 53

When Dio returned from his office, Lydia could tell by the look on his face that he had something important to say. "I was planning on taking you out to dinner tonight, but I thought it might be best if we order in as we've got a busy day tomorrow."

Lydia knew that he was deliberately drawing out what he wanted to tell her, like a parent holding a surprise toy behind their back. "Oh come on, D. Tell me, *please.*" She playfully snuggled up next to him and pressed her body to his. "If it's something good, I'll be very, very appreciative, if you get my drift." She placed her hand on his crotch. Dio was surprised at how quickly he responded and how for the first time he did not think about his deceased wife as he started to undress Lydia right there in the living room.

They made love on the sofa and after they both came, they rolled onto the floor, sweaty and panting. "So what did you want to tell me now that you've had your way with me?"

Before he answered Dio got up and walked into the bedroom. It was the first time that Lydia had seen him walking naked. She hadn't realized that Dio's body was pretty tight for a guy in his early sixties. His butt didn't sag, and he had very little body fat. When he returned from the bedroom, he was wearing a pair of gym shorts and a T-shirt. Very, very unlike him she thought.

"So today Kurt and I had discussed the cross-referencing of unsolved murders of young women during golf tournaments that Messerschmitt competed in. Kurt started his search with the first tournament the two played in. It was the 1999 European Junior Amateur Championship held in Troon,

Scotland. It seems that during that tournament, two women were killed in a horrific car accident. Their bodies were burned beyond recognition. Dental records had to be used to make a positive ID. There was no DNA or other forensic date retrieved at the scene, but the report Kurt read to me stated the two women had been seen earlier in the evening drinking with two young Germans who were playing in the tournament. According to the report, they were all pretty drunk when they left the pub. Kurt gave me the name of the assistant chief constable, Ian Hutchinson, with whom I took the liberty to call." Lydia was a bit taken aback by this. On the one hand she was pleased that Dio was able to reach out and find out so much in a short period of time; but on the other hand, she was thinking, is he going to co-op my investigation again?

"Anything else, D?"

"Yes, there were only six German golfers in that tournament. Two of whom were Messerschmitt and Spunkmeyer. This puts them both at a location where another horrific crime was committed."

"But you just said these girls died in a car crash."

"Yes, I did."

"However, Hutchinson told me he always believed that the Germans were somehow involved. He was a constable then and was assigned to a different area. But he was sent to the scene the next morning to assist the locals with the investigation. "The case was closed as a traffic accident caused by the driver of the vehicle being drunk."

"That's interesting, Dio. Go on."

"Hutchinson told me that even his superiors wanted to speak to the German players to see who might have been with the deceased the previous evening, but the tournament officials threw cold water on that suggestion. Sound familiar?"

"Yeah, just like my case in Florida."

"But we'll hear more tomorrow." He handed her a small gift-wrapped box from Hobbs.

"What's this, D? It's not my birthday."

"Open it. You'll need it in Scotland."

"Scotland? We're going to Scotland?"

Lydia opened the Hobbs box and found a pair of black fur-lined leather gloves.

"Thanks, D. No one has ever given me gloves before. I guess being a lifelong Floridian I had no need for them."

"Well, you're gonna need them in Scotland. The weather there can be tricky, to say the least. You'll want to pack a sweater and some warm undies. We may be there a few days. Hutchinson has agreed to meet with us tomorrow, so I've arranged for the company jet to fly us up to Glasgow. The flight takes about ninety minutes and another hour or so by car to Troon in South Ayrshire. I think if we leave here by 8:00 a.m., we should be there for the 11:00 a.m. meeting." Lydia didn't say anything, and this caught Dio by surprise. He expected her to respond in a more positive way.

"Lyd, is something wrong? I thought this would be great news. We have an actual solid lead that may put *our boys*," as he was now referring to Messerschmitt and Spunkmeyer, in the same place as another suspicious homicide. I thought you'd be pleased."

"I am, Dio. I am. It's just that," she paused, "you know, it's like the last time. I caught the case, but you solved it."

"No, Lydia, *we* solved it. We worked on it together, each using our skills and contacts. Just like we're doing now." He was trying to ameliorate her feelings.

"I can't do what you do as far as getting these creeps extradited. I can't go to the police in an official capacity. Only you can do that. Sure, my contacts and position are helping us make progress, but this is your case. You developed the leads. You conducted the interviews and you collected the evidence that your lab people used to connect the perps to the victim. No babe, this is totally you. I'm just doing what I can to help you."

Lydia still had a sheet wrapped around her body as she had not put her clothes back on. "I'm going to take a shower. I feel like pizza. Are there any good pizza take-outs here?"

"This is London. They're called take-aways, and I do happen to know of a good Italian restaurant. And the owner is a friend of mine. He will make us a pizza and deliver it too. Do you want a salad too?"

"Yep, sounds good, I'll be out in a bit."

Dio felt bad. Did he go too far in helping her? He didn't think so. Crime solving is a team effort. Many a time his best detective, Joe Pollicino, was the one who broke their big cases. Shit, he thought, I haven't spoken to Joe P. in a while. I wonder how he's enjoying retirement. I've got to give Joe a call—see how he's doing.

CHAPTER 54

The delivery pizza was fresh and quite tasty. Even Dio, who was a self-admitted pizza snob enjoyed the pie. Small talk was made as they ate and drank a bottle of Ponzi Pinot Noir. When they finished up and cleaned the table, Lydia decided she wanted to lay down and read. Dio had some work to do so he stayed up for a while.

As Lydia lay in bed she began to think about Jasmin Dollbee and her family and what they were going through. She thought about Karl Messerschmitt and his arrogant, self-important, entitled attitude. She wondered about this Dieter Spunkmeyer and how he was ogling poor Jasmin in the video Dio showed her. Finally, she thought about her future with the PBSO. If she fell on her face after the shit she pulled here, she would be back on road patrol.

Finally, she thought about Dio. Did she enjoy being with him? Yes. Did she enjoy the sex? Yes, more than she thought she would. Did she love Dio the way he professed to love her? And could she see herself spending the rest of their lives together? Of those last two thoughts, she was not sure. She fell asleep and stirred when Dio came to bed and spooned next to her. He fell asleep in a matter of seconds. Snuggling next to him she wanted to tell him that she loved him, but she could not bring herself to say the words.

CHAPTER 55

The next morning was cold, and a misty rain greeted them as they awoke. Dio had programmed the coffee pot the night before so the smell of fresh-brewed coffee permeated the condo. Dio was up and dressed and offered Lydia a bagel.

"No time for a fancy breakfast today, Lyd."

"This drizzle will turn to rain, and these pilots we have do not like flying in bad weather."

"Why the hell are they working in England then?"

"Good point. Most of our pilots are ex-RAF, but there is very little opportunity for them after their service, so most blokes stay the full twenty-five years to earn a pension."

"Excuse me. Did you say blokes?"

Dio smiled. "I guess I've been here too long, eh Lyd?" He loved the face she made when she threw him a zinger. A sort of wry smile that touched his heart. God, I love this woman.

Dio's driver and Bentley were waiting for them, and the ride to Gatwick was uneventful. It was not Dio's regular driver, Charlie, who was visiting family in Ireland.

"Good morning, sir, Madam."

Dio introduced him to Lydia, "This is Chairman Power's driver, Bev Miller." Lydia just smiled a hello and got into the Bentley.

Miller, like Neligan, was a retired constable from the London metro police. Dio had hired him and liked the fact he was an ex-LEO and did not talk unless he was asked a question. As a matter of fact, Dio replaced all of the executive drivers with retired police officers. They were sharp, knew their way around town, and most importantly kept their mouths shut.

Lydia, whispering, commented to Dio about his name. Dio told her that Bev, like Vivian, is a gender-neutral name in England. She just shook her head.

The flight was quick too. Dio introduced Lydia to the pilot, a different one from the flight to Frankfurt. His name was Daniel Carbone.

"Any reason why you introduced me to this pilot and not the one the other day?"

"Did you not recognize the name Dan Carbone?"

She thought a minute. "Wasn't there a Carbone in the crew who did that big hotel caper you solved back in the last century?" Again, the zinger smile.

"Exactly, good for you, Detective Martinez. We collared Carbone on an unrelated drug charge and before we could flip him, he gets clipped. Probably by those Russians."

"They're not related, but I thought you would find it interesting." Lydia didn't say anything, just patted his hand as the Gulfstream took off.

CHAPTER 56

When they landed in Edinburgh, they were met by DCI Hutchinson, a burly man of about late forties with a full head of red hair. A female uniformed constable was positioned behind the wheel of a black checker-marked vehicle. During the flight Dio had explained to Lydia the different police agencies in the United Kingdom. "However, he said, in Scotland the official name is the Police Service of Scotland (PSS). There are also some local constabularies, but the PSS handles most major crimes."

"What about Scotland Yard?"

"That's in London, along with the Metropolitan Police Service and the London City Police."

"So there's no Scotland Yard in Scotland? You call guys blokes. Take-out food is take-away. The bathroom is the loo. French fries are called chips. Chips are called crisps. Men have names like Bev and Vivian. Strange, don't you think? If I move here, I'm going to have to learn all these terms," she said with a chuckle.

Dio just nodded and smiled. They both enjoyed this back and forth banter. It seemed to bring them closer.

CHAPTER 57

During the drive from the airport to Ayr, DCI Hutchinson, who sat in the front and talked looking straight ahead, explained that he was in charge of the Historical Crime Unit.

"I guess it's what you folks back in the states call a Cold Case Squad."

Lydia just rolled her eyes at Dio, who smiled. His Scottish accent was so thick they both had hoped he would not go into details of the case until they were seated face-to-face.

"We'll be going to Royal Troon," he continued. Lydia had no idea what he said or meant. For the rest of the ride DCI Hutchinson told them how Troon was granted *royal* designation in 1978, during its centennial.

"Jim Montgomerie, the former club secretary, was a mate of mine, so I've played all forty-five holes on numerous occasions. His son Colin, as you probably know, is now playing on the Champions Tour in the states."

She thought to herself, What's the deal with these golfers? Do they really think the whole world gives a rat's ass about golf?

Lydia tuned Hutchinson out and was looking at the passing landscape. Never before had she seen such a place. The beauty of the land—rolling hills of green and heather. It started to rain, and the wind picked up. Still the beauty of the land relaxed her.

"This landscape is beautiful," she said to no one in particular.

"Aye, been here all me life, and I'm still amazed by the beauty of the countryside. Ya live in the city, do ya lass?"

Lydia was not sure what Hutchinson said. She looked at Dio and shrugged.

"Both Detective Martinez and I are city folk. Although New York is nothing like south Florida. Isn't that right, Detective?"

Taking her cue Lydia continued the dialogue.

"I've lived in Florida all my life. Palm trees, the beach, warm weather. But this, this countryside as you called it, it's very different. It's truly beautiful."

"Aye so it tis, so it tis."

Lydia wondered why Dio never took her for a ride in the English countryside. Each time she visited they stayed primarily in London, which by the way she did not mind. Maybe he's saving the road trips until I retire, she mused to herself. She looked over at Dio, who was still in conversation with Hutchinson, but she could tell he too was having a difficult time understanding the Scott.

After about thirty minutes, they pulled off the road into what seemed to be a one-lane dirt path leading up to what appeared to be a huge hotel.

"Aye, there she is—the Royal Troon Club House. Beautiful she is, is she not?" I'll be taken ya on a tour if ya fancy after we talk to Neil."

Neither Lydia nor Dio asked or cared who Neal was. They both wanted only to be able to speak to someone face-to-face so they could understand Hutchinson a little better. She hoped this Neal guy had a better command of their English.

The police car pulled up to the circular driveway. Lydia noticed the parking lot was full and wondered if people were actually playing golf in the rain. It started to rain harder as they exited the checker. A valet appeared with an umbrella and only used it to shield Lydia. Ah, she thought, the age of chivalry is alive and well in Scotland.

They were led into the building. Straight away you knew you were in a place where golf was king. Pictures, both old and new, mostly black and white adorned the walls along the long corridor. They were greeted by a gentleman who Hutchinson introduced as Mr. Donald Ross, the club secretary. As he approached, he extended his hand toward Hutchinson.

"Good morning, Chief Inspector. These must be our guests from the states?" His accent was as thick as Hutchinson's.

Hutchinson made the introductions and mentioned that Mr. Ross was the great grandson of *the* Donald Ross, but the reference was lost on both Dio and Martinez. Lydia commented that there was a Donald Ross Road in Palm Beach Gardens, but she added that it was named for the first local soldier killed in World War I.

The group was escorted halfway down the corridor to a door with a sign that read "Neal Lockie—Head Professional." Ross knocked lightly on the door and opened it. A nice looking man of about thirty-five with sandy hair and a scraggly beard got up from behind a large mahogany desk, and introductions were made all around. Neal asked them if they wanted coffee, tea, or somethin' a wee bit stronger. Thank God, Lydia thought. I can understand this bloke (she chucked to herself).

"Coffee would be great. Milk and honey," said Dio. "Me too, please," added Martinez. Lockie looked over at Hutchinson who just held up his thumb and index finger about three inches apart. Dio remembered this from his rookie days in the NYPD. The old timers would stop into a local saloon and make the same gesture—meaning three fingers of Four Roses.

Lockie directed them to a small round table where the four of them sat. Mr. Ross brought their beverages, and the uniformed female driver handed Hutchinson an old, battered, leather briefcase. He pulled out a tarnished yellow folder and placed it on the table.

"This here is the file we have on the accident that took place in town during the 1999 European Junior Amateur Championship tournament that was held here." Pointing toward Lockie he continued, "Neal won that event, which is why I suggested we meet here. But we will get to Neal's part in a bit."

197

Lydia was thankful she was sitting facing Hutchinson and was sure Dio was too. He was much easier to understand. Maybe the shot of whiskey slowed his speech down she thought.

"So on the night in question," he said opening the folder, these two ladies from Ayr are pub-crawling. Now keep in mind the town back then is not much different than it is today, some twenties years on. The victims, again he leafed through the folder, were twenty-five-year-old Barbara Maples and twenty-eight-year-old Susan Thorp. They both lived in Ayr and worked in a women's clothing shop. Thorp was a divorced mom and had a two-year-old. We could only ID them through dental records—their bodies were so charred. As I said on the phone, I was only a constable then and had no input into the investigation. I only became aware of this case about two years ago when I was put in charge of the Historical Crime Unit."

"If it was an accident, why then was it given to your unit?" Dio asked. Lydia thought the same thing.

"Well you see about five years ago, one of the victim's family members persisted in getting us to look at it again. You have to understand that prior to the merger in 2013, there were eight different police agencies here. Technology was also slow a comin' to these parts so we didn't have that nor the trained manpower to conduct the kind of investigation we would do today in a similar case."

OK, enough of the history lesson, Lydia was saying to herself, let's move on here.

Hutchinson pointed at his empty tumbler and gave Lockie a smile. Lockie picked up the phone and placed an order, "More tea? Coffee?"

"I'm good," said Dio. "Me too," added Martinez.

Martinez looked out the large window behind Lockie's desk and noticed the rain had stopped and the sun was shining. Lockie looked at his watch as a way to get Hutchinson to continue.

"After the merger the Historical Crime Unit was formed. Initially I was second in command. We had about fifteen

198

experienced DCs (detective constables), DSs (detective sergeants), and DIs (detective inspectors). I was the DCI and reported to a chief superintendent." Lydia recalled Dio telling that all the police agencies in Great Britain did not use military ranks, with the exception of sergeant, for their respective officers.

Hutchinson continued, "So after we settled in and we began to review cases, two of our DCs, again flipping through the folder, yes, here it is, DCs Teresa Price and Donna Harran, both females I might add." He said this looking at Lydia in a patronizing way. They discovered that in the autopsy report, both of the victims had signs of blunt force trauma to the craniums. He read on. The original report stated the gas tank exploded when the vehicle crashed into the ditch, but my team noticed that the gas tank gauge (one of the few salvageable pieces of the vehicle) indicated the tank barely had enough petrol to get them back to Ayr. He indicated that he was not confident that small amount of petrol would have caused such damage. He believed an accelerant had been used. They also found an object in the burnt out vehicle, some sort of rock that was used to keep pressure on the gas pedal."

"Why wasn't any of this done originally?" Martinez asked.

"Like I said, we didn't have the manpower or expertise back then, plus very little crime happened here. Mostly stuff related to alcohol—ya know, fights, domestic disturbances, maybe a DWI. People come here for one reason and one reason only—to play golf. Ain't that right, Neal, old boy?"

"Aye, it tis, it tis."

"So how are you involved in this, Neal?" asked Lydia.

As he was about to answer, Hutchinson held up his hand to cut him off. "We'll get to that anon. But first let me continue on with what we did at HCU. We had the family give us some items of the victims that might contain DNA—you know a toothbrush, lipstick, and the like. So we at least have their DNA on file now." He was rumbling through the file again.

"Most of this is on computers now, but I still like the old way, eh," he said with a smile. He pulled out a smaller envelope from the file, opened it, and handed the contents to Dio and Lydia.

"These are the photos we have of the remains. He handed her two other photos. "These are the photos from the motor vehicle agency. Copies, their licenses were not recovered, probably burned in the fire."

Lydia looked at the charred bones laid out on a morgue gurney and several photos of the burned out vehicle. She and Dio passed them back and forth. Looking at the photos from the driver's licenses, Lydia saw the pretty faces of two young women who died a horrible death. Could Messerschmitt and Spunkmeyer be involved? she wondered.

"Was there any evidence of sexual assault?"

"Again, Detective, as you can see from the photos, the victims' bodies were burned beyond recognition. I don't think we had the technology to make such a determination at that time."

"Of course," she replied, "DCI Hutchinson, would we be able to talk to your detectives who did this investigation?" Looking at her notes, "DCs Price and Harren?"

"Well, nae, ya see, Terry Price retired and moved to New Zealand, and Donna married a Yank she met here playing golf. As a matter of fact, I think she lives in Florida. Anyhow, I got all the files ya need right here and when Neal here tells you his side of this story, you may not need to speak to anyone else. Go on now lad."

Lockie looked directly at Martinez and began his story. "Well ya see ma'am."

"Lydia, please."

"OK, then Lydia. In 1999, I was a lad and I played for the Scottish national team in the same European Junior Amateur Championship tournament against Karl Messerschmitt and Dieter Spunkmeyer. We, the Scottish and the Brits, called him 'Spunky,' but not to his face. He was a scary dude but a very good player. Nothing seemed to bother him on the golf course. We were playing on our home course and were heavily favored. Spunky never played either course here. Not sure about Messerschmitt, who by the way was another loner kind of guy. So there are six countries represented and each team has six players. So the first two days we played stroke-play elimination with the two teams with the lowest scores to par go on to play head-to-head in a traditional Ryder Cup format. You know what that is?"

She had no clue but nodded yes just to get him to move on. " Our team comes in second to the Krauts. Oops, sorry I mean the German lads."

"Could you just get to the part about the German players?"

"OK, yeah sure, but I forgot most of the details. It's been nearly twenty years. But I remember we go into the final match-play round and it's me playing Messerschmitt and another lad," he paused to recall the name.

"Richard Nolan?" asked Hutchinson.

"Aye, Richard, good player he was. I think he moved to the states too. Anyway, we have to win only one match to win the championship. Spunky blew Richard away and I was losing to Messerschmitt, until we got to the twelfth hole." He went on to describe how Karl's game fell apart after twelve.

"Were you aware of the accident that happened the night before?"

"No, not at tee-off time. But that's just the thing. When we got to the twelfth hole, which is just off the road from where the accident occurred, we could see the police vehicle and a tow truck. I remember Karl looking over there and his face went white, whiter than it already was, I mean."

"Go on, Neal."

"Yes, well from that point on, Karl fell apart. He made some terrible shots. Spunky beat Richard four and three, so at this point I had to win my match, which I did to win the championship. I remember asking Richard if he thought anything strange happened out there and he said the same thing."

"Spunky was definitely hungover, but it never showed. The only time he showed emotion was when I mentioned to the official that a tee marker was missing from the twelfth tee."

"Anything else, Neal?"

"No, not that I can think of. Does this have anything to do with the medical leave?"

"What leave? What do you mean?"

Lockie reached into a letterbox on his desk and handed a paper to Martinez. "This came in earlier today via email. I printed it out in case you wanted to see it."

Lydia read the note on PGA Europe letterhead. To all PGA Europe professionals and PGA Euro golf facilities. Effective immediately, PGA touring professional Karl Messerschmitt will be placed on medical exemption for the remainder of the season.

Lydia passed the memo on to Dio, who just read it and passed it back to Lockie.

"Interesting," said Lydia.

As she stood up, she thanked both Lockie and DCI Hutchinson for their assistance in their investigation. She wanted to get out of there and call back to tell ASA Heichemer what she had just learned, maybe help strengthen her extradition application. She wondered how the smug entitled Messerschmitt would respond to this.

Dio had booked a room for the night at the Lochgreen House Hotel. Dio had mentioned to Lydia that he had some business to attend to in nearby Prestwick and rather than rushing back to London, they could spend a night or two in Scotland. Lydia was pleased to have packed an overnight bag.

"Well as long as they have Wi-Fi and a cell tower, I'm in. Plus I've never gotten laid in Scotland. Have you, Mr. Bosso?" Dio just gave her a smile.

CHAPTER 58

The year was 1999 and after playing in Berlin the previous year, Dieter was now being driven all over Germany and by Herr Rhienhardt to compete. Although he had never beaten his new friend Karl, he always faced him in the finals only to lose by one or two holes. When they played in team events, they easily won. It was time for them to play on the international amateur circuit. When they traveled abroad, either Dieter's coach Rhienhardt or Karl's coach Herr Van Boven would coach both boys; rarely did both coaches travel.

While Karl's family had the financial resources to support Karl's golf, Rhienhardt on the other hand had to scrounge funds through the Saxonwalt club members to support Dieter's golf. Their reward would come in the publicity that their club would get by having the number-two-ranked junior amateur in Germany. They had hoped, like Van Boven, when their protégé became a professional they would receive some form of payback in the agreement they made with Rhienhardt without Dieter's knowledge.

The 1999 European Junior Amateur Championship was being held in Troon, located on the west coast of Scotland and about a one-hour drive from the Glasgow Prestwick airport. It was only the second time Dieter had flown and his first playing in Scotland, considered to be the home of golf. Previously he had played in England and had flown from Berlin to London to play in a tournament in Sandringham. Karl missed that tournament, so Dieter had won. This was to be a team format event with each team consisting of six players. Besides Karl and Dieter, the four other boys were not as well known.

The teams from England, Ireland, and Scotland were heavily favored. The format for the tournament would be two days of stroke play. The two teams with the combined lowest scores would meet in match play, with each team playing its two best players. After the stroke play rounds, all of the other teams were eliminated except for the Germans and the Scots. On Saturday evening Herr Van Boven took the boys into town, which was only a short distance from the hotel and the golf course. Like most of Europe, Scotland had no drinking age, so the team members all were permitted to have some ale with dinner. After dinner coach Van Boven told the lads to head back to the hotel, as they needed their rest. He had his eye on a young lady who was one of the officials at the tournament.

As the team members walked back to the hotel, Dieter and Karl lagged. Karl had a low tolerance for alcohol and Dieter could see he was a bit tipsy. They let the other team members get ahead and they went into another pub. Karl of course had plenty of cash, so they had a couple of more beers and starting to buy rounds for some of the people at the pub. They made it known who they were and were met with good cheer, as the Scots knew their boys would prevail on Sunday's single matches, especially if these *two krauts* kept drinking. As Dieter and Karl sat at a table, they were joined by two pretty young ladies who introduced themselves as Barbara and Susan. They were both hitting on Karl as he was easier on the eyes and more talkative than the gangly curly haired Dieter.

"You don't look like a German," Barbara said to Dieter. "I've never seen a kraut with such dark hair and dark features. You on the other hand," she pointed to Karl, "look like someone out of a Nazi World War II movie." They both giggled and asked the boys if they wanted to do shots of good scotch whiskey. Karl waived the bartender over and ordered.

"Four shots of your best whiskey." The barman complied.

After about three rounds, it was obvious Karl and the girls were in their cups. Dieter said to Karl in German that it was time to go.

"Hey, no speaking German," said Barbara, the drunker of the two.

"We have to play golf tomorrow and need to get back to our hotel."

"Yeah," slurred Karl, "golf tomorrow, golf, golf, golf."

The girls were drunk too, and Sue said, "We should go too, Barb. We have a ways to drive back to Ayr."

"You don't live here?" asked Dieter.

"No, Ayr," replied Sue. "My car is parked down the road a bit. Will you walk us to the car?"

"Yes, good idea," replied Dieter. The party got up and Dieter had to help both Karl and Barbara to their feet. They were both giggling and walked out of the pub arm-in-arm. Susan reluctantly held Dieter's arm feeling once again her friend got the better-looking guy. Susan was not as attractive or outgoing as her friend. Barbara was prettier, friendlier, and flirtier. It was not the first time Susan got the second prize.

They made their way along the darkened street back to where Susan had parked her small Ford Taurus. Giggling, Karl and Barbara made their way into the back seat and immediately started to make out. Susan started the car and Dieter reached over to kiss her and she reluctantly kissed him back.

"What's wrong? Don't you want to make out like our friends in the back?" By now Karl and Barbara were both panting feverishly—Karl running his hand under Barbara's skirt and unbuttoning her blouse.

"Let's give them some privacy," said Susan and they both got out of car. Their car was the only car on the dark unlit street, and Dieter walked with Susan to a secluded area that appeared to be a park. Then Dieter realized they were on the back end of one of the golf courses. He grabbed Susan and drew her into him and this time she responded better than in the car. Dieter put his hand on her breast, which felt firm, and he started to get an erection. This was his first encounter with a girl since Dagmar/Edletraud/Maria in Berlin, and when Susan felt his hardening cock, she pushed him away.

"Oh no, you're not. I'm not letting you have me then never see me again when you go back to Germany." She was fishing for him to say something sweet and romantic, as she too was feeling a bit randy. However, Dieter did not pick up on her coyness. Why would he? It didn't take long for the perceived rejection to take control of Dieter's emotions nor the rage in him that seemed to grow within seconds of Susan's words.

He struck her with his fist so hard that she almost passed out. He hit her again and dragged her further away from the road. He hit a third time, knocking her unconscious. All the while he could feel his cock getting harder and harder. As Susan's unconscious body lay on the ground, Dieter ripped at her skirt and pulled her panties down to her ankles and dropped down on his knees—rolling her over, entered her from behind, and had no need for a lubricant. He thought that this slut had fucked many men, as she was not as tight as he expected. What he did not know was that she had had a child and in fact was in her late twenties, ten years older than he was. She started to stir as he pumped away at her limp body. She tried to move and started to scream. He punched her again in the back of her neck, then feeling around the ground he found a rock and started to bash her head all the while fucking her from behind. Dieter exploded into her fully knowing she was dead.

Panting like a wild animal he stood up and looked back toward the Taurus and could tell by the rocking of the small car that Karl and Barbara were going at it. Looking down at the body of the thing that was only minutes ago a living human being, Dieter pulled up his own pants and started back toward the car. Rage still filled him. He opened the door and yanked the humping Karl off the blonde. Both were shocked, and Karl yelled in German.

"Dieter what are you doing? Are you crazy? What are you doing?" He threw Karl to the ground and started to drag a screaming Barbara from the car. He punched her hard in the face and she fell back into the car. Karl was grabbing and screaming at him.

"Dieter why are you doing this? What is wrong with you?"

Dieter, in German, said, "Quiet. You will wake the whole town."

Barbara was screaming and crying, and Dieter finally got her out of the car. He realized he had the object that he bashed Susan's head in within his hand still and he used it to strike Barbara on the head. She immediately fell to the ground. Her skirt still around her knees. Karl was starting to get up and was obviously in shock. He had never seen his friend or anyone for that matter in such a state of rage. Dieter meanwhile could feel his cock still hard in his pants. He snapped at Karl, "Did you finish?"

"What, what are you talking about? Finish what?"

"Finish fucking her," Dieter screamed. Karl could barely get up. His head was spinning from what he had just seen his friend do, plus the effects of the alcohol he had consumed. He felt himself getting sick, then he vomited all he had drank and ate today. When he finished, he could not believe what he was witnessing let alone what he had just seen. Dieter had his pants down and was humping the lifeless body of Barbara.

"Dieter, what are you doing? Why are you doing this? I don't understand," Karl was now in shock and tried to get his head to stop spinning. Dieter moaned as he came again into dead Barbara.

Karl staggered away, his head spinning, his stomach spewing out more vomit, and his eyes burned.

"Quick, help me get her back into the car."

What, thought Karl, "what are you saying"?

"They can't drive. Are you insane?" Dieter just looked at him and stared. Karl was frightened that Dieter might take that object and bash his head in, so he helped Dieter put Barbara's lifeless body into the passenger's seat. He then took Karl by his shirt collar and marched him over to where Susan's body lay. A light rain started to fall.

"She is still warm, so you can fuck her if you want," Dieter said as if telling Karl it was the most natural thing to do. Karl didn't say a word. He helped Dieter put the lifeless body of Susan into the back seat. Dieter told Karl to get into the back seat. Karl was incredulous.

"You want me to sit back here with this dead girl?"

"Well you can drive, and I'll sit back there." Karl who was in shock just complied and got into the back seat trying to avoid eye contact with Susan, whose head was still oozing blood from her skull. Her eyes were open, and this made Karl feel like he wanted to puke again. Dieter got behind the steering wheel and put the car in drive. He drove toward the city of Ayr. He asked Karl once again if he fucked Barbara. He asked this in the same manner he would ask, did you practice putting? or Did you have lunch?

About a mile out of town Dieter pulled off the side of the road next to a ditch about two meters deep. He told Karl to get out and asked him once more if he wanted to give either girl a final fuck. Karl just shook his head, still in disbelief of what he had witnessed.

Karl once again became ill and vomited on the side of the car. While he was doing this Dieter took Susan's lifeless body and placed it behind the wheel of the Ford and buckled both girls in. He removed their driver's licenses from the pocketbooks. He found some rags in the boot of the car and stuck one of the rags in the gas tank. He pulled it out and, taking a Bic lighter, lit the rag. He threw the rag in the front seat; it landed on Barbara's lap. He took a second rag and did the same on Susan's lap; they both caught and flames started to grow inside the car. Now he put the car in gear and told Karl to help him push the car forward heading for the ditch. He placed a third rag in the open gas tank and lit it. The car rolled forward, and Dieter placed the murder weapon on the gas

208

pedal and the car accelerated. As it rolled toward the ditch, he patted Karl on the back and said, "OK, partner, let's get out of here. We got golf to play in the morning," and just like that he was the same old Dieter that he was before they left the pub. Karl, still in shock, just walked along.

As they walked back toward Troon, they heard the gas tank explode. Boom thought Dieter. Just like Berlin last year, only this time there would be two bodies instead of one. Two drunk girls driving home after a night of partying. There would be no evidence of foul play, no prints, no DNA, and no Dieter and Karl. *Auf Weiderschen*. The boys walked back to their hotel and did not see or hear a thing, not even a fire engine responding to the flames of the burning Ford.

The next morning as the teams assembled for the final matches, Karl was hungover and sick from what he witnessed the previous evening. He thought any minute the cops would appear and arrest both him and Dieter for the brutal murders committed by Dieter. He thought of telling Coach Van Boven but then erased those thoughts, as he knew he would be considered as guilty as Dieter.

The early matches on Sunday proved uneventful. The teams from England, Ireland, Northern Ireland, and Sweden did not score well enough to make it to the match-play finals. It would come down to the two remaining teams, Scotland and Germany—Lockie and Nolan for Scotland and Messerschmitt and Spunkmeyer for Germany. The Germans needed to win both of their matches while the Scots needed only one victory to win the championship. Coach Van Boven knew both his star players would be up to the task. Of course, he was not aware of last night's atrocities.

The teams would play their matches on the East course, which was closer to town. This course was not played during the previous matches and would give the Scots an advantage. Coach Van Boven complained to the tournament officials to no avail. Dieter who acted as if nothing had happened the night before was selected by Coach Van Boven to play the first match against Nolan. He won the first two holes and remained two up until they reached the twelfth hole. Both ten and eleven played into the wind and toward the town where they had partied and murdered the night before.

On the twelfth tee, Nolan commented to the official that there was only one tee marker. Looking at the tee marker with the official, Dieter realized the object that he used to bash in the skulls of his victims was the missing tee marker. He looked around to see if Susan's blood was visible, but the steady rain had apparently washed it into the ground. Dieter won the twelfth hole, a par five by sinking a ten-foot putt for birdie. They halved thirteen and fourteen, and Dieter won fifteen to close Nolan out four and three (four up with three holes to play). The German team was now even with the Scots.

Although hungover and still somewhat in shock from what he had witnessed the previous evening, Karl played OK. He was two up on Lockie until they got to the twelfth tee. Karl recognized the adjacent area as the place where Dieter's evil deeds the night before took place. He also realized that the missing tee marker was the weapon used to bash in the skulls of Susan and Barbara, two young ladies just out to have a good time. He could not get them or the events of the previous night out of his mind. Karl had never lost a match that he had a lead going into the back nine; however, this time the results were going to be different. Lockie won twelve and thirteen with pars while Karl made bogey on both holes. Karl had gone from plus two to even in two easy par fours. Van Boven, watching from the sidelines, could see his player was visibly upset. He tried to bolster his spirits.

"Come on, Karl, you're better than this guy. Refocus, refocus," he pleaded. Karl just shrugged him off. "I don't have it today, Coach. I feel sick."

The pep talk from his coach did not help Karl. His concentration was lost. All he could think about was how his friend had brutally raped and killed those two women and then go out and win a golf match. He lost the next two holes and was two down with two to play when they reached the par three, sixteenth hole. Lockie hit his tee shot on the green ten feet from the pin. Karl drove his tee shot out of bounds and conceded, and the jubilant Scots won the match. Karl just wanted to go home.

On the flight back to Germany, Karl could do nothing but think about what he had witnessed the previous night and the horrible actions of his best friend. He thought of approaching Dieter, who sat alone reading a golf magazine, and talk to him about last night but did not. When they arrived at Tempelhof Airport in Berlin, Dieter was met by Coach Rhienhardt. Except for Karl, the rest of the boys on the team had to catch a train back to their hometowns. Karl had a private plane waiting to take him back to his parents' home outside of Frankfurt. After all his name was Messerschmitt, synonymous with flying.

Over the next several months, the boys played in several amateur tournaments, both on the continent and in Great Britain. While Karl and Dieter won most of their doubles matches, Karl made it a point to not socialize with Dieter alone. Neither boy mentioned the events that took place that night in Troon.

One evening while playing a tournament at Le Golf Club outside of Paris, Dieter asked Karl to join him for a few drinks in the city of lights. Karl feigned illness and declined to go, even though Dieter persisted. Dieter left on his own. Karl stayed in the room he shared with Dieter and could not sleep thinking about what his friend, who he now feared yet loved, might be up to.

Around 3:00 a.m., Karl could hear some noise coming from the outside of the hotel and got up and peered from his window. He saw a gens d'armes vehicle parked in the driveway and Coach Van Boven standing in his robe talking to a French policeman. He also noticed Dieter sitting in the back seat. Van Boven was gesturing with both hands speaking in German while the French cop was speaking in French. Finally the hotel manager appeared and was able to translate for the coach. After a few minutes the French cop and Coach Van Boven shook hands and nodded heads. The cop opened the rear door and Dieter stepped out, his right hand heavily bandaged and in obvious pain. Karl scooted back to his bed and pretended to be asleep as Dieter entered the room.

"Karl, are you awake?"

"I am now." Looking at his bandaged hand, he asked what happened.

"I was stabbed. A couple of punks tried to mug me, and I got stabbed right through my hand. It hurts bad. Have you got any of those pain killers?"

"Er, yes, I do. Wait, I'll get some." A skeptical Karl got out of his bed and reached into his duffel bag and pulled out a bottle of painkillers. He tossed the plastic bottle of pills to his friend, wondering what really happened.

"Dieter, is there anything you want to tell me about tonight? Were you up to your old tricks again? You know you can trust me."

Dieter just looked at Karl and smirked.

"Trust you, sure I can trust you. Remember you were with me last year in Troon. And you will be with me, or I with you (he raised his bandaged hand) for a long time my friend."

"Now let me go to sleep. I don't think I will be playing golf for a while."

Over the next several weeks, Dieter saw doctors in both France and Germany. Apparently the injury he sustained severed the ligaments and tendons in his right hand, and as a result he was unable to grip a golf club. He had several surgeries and therapy, but once he started to practice again his game was not the same. He tried to compete but was unable to win. In fact, over the next two years his game got so bad that he lost his sponsors from the Saxonwalt golf club.

Eventually coach Rhienhardt told him that he could no longer qualify for the German national amateur team. Dieter was disappointed but not overly so. As Karl Messerschmitt's

212

game improved and he moved on to the European semiprofessional tour, Dieter became his caddy. Karl was still frightened of his friend, but he believed nobody knew his game better than Dieter, and in fact he credited him for his rapid rise on the mini-tour and his eventual goal of playing on the European PGA tour.

Dieter had several more surgeries on his right hand but as time went on, his hand started to close and he could no longer open it enough to properly grip a golf club. It was strange to Karl how this didn't seem to bother him as much as it would have bothered Karl if the situation was reversed. No, Dieter seemed to be content being Karl's caddy and traveling first-class all over Europe and Great Britain.

Karl's game with Dieter's help continued to improve and by the time he was twenty-three, in 2007, he had gotten his PGA European tour card and was making close to a million euros a year. The agreement he had with Dieter was the standard player-caddy agreement most pros employed. A straight 10 percent of earning plus expenses for travel, clothing, and a per diem for food and beverage. Karl's father had his attorney drew up the contracts, as Karl never discussed financial matters with Dieter.

After the "mugging" in France, Karl seemed to think that maybe he had learned his lesson as he was sure that Dieter's stabbing was the result of a potential victim fighting back rather than the alleged mugging. Although the French police interviewed Dieter several times about what transpired that evening, Dieter stuck to his story. He was attacked by two men, who appeared to be Middle Eastern. They demanded money and when he told them he did not understand, one of them came at him with a knife. He raised his hand to defend himself, and the knife went through his hand. His assailants ran off.

CHAPTER 59

ASA Heichemer called a meeting with her boss, State's Attorney Ed "Mickey" McDonald, and Sheriff Rick Romain to discuss the Dollbee homicide. McDonald was a standout college basketball player for the Miami Hurricanes and had a brief NBA career. Having gone to law school at night he decided to pursue a political career and was elected state's attorney the first time he ran. Everyone knew he had his eyes on Tallahassee. The current governor, Denis Biglin, would be unable to run next in 2020, due to term limits. A high-profile prosecution and conviction in this case could catapult McDonald right into the governor's mansion. The meeting was held in Romain's boardroom and in addition to a stenographer, Major Adams and Lieutenant Cashin were present.

Romain started the conversation and looking directly at Lieutenant Cashin said, "Looks like your detective is stirring up shit over there in Europe."

"As far as I know she's on vacation, Chief. But we both know she's not going to let this go."

"Nor should she," said Major Adams. Addressing the room Adams continued, "Look, we all know Detective Martinez can be a little strong-willed and has a history of doing things, er, let's say, her own way. But she gets results. Lieutenant Cashin, what's her clearance rate?" she asked looking at Cashin.

"Well, since I've been the CO, it's been 100 percent, but she's only had the one homicide prior to this one."

Looking at Romain he continued, "You know, Chief, the homeless vet that got roasted by the gangbangers."

McDonald was next to speak, "ASA Heichemer briefed me on this case earlier this morning, and I must say I've read the coverage in the papers. Why did you reassign this to Cold Case, Sheriff?" He was looking at Romain, who in turn looked at Lieutenant Cashin to give an answer.

"Well you see, Mr. McDonald, I felt that Detective Martinez became too emotionally involved in this homicide, so I suggested we have fresh eyes look at it. The rest of my team had other cases to work on, so the next logical choice was the Cold Case team." Cashin pushed back in his chair and glanced over at his boss. Romain just looked ahead and Cashin thought that his time as a detective commander might be coming to an end.

The group once again discussed all the facts and evidence of the case and after about a forty-five minute back-and-forth, it was decided that ASA Heichemer will empanel a grand jury and seek an indictment of Messerschmitt and Spunkmeyer. Once indicted they could start the extradition process through a local magistrate. McDonald said he would personally contact the lawyer MacLeod and arrange for an interview with Messerschmitt and possibly Spunkmeyer. Sheriff Romain would contact Martinez and the German federal police and advise them of Martinez's now official position and request assistance from them. Romain also suggested that both the state's attorney and his office have their respective public information sections make a joint statement to the press and update them on the investigation. It was suggested that they notify George Goll at The Florida Classic of what they were about to do so that he could get ahead of the backlash from the public that one of *his golfers* is a suspect in the murder of Jasmin Dollbee, a volunteer.

"This is gonna cause a shit storm at the PGA, AMC, and the other sponsors," added McDonald. "But what the hell, I drive a Chevy, and I don't play golf. So let's not let our personal

215

relationships get in the way here." He was looking at Romain as he made this statement. "Let's go full-bore here and do what's right. Major Adams, could you give me Detective Martinez's cell? I might want to speak to her myself."

CHAPTER 60

The next day State's Attorney McDonald along with the PBSO held a joint news conference on the Dollbee homicide. It was scheduled for 4:00 p.m. McDonald, in his fifties, who still had an athlete's build was dressed in a dark blue suit. He stood behind a podium and was flanked on either side by Sheriff Romain and Dr. Debra Widman of the ME's office. Next to each of them was Major Adams and ASA Heichemer. McDonald was ready to address the assembled members of the media. He looked over at Dr. Widman who was still eating the complimentary bagel that was customarily served with coffee at press conferences.

"We're going to start now, Dr. Widman," he said pointing at the bagel.

"Em, sorry sir. I had to stop by the office before I came here and had no time—"

McDonald raised a hand to cut her off.

From the back of the room the director gave the countdown, "In five, four, three, two, one." He pointed at McDonald.

"Good morning, ladies and gentlemen. Over the last forty-eight hours we have developed new information concerning the brutal murder of Jasmin Dollbee. Information gleaned not only from the diligent investigation by the Palm Beach County Sheriff's Office but also evidence from the medical examiner's office and PBSO crime lab that strongly implicate professional golfer, Karl Messerschmitt, and his caddy, one Dieter Spunkmeyer, as persons-of-interest. Witness and forensic evidence place both men at the scene of the

217

crime." McDonald paused for a second, "I have assigned Senior ASA Nancy Heichemer, a seasoned prosecutor, to this case. Ms. Heichemer, please." He gestured for Nancy to step forward and she did. She had to adjust the microphone to meet her five-foot-three height. McDonald stood at about six-foot-four.

"Good morning, ladies and gentlemen. Yesterday afternoon I empaneled a special grand jury with the purpose of presenting evidence and testimony on behalf of the county of Palm Beach in order to seek an indictment of first-degree murder and other charges on the two men that State's Attorney McDonald mentioned in his remarks. Witnesses have been subpoenaed. I am confident upon presentation of the evidence and testimony of the witnesses that an indictment will be issued. I also went before Judge Matthew D'Emic and started extradition proceedings against Messrs. Messerschmitt and Spunkmeyer. While the process is cumbersome, Judge D'Emic assures me he will issue the order once we have an indictment. However, we may face some difficulty with the German courts."

As she stepped away Sheriff Romain took the podium. "The PBSO has sent the lead detective on this case, Detective Lydia Martinez, to Germany to work with their federal police in continuing the investigation and interviewing the suspects." He went on about the sheriff's office's commitment to solving this horrendous crime. Major Adams knew that he along with the others were just saying what they wanted the press to report. She knew the only way they will get results would be due to Martinez's tenacity and unwillingness to let justice not be served. She wished all cops she knew were as dedicated and ballsy as Lydia Martinez.

As soon as Romain finished McDonald retook the podium. "I know you all have questions, and we will try to answer them. Please, one at a time."

The questions were routine, and the responses were for the most part a repetition of what was said from the podium. Before McDonald left, he instructed Heichemer to continue on with the extradition paperwork. He would call Judge D'Emic and contact the M&M law firm in Europe as well as the Corcoran, Denihan, and O'Shea firm here. Heichemer smelt a deal in the works.

CHAPTER 61

At PGA of America headquarters, PGA President Sean McCooey was on a conference call with George Goll and Eric Strumza, vice president of sales for AMC. Strumza was fuming that the PGA and Goll did not get on top of this situation. Neither of them knew what they could have done to short-circuit this situation. Strumza was threatening to pull the AMC sponsorship or move the tournament to another state. McCooey let him vent as did Goll. After he calmed down, he said, "OK, let's do some damage control here."

It was now McCooey who spoke, "The PGA of American and the PGA Europe will issue a statement saying that we have temporarily suspended Karl Messerschmitt's playing privileges at our events. In my statement I will attempt to absolve both American Motors Corporation and The Florida Classic of any malfeasance on their respective parts. After all, how could any of us know what a tour player does off the course?"

It was Strumza who broke in, "By the way, do either of you know this guy personally?"

McCooey answered first, "I met him a few times. Never really had a conversation with him."

"How about you George?"

"I've meet him a few times also. But he has a reputation of being a loner. Doesn't pal out with any of the other pros as far as I know. Not even Kaymer or Cjeka, the other Germans on the tour."

"It seems to me that walking away from this year's Classic, when he was in the top ten, and he was scheduled to play in Doral and Bay Hill tells me something is not kosher with this guy."

"I agree, Eric," said Goll.

"OK, I'll get my PR people at AMC to get ahead of this. I have no problem throwing this guy under the bus. Christ, if he did do this, he must be some sicko anyway."

"I agree with you, Eric. George, let the PGA put out a statement. I don't think we need for The Classic to say anything about Messerschmitt just yet. You may want to personally contact the Dollbees and offer them your support."

"We already did, Sean. I had our media people contact Mr. and Mrs. Dollbee just after their daughter's funeral."

"I'm thinking more of a personal call from you, George. Don't you agree, Eric?"

Strumza said he agreed and suggested that maybe American Motors might do something next year at The Classic to honor Jasmin.

Just as McCooey finished his office door opened and his assistant handed him a note. He read it for a moment then said to the others, "Looks like the Euros beat us to it. I'll fax this over to you now. They put Messerschmitt on the medical exemption list."

"Those fuckers," said Strumza. "So what now Sean?"

"We can still suspend him. The alleged crime happened here, not Europe, so we can take a harder stance."

"Alleged, what the fuck you mean alleged? That girl is dead."

"Yeah, sorry Eric, it must be the lawyer in me."

"In your press release Sean mentioned that the PGA will assist in the investigation in any way it can. I want the cops to know we're not responsible and we will cooperate."

"What about that lady detective? What's her name?"

"Martinez."

"Yeah, Martinez. Has she been around again, Sean?"

"No."

"How about you, George?"

"Last I heard she's on vacation and the case was reassigned.

They continued their three-way conversation discussing other less important matters. They all agreed that Messerschmitt, although popular in Europe, was a relative unknown here in the states. Assuming he was guilty, there would be a minimal ripple effect outside of Florida.

It was Strumza who made the end statement, "PGA of America will be the only entity making any public statements on this matter for now. We will announce that AMC is severing its sponsorship of Mr. Messerschmitt. I'm sure his other sponsors will follow suit. As for you, George, you'll have to deal with your other sponsors, charities, and the authorities. Let's do our best to let nature take its course here and hope this is all behind us next year."

The conversation ended and Sean McCooey turned on his computer and started to craft the memo that would announce Messerschmitt's suspension.

CHAPTER 62

It was raining and chilly when Dio woke up. Lydia was still soundly sleeping next to him. He had hoped to take Hutchinson's suggestion of taking Lydia on a drive through the countryside after his business in Prestwick. Maybe drive to Edinburgh to see the city. Last night, after making love she talked about how much the cold, rainy weather made her feel more alive.

"You sure it's not the sex?"

"You're not gloating are you, D?" He smiled.

"Try living here. After a few months of this you'll want to swim back to Florida."

"Oh, I don't know, Dio. It's different. The landscape, the wind-swept rain. I like it and I can wear the lovely gloves you gave me all the time." She reached over and kissed him good night. They both were asleep in a matter of minutes.

Dio was about to snuggle next to Lydia when his cell phone rang. Getting out of bed, he picked up the phone and was greeted by Polizeidirektor Boser.

"Good morning, Dio. I also left a message for Detective Martinez. Messerschmitt's lawyer had agreed to another interview. From what I understand, he spoke to a prosecutor in Florida and some tentative deal was made. The interview will be conducted at Bundespolizei office in Wiesbaden at 1300 the day after tomorrow."

"That's great news, Walter. I'm sure Detective Martinez will be pleased when she hears this news."

"Come on, Dio, I'm sure she is with you now. I'm a detective too, and I can tell by your body language that you two are, how you say, doing it," he laughed. "But be careful, my friend. An old guy like you can only take so much," he laughed again, this time louder.

Dio thought, Now I got this guy busting my balls. Dio didn't mind the ribbing. The good news from Boser was just that—good news. Now he wanted to wake Lydia and share this with her. Plus he would have to make arrangements to fly back to Frankfurt.

Having made some calls he found out that it would be easier to fly commercial from Edinburgh direct to Frankfurt. He had miles to spare and he didn't want to abuse his flying privileges with Lloyd's. When he woke Lydia and told her the good news, she did not react the way he thought.

"Why would Boser tell you and not me. It's my case, is it not? What's wrong with these guys here? Do they think I'm just some girl along for the ride?"

"Hold on, Lyd. Hold on a second. Check your phone. Walter called you first, left a message I believe."

Lydia picked up the phone, scanned the messages, and held it to her ear listening to Boser's message. Looking at Dio, she just smiled. "I guess all this sex is making me a little sensitive. Maybe we should abstain for a few days, so I get back to being my old hard-ass self."

He pushed her back on the bed and grabbed her butt with his hands and said, "I love this hard ass of yours." He kissed her hard on the mouth and she responded but for only a second.

"Ugh, my breath must stink, let me up."

"We've got to be back in Frankfurt in two days. I booked us a flight on Lufthansa for Wednesday morning, direct to Frankfurt. Boser will arrange a ride to BPOL headquarters in Wiesbaden."

"What, no private plane? This is bullshit, Dio. I'm outta here," she said mockingly with her hands on her hips.

"Go brush your teeth and get dressed. We'll grab some breakfast downstairs. Hutchinson arranged for a car, so we can drive out to the countryside, maybe hit Edinburgh for dinner."

With that Lydia gave him a hug and kissed the side of his face as she trotted off to the bathroom. Dio watched her go and loved the sight of her naked butt.

CHAPTER 63

They were enjoying the scenery of the Scottish countryside, driving north through several small villages, stopping once for a coffee and a snack. Just as they got back into the unmarked police car Hutchinson secured for them, Lydia's phone rang. The call was from Nancy Heichemer.

"Lydia, how are you?" Her voice was exuberant, and Lydia hoped this would be good news.

"I'm fine, Nancy. Any news?"

"Any news? Where you been girl?"

Lydia was surprised at Nancy's relaxed tone. She had always been so formal. "I have a grand jury empaneled and I've got several witnesses ready to testify. I am going before it tomorrow. Originally I thought I would need you but based on your reports and your witness statements I think I will have enough for an indictment of both Messerschmitt and Spunkmeyer."

"That's great, Nancy, but can you hold off a day or two? Messerschmitt has agreed to an interview with me and if he and his high-priced lawyer in the three-thousand-euro suit get wind of that he may decide not to talk."

"Well I have the ME, Doc Widman, and the lab tech Stack on for tomorrow morning, followed by the security guys from PGA National, Dansky and Kriegsman. The following day I have those teens you interviewed," she paused, and Lydia could hear her riffling through her files, "yeah, Tricia Maddox, Michael Pierce, and Mark Van Hooey. Pierce's girlfriend is back in San Antonio in the air force. I don't think I'll need her or you for that matter. Your lieutenant said he would have one of his detectives, I think he said Detective Kiers, give testimony in your stead. Hell, it's only a grand jury right? You can get a ham sandwich indicted here in the sunshine state."

"By the way, Detective, did you place a magic spell on the Van Hooey kid. All he could talk about was you and wondered where you were or if you would be at the grand jury."

Lydia knew she was teasing and played along, "Yes, we Latinas have an alluring power over young white boys."

Getting back to business, Nancy continued, "My boss, Ed McDonald, spoke to Messerschmitt's lawyer. I wouldn't be shocked if some deal was already in the works."

"Really? That was quick, don't you think?"

"Maybe but nonetheless you do your interview. Go at him with all we have. If he's guilty of Jasmin Dollbee's murder then I want his ass here, so I see that he gets a needle in the arm."

Wow, Lydia thought, where did that come from?

"I feel the same way. I will call you as soon as I complete my interview. If you hear of anything else that would be beneficial to me, please call."

"No problem. By the way, Lydia, where are you now?"

"In Troon, Scotland, following a lead. Back in 1999, during an amateur golf championship, two women were killed in a horrific car crash. Witnesses back then saw the two drinking in pubs with members of the German team. Messerschmitt and Spunkmeyer were on that team. The case was not thoroughly investigated for many reasons. However, the newly created Historical Crime Unit has recently been looking at this case," she felt she said enough and wanted to end the conversation.

"OK, so let's talk after you interview Messerschmitt." They each ended the call, and Dio looked over his left shoulder wanting to say "So," but didn't. Lydia was staring straight ahead thinking to herself.

Finally after a few minutes she looked over at Dio and said, "How the hell can you drive on that side of the road?"

CHAPTER 64

They continued driving in silence both enjoying the scenery and thinking about each other.

"Lyd, so what do you think? Edinburgh?"

"Yeah, sure D, I'm sorry I was daydreaming."

"So I know this great little Italian family restaurant in the Old Town section of the city."

"You're putting me on, D. Italian restaurant in Scotland—what do they serve? Haggis Bolognese? Sheep primavera?" He was happy her mood lightened up.

"No, this guy from Italy and his wife moved here about ten years ago. He imports or grows his own veggies and makes his own pasta. I always go there when I'm in Edinburgh on business. I'm one of their few Italian regulars and they treat me like family. You'll see."

"How can you grow veggies in this climate?"

"This guy's amazing. He built his own greenhouse. I believe you'll hear the whole story after we eat, that is if you want to go."

"Sure, I'm in. Can't wait to have Italian, in Scotland."

Dio phoned ahead and made an 1800 reservation. Lydia was getting used to the military time used in Europe, having been in the military. It was Dio, also a veteran, who still had to do the math when it came to time.

The restaurant, Colello's, was at the end of a cul-de-sac in the medieval Old Town section. When you entered the street, you could not miss the green, white, and red awning under the neon Colello's sign. They were greeted by an attractive young woman who Lydia thought looked nothing like the fairer, light-haired girls she had seen in Troon.

"Signore Bosso, so nice to see you again."

"Hello, Brielle, *come'sta*. This is my friend Lydia."

She extended her hand to Lydia and they shook.

"Come right this way." She did not have a Scottish accent but more like an Italian-speaking US English. Brielle led them to a table in the back of the room. As they were about to sit, an older attractive woman came rushing over, arms extended.

"Signore Bosso, so good to see you again." She hugged and kissed both his cheeks. "Dominic is so excited too, but he's out back in the greenhouse."

Turning to Lydia, Dio said, "Donna, this is my dear friend, Lydia Martinez." Lydia put out her hand, but Donna was not having any of that. She threw her arms around Lydia and kissed her on both checks. Lydia was not offended but felt rather welcomed by the nice gesture on the part of her host. The restaurant was not crowded but the aroma of a thick Bolognese sauce permeated the small room. The room had maybe twelve tables, mostly fours with the traditional red-checkered tablecloths. As soon as they sat Brielle reappeared with a bottle of red wine and three glasses.

Donna pulled up a chair. "Dio, I want you to taste this beautiful vino my brother-in-law Joe made in his vineyards back home in Sicily. Lydia, you do you like red?"

Lydia just nodded.

Brielle opened and poured. The wine was delicious. Donna drank her wine, stood, and with a smile said, "Got to get back to the kitchen." Looking around the sparsely filled room she continued, "Not too busy tonight. I can make you your favorite, signor Bosso, peppers Monaghina." Looking at Lydia she said, "How about senora, anything you don't like?"

"Haggis."

"Just took it off the menu," she joked.

"Peppers Monaghina it is, Donna, for two." Looking at Lydia he said, "You'll love this—homemade sausage, peppers,

229

and onions in signora Colello's special sauce. It's the best, right Donna?" Donna just smiled and walked toward the kitchen. As she left Lydia noticed Dio's eyes following Donna's ample bottom.

"Why, Dio Bosso, you are an ass man, aren't you?"

He smiled. The meal Donna prepared was wonderful. A salad of fresh baby lettuce, cucumber, olives, and scallions in a tasty vinaigrette. The main dish was spectacular. Lydia had never tasted sausage and peppers like this before. As they ate, they made light conversation about the food, the area, and the people they met these last two days. They truly enjoyed each other's company. Dio had known it for a long time. Lydia was learning it more and more each day.

Just as they were finishing their meal, Lydia saw a tall, muscular, bald man approaching their table. She knew it was Dominic as Dio got up and they hugged. She got the same hug and double-cheek kiss from Dominic that Dio had gotten. Dominic sat down and Brielle appeared with three fresh glasses and another bottle of wine. They drank and Dominic told them all about his latest project. He was determined to grow tomatoes, basil, and other herbs here in Scotland. "Sure, I can get the cheaper from my brother Joe back home. We get all of our provisions from his company. But it's a challenge for me, plus Donna and Brie run the restaurant. A couple of the regulars tried to get me to play golf, but every time I go out it rains. It doesn't bother the locals, but it kills my old legs."

They finished the meal and the second bottle of wine. Dio excused himself from the table and when he returned, Lydia was sitting talking with Donna and Dominic.

"I called an Uber and got a room down the road at the Marriott." He sat down and asked Donna to get him his check.

"Check? What check, Dio? When is the last time I had two Italians eating in my restaurant? Martini and Bosso— sounds like an aperitif." Donna must have misunderstood Lydia's last name and Italianized it. They bickered about the bill and finally Dio relented and thanked Dominic for his hospitality. Leaving, he threw a hundred pound note on the table.

When they arrived at the hotel they were both tired and a bit tipsy. They undressed, made love, and went to sleep. They had to drive back to Troon and return the unmarked police car to Hutchinson before they left for Frankfurt.

CHAPTER 65

When Dio and Lydia arrived back in Germany they were met at the Frankfurt International Airport by a uniformed officer from BPOL. He introduced himself as Poliziemeister Wilhelm Werner and would be their driver for today.

"Poliziedirektor Boser will be meeting us at Kronberg," he said with a thick German accent. "We were supposed to go to headquarters but that was changed."

After that he didn't say too much as Dio and Lydia reviewed the questions she would ask Messerschmitt. She expected that his lawyer in the three-thousand-euro suit would be instructing his client on when and what to answer. She was confident she could get Messerschmitt to talk.

Dio reached into his briefcase and pulled out the notes they made after Messerschmitt made his statement the previous week. He also handed her the questions they drew up. "Here Lyd, I brought these along. You can review them before the interrogation."

Lydia was surprised that he did not give her these on the plane and disappointed that she did not think of bringing them herself—more self-doubt.

They were met at Kronberg Castle by Boser who was in uniform and, as Lydia noticed, posed a handsome figure in his green and white. After handshakes all around Herr Inge, the butler, led the group to the same room where the first interview took place. Looking at Dio, Boser said that only he and Martinez could question Messerschmitt, "But you can take notes if you'd like."

Dio just nodded and looking at Lydia said, "Detective Martinez is quite capable of conducting an interrogation without any assistance from me or anyone else for that matter."

"OK, OK, Dio, I am sure Detective Martinez is quite capable. We will be joined by an Anklager," he paused, "what you would call a prosecutor from the office of the public prosecutor. They will be the people who will decide on the extradition."

Looking at Dio she said, "I can handle Messerschmitt and Mr. MacLeod on my own Walter."

"Oh, MacLeod is not here. One of his associates in the criminal defense division of his firm will be with their client."

As they entered the interview room, Lydia was surprised to see a different Karl Messerschmitt than the one she met at his home just last week. Gone were the golf clothes, replaced by jeans and a dress shirt opened at the collar. The smugness he demonstrated last week was now replaced with an actual look of concern. He stood up and extended his hand when Lydia and Boser entered the room. The first to speak was the new lawyer—a small, white-haired gentleman in an off-the-rack blue suit.

"My name is Gunther Minglemeyer, and I represent Herr Messerschmitt," he said in a thick German accent. "Herr Messerschmitt is here on his own to help you resolve some issues and events that occurred in Palm Beach County, in the state of Florida, USA, on 27 and 28 February this year. Herr Messerschmitt is not obligated to answer your questions or make any statements that may incriminate himself. But he has expressed to me his willingness to help you." He sat down and Lydia brought out a tape recorder and placed it on the table.

The door opened and a woman in her mid-forties entered the room. "Sorry, I am a bit tardy," she said with a perfect English accent. Looking around the room, she continued, "I'm Doris Bodenbender. I am here on behalf of the public prosecutor's office."

233

It was Boser who spoke next. He noticed a gold wedding band on her right finger. "Good Morning, Frau Bodenbender. We have not yet begun."

Introductions were made all around and once again Minglemeyer repeated what he had said prior to the prosecutor walking in. Lydia took the initiative as she wanted to get started before someone suggested coffee, tea, etc. Pressing the record button, she began, "I am Detective Lydia Martinez of the Palm Beach County Sheriff's Office, and I am here to question Mr. Karl Messerschmitt about the events that occurred in Palm Beach County on February 27 and 28, 2017," She looked at Minglemeyer when she said events.

For the next two hours she questioned Karl about his statement and what transpired during the first two days of The Florida Classic and especially the Friday night Jasmin was murdered. He seemed to wince whenever Lydia mentioned her name.

"It all started as soon as we arrived in Miami. Dieter was feeling ill and did not want to caddy. It was no big deal. I played Doral with a local caddy. After I finished, we hired a limo to take us to PGA National. I registered for the tournament and picked up our credentials, gift bags, and hotel and car assignments. We played the pro-am on Wednesday. I was playing well, but Dieter," he paused and looked at his lawyer who just nodded and said, "Go on, Karl."

"Dieter seemed distracted by this girl who was carrying the" he struggled for the word and said in German "vas is das thing with the names and scores?"

"Standard bearer," answered Gropp.

"Ya, standard bearer. He could not take his eyes off her. I had to remind him to pay attention to my game."

"Had he acted that way before?" Martinez asked.

"Well, yes, many times but not in a while, not since his accident."

"What accident is that, Karl?" Lydia was speaking softly, sort of in an understanding motherly way.

"In France, a few years ago. We were in a tournament. He was not my caddy then, only my playing partner. He was assaulted in town and was stabbed through the hand. It ruined his golfing career, but he became my caddy. It worked out OK for both of us." He continued on,

"Well this young girl, I forget her name, she was with us for the pro-am and the first two rounds Thursday and Friday. I was playing well. I was only a few shots back of the lead. I had a chance to win. Certainly the way I was playing, a top ten was very likely." His voice was becoming animated and Lydia could tell he was uncomfortable.

"But you withdrew and returned home, here to Germany, why?"

Again, he fidgeted and looked over at his lawyer. "After the round I saw Dieter go over to the player hospitality tent. I said to him, 'Dieter, what are you doing?' He had that look, the look I had seen before, and I knew it was not good. He said to me in German that the young girl gave him her address and phone number, but he misplaced it and asked the volunteer if she could help him."

"So he got Jasmin Dollbee's address?"

"Yes, he told me after I practiced that he wanted to drop by her house and give her some of the gifts we got. We get so much stuff, that a lot of guys give them away. You know, gloves, shoes, bags, balls, all kinds of stuff we don't need."

"So after golf you, what, you drove to her house?"

"I practiced for about an hour then we went back to the hotel, ate dinner, and you know, changed clothes. But Dieter was drinking, and he is not good with alcohol."

"What do you mean?"

"He gets nasty and scary. Especially if he thinks a woman or girl is making fun of him. I stopped going out with him when we are on the road. At home he lives in our guesthouse, so I don't know what he does when he's there."

"Go on Karl, what happened next?"

"Well we got into our courtesy car and he tried to program the address of this girl's house but for some reason we got lost. We pulled over in a park area of some sort. He said he had to pee and got out of the car. He was gone for a long time, and I don't know where, and I was getting frightened. I was about to get out, but he came back. I asked him why he was gone so long, and he just said that we are in some natural area and went on about the pond and canoeing and bird watching and stars. I finally had enough and told him to get me out of there."

"Did he get angry with you?"

"No, but sometimes I have to remind him what our roles are."

"Did he seem resentful or jealous?"

"No, but sometimes if I made a bad shot, he would say that if he was playing, he would not make a stupid shot like that." Continuing on he said, well we made our way back to PGA and he got directions to this girl's house from the security guard at the gate."

That would be Stan Kriegsman, she thought to herself. "So you drove to Jasmin Dollbee's house?"

"Yes."

"Were you sitting in the passenger's seat, Karl?"

"No, I sat in the back seat. I don't like the way he drives when he drinks. I feel safer in the rear."

"He was drinking before you went out?"

"Ya, he had a couple of shots of brandy before we left the hotel. I told you that!"

He stopped for a second and took a drink from the water bottle that was on the table. Dio was in the room on the other side of the glass and was sitting next to another uniformed officer. He thought that Lydia was doing fine and could see Karl was very nervous and animated.

"So, Karl, tell me what happened next."

"Well, we find the address and just as we pull up, Dieter sees this Jasmin girl get into a car with an older woman."

"Go on."

"He starts to follow them and turns back to me and said, 'Ah, two. One for me and one for you.' And he made the laugh, that scary laugh. We followed them a few miles and he made a comment when we passed that area where he peed. I was starting to feel sick. I knew he was up to no good, but what could I do?"

"Did you tell Dieter that you wanted to go home?"

His voice raised, "You don't understand. When he's like this, you can't say anything. You just have to hope something happens and, and" he paused, "whatever he's thinking just passes and we go home."

"What about that night, Karl?"

He put his head down and was wringing his hands. "I don't know. I don't know. I kept telling him we should go home. We have golf tomorrow. He just pointed out the window and said, "Look at the sky, it's going to rain. There will be no golf tomorrow"

Lydia had to coax him to continue.

"We followed them to another house. The girl got out and the other car took off. Dieter made some comment, but I wasn't paying attention." He looked up at Martinez and the others. His voice was now quivering, and Martinez thought he was going to burst out in tears. "This is not what I want. I only care about one thing. One thing. I work very hard and trying to get better every day. And now," he looked at Martinez, "you want to take it from me."

She tried to maintain her cool. It was difficult. She knew this was not Florida, where she could get into his face, maybe smack him upside his head just to get his attention, as Dio would say. No, she had to lead him along like a puppy dog. "It's OK, Karl, I understand. Just tell me what happened next."

Mingelmeyer cupped his mouth over Karl's ear and whispered something to him. Karl just nodded his head. "I was telling Dieter we should go because those girls were going to be hanging out all night and just when I thought he would go a car pulls up and Jasmin and some other girl get in. I told him they are probably going to a movie and we should go home. We have a big day tomorrow. He didn't seem to hear me. We followed them for a short while and they got out of the car and went into another house. You could tell there was a party going on—you know, cars in the driveway, kids on the lawn. I was thankful. Now we can go home. Dieter said, 'Maybe we should crash the party. Maybe they see you, a big-time PGA golfer, and we both get laid, ha, ha." I said "are you nuts, Dieter? They are all teenagers. They have laws here about that. I told him it was time to go and we must go *now*. "OK, OK, we go," he said to me. I could tell that he was angry with me. I became afraid he would hit me."

"Had he done that before?"

"Only once. About a month after the Troon incident we were having dinner in my house. We were alone and I asked him if he ever felt bad about what he did to those girls. He became very angry, grabbed me by my neck, and smacked my face several times. He told me that "*We* did it. You and me, Karl, you and me." "After that I never mentioned it again."

"So you're at the house where Jasmin and her friend are at a party. What happened next?"

"I decided to lay down in the back, but it seemed to me we were going in circles. The car stopped and I got up and saw we were in front of the same house. I said, Dieter what are you doing? Before he could answer, I see him pull up to the curb and I see this girl, the girl from the golf tournament, Jasmin."

"What did you do?"

"I laid down in the back and stayed there. I was scared."

"Did you hear what Dieter said to Jasmin?"

"No."

"Did you coax Jasmin into the front seat?"

"No, no."

"Did you and Dieter kidnap Jasmin Dollbee, take her to the natural area, and rape and kill her?"

238

Lydia's voice gradually raised and for effect she pounded on the table.

"Tell us, Karl, tell us you killed Jasmin Dollbee. You raped Jasmin Dollbee. You put Jasmin's lifeless body in the pond. You, Karl, you and Dieter did this together."

"No, no, no, it was not me. It was Dieter. It is always Dieter," he shouted.

The room fell silent as Karl put his head down on the desk and was sobbing. Minglemeyer suggested a break. Martinez was totally against this. She had him where she wanted him, but the prosecutor Bodenbender and even Boser agreed on a fifteen-minute break.

Dio met Lydia outside the interview room and handed her a coffee.

"Is it regular?"

He just smiled. Only she could make a wisecrack in the middle of an intense investigation.

"You got him, Lyd. Nice work in there."

"I'm not done yet. But I now know he isn't the major player here. This Spunkmeyer dude has some kind of power over him. Like a mind-control thing."

"Like a Svengali."

"Sven-who?"

"Never mind. Just go back in there and reel him in."

CHAPTER 66

When they returned to the interview room, Karl was more composed. During the recess Minglemeyer spoke to Bodenbender and they agreed that the allegations made by Detective Martinez are serious crimes. However, they were not committed in Germany. Like Martinez both Bodenbender and Minglemeyer were appalled by what they heard. Minglemeyer knew his firm had been in contact with the state's attorney in Florida and that a deal was in the works. For her part Bodenbender was not a big fan of extraditing German citizens for any reason. When Mingelmeyer related this to Karl, his response made the lawyer think his client was delusional.

"So, Herr Minglemeyer, you think I can get back out on tour soon?" Apparently, Karl had not been informed of the decisions of the PGA Europe and America.

Confident his troubles would soon be behind him, Karl told of how Dieter coaxed Jasmin into the car and drove her to the natural area.

"Did she resist?"

"No, I think she wanted to go. I think maybe she liked Dieter," he lied.

"Liked him? I don't think so. We have evidence to the contrary." She pressed him about the shoe bag placed over Jasmin's head and the bruises on her neck. He denied any knowledge of that.

"It was the same other times. I was there, but I did nothing."

Now Lydia had him talking of other times. So she and Dio were right. This was not a first kill. But which line of

240

questioning should she pursue? Continue on with the Dollbee case, where he seemed reluctant to implicate himself, or should she let him go on about the other times?

"Karl, before we get to the past. It's important that you tell me what happened after Jasmin got into the car."

"I told you. I was laying down. We drove for a while. They got out and after a while Dieter came back and we went home."

"Just like that? You didn't ask about the girl? You didn't ask what happened? I find that hard to believe." Lydia pressed him about the muddy shoes but did not give away the incriminating evidence about the diatoms that Stacey Stack discovered. Nor did she talk about the shoe bag and the flakes of matching material under Jasmin's fingernail or her DNA on the bag found in their hotel room at the Marriott. She had him, at least as an accessory and she could tell by the others in the room they knew it too. She wondered what Dio thought.

"Karl you just told me that you stayed in the back seat of the courtesy car the entire time. Yet we found mud in the back seat that could only come from the pond area, which means you got out of the car and helped Dieter rape and kill Jasmin Dollbee, didn't you?" again she raised her voice for effect. She had him cornered and felt now is the time to pounce. She continued in an accusing tone, "You did this, Karl. We know you did this with Dieter. Did you rape the victim too?"

Karl was now almost in tears. "I don't remember what happened, I might have gotten out of the car to pee, but I never hurt that girl. I never hurt any of them," he shouted. The room fell silent again as Lydia looked over at Bodenbender who was busy taking notes. Boser just raised his eyebrows.

Karl looked up at her and then scanned the others. His wide eyes betrayed his fear. "Rape? No, I never touch them," he paused. "He has sex with them as he is killing them or after they're dead. The girl in Florida, after Dieter knocked her out, he took her to the pond. He put her head under the water and then he pulled her pants down and raped her as she struggled."

241

"You saw him do this and did nothing?" She was trying hard not to lose it.

Boser could sense the tension and jumped into the conversation. "Karl, how many others did Dieter do this do?"

"I'm not sure. Just the time in Scotland was the only time I was with him before this. I've seen this look in his eyes before and how he is different after."

"How do you mean?"

"After, like the Saturday during The Florida Classic, he acted as if nothing happened, as if a different person had done what he'd done the night before. When I told him we had to leave, he acted surprised. He said, 'Leave? Why Karl? We are only five shots back, and we have Doral and Bay Hill coming up. I lost it on him. I said, "Are you out of your mind? You just raped and murdered a young girl who was with us for the last two days. You think the police are not going to figure this out? This is not Scotland twenty years ago."

"What was his response?" asked Martinez.

"He shrugged his shoulders and said, "you're the boss."

For the next two hours he told the story of what happened during the 1999 European Junior Amateur Championship at Troon. His story was consistent with what she had heard just a few days ago from Chief Inspector Hutchinson and the golf pro Lockie. He also mentioned that he always believed that the injury Dieter sustained in France was the result of a potential victim fending him off.

Both Lydia and Boser were drained by the time Karl finished. He gave them four or five instances where they were playing in tournaments where he became suspicious of Dieter's behavior. Boser asked Karl if Dieter had ever raped or killed in Germany.

"No, I don't think he would ever do anything in Germany. I am certain of that."

Martinez knew she had enough from his statement that he could be indicted, tried, and convicted at the very least as an accessory. The difficulty would be in the extradition.

Mingelmeyer called for another break as he could see his client was visibly distraught.

CHAPTER 67

Dio and Lydia were not aware of the sanctions placed on Messerschmitt by the ruling golf authorities. Several of his sponsors—Lufthansa, Deutsche Bank, and Puma—also sent letters terminating their relationships as per the personal character clauses in their respective contracts. During the break the elder Messerschmitt approached Mingelmeyer and Bodenbender and showed them the telegrams and faxes he received canceling Karl's sponsorship. He was furious and expressed concern about how Karl would handle this news.

It was the attorney who responded. "Sir, with all due respect, your son just implicated himself in a number of brutal rapes and murders committed by Dieter Spunkmeyer."

"Your son committed no crime here in Germany," added Bodenbender. "It will be a challenge for us with regard to the extradition. The Americans still have capital punishment for such crimes such as this," she looked disdainfully at Karl, "but we do not extradite our citizens to places where they practice that barbaric form of punishment."

It was Minglemeyer who spoke next. "My boss, Mr. MacLeod, has been in contact with the prosecutor in Florida. We are trying to work out some sort of deal, whereby maybe Karl could plead to a lesser charge and be incarcerated here in Germany." Karl reentered and heard what Minglemeyer said. Before he could finish his narrative Karl was in his face.

"Incarceration? Germany? Are you out of your fucking mind?" Minglemeyer backed off. He actually thought Karl was going to strike him. He looked toward Bodenbender hoping she would say something to calm Karl down.

"Herr Messerschmitt, you must see that your attorney and the German government is trying to protect your rights, but you have to understand," before she continued he cut her off again in a loud voice.

"Understand? What do I have to understand? I gave that bitch what she wanted. I gave her Dieter. He did this, not me. He's a murderer, not me. I just want to play golf."

After knocking on the door, Herr Inge reentered the library and handed the elder Messerschmitt several sheets of paper.

"*Auch du lieber,*" he cried. Handing his son the faxes he said, "I don't think you'll be playing golf professionally for a while I'm afraid."

Karl scanned the notices and after crumbling them up, fell to his knees screaming, "*No*, no, no, they can't do this to me. I didn't do anything. It was Dieter, that fucking Dieter."

The elder Messerschmitt helped his sobbing son to his feet. Herr Inge, along with a maid, took the visibly shaken and distraught Karl out of the room.

"I will give him a sedative to settle him down. What do you think?" he asked looking at Minglemeyer.

It was Bodenbender who answered, to Minglemeyer's relief. "It's obvious your son has some problems, Herr Messerschmitt. Is he under the care of a doctor by any chance?"

"No. I mean, he has a sport doctor and, you know, a massage therapist, a fitness trainer. All the things you need on the tour, you know."

Well he won't be needing them anymore, thought Minglemeyer.

"Maybe you should have him see someone. It seems to me that if the Scots or Americans seek extradition, the fact that he is in therapy might work in his favor. Isn't that right, Herr Minglemeyer?"

"Er, yes, yes, I was just about to suggest the same thing."

"Do you think he is, you know, mentally ill?"

"Well, Herr Messerschmitt, let's look at his reactions. He seemed more upset about the suspensions than the possibility of going to prison in, of all places, Florida."

"Yes, you're right, Frau Bodenbender. I guess you just don't see it when you're close to someone."

"I always suspected that Spunkmeyer was a little off. I let him stay in the cottage because he is good for Karl's game."

Actually, thought Minglemeyer, you let him stay here because it's in his contract, which I drew up.

"I suggest we call it a day. I need to review Karl's sponsorship contracts and see if we can challenge their decisions or get a settlement."

"Yes, I want to check on him too. Thank you both so much. It would be a shame if Karl was not able to resume his career at some point in time."

They just looked at one another and left the room. While all this drama was going on, Lydia and Dio just sat quietly. She knew that she got what she needed from Messerschmitt. She just could not comprehend how he did not feel any remorse for his actions.

Bodenbender looked at Minglemeyer with a look of disdain. "How can you work for these people? Do they live in the real world or not?"

Minglemeyer gave a snarky reply, "I'm just a soldier in the army of the M&Ms. And I'll do my best to see that my clients get the best deal possible, even if I think he is a sociopath."

He winked, and they shook hands goodbye.

CHAPTER 68

They reassembled in the front hall and Bodenbender was the first to speak.

"We need to find Dieter Spunkmeyer. Do we know where he is?"

"No, Frau Bodenbender, we do not," answered Boser. "When I asked Karl of his whereabouts, he just shrugged his shoulders. I will put out a BOLO," he looked at Lydia. "Yes, we use that term here too, Detective. And we should get a warrant to search his quarters here. Can you arrange that, Frau Bodenbender?"

"*Naturlisch.*" she answered in German. Extending her hand to Martinez she continued, "You did a nice job in there with him. I always thought you Americans beat confessions out of suspects," she said with a wry smile, obviously joking.

"I couldn't get my billy club and electric cables through your customs."

They all laughed and Bodenbender continued, "Let's see how this plays out. You understand, Detective, that if Scotland wants to prosecute, they will have the opportunity to do so even before we discuss extradition."

"I understand, Frau Bodenbender." Lydia wished she would say, Hey call me Doris, but she was very formal and very professional. Other than the remark about confessions, she kept a strictly businesslike demeanor.

"One more thing, Herr Boser."

"Yes, Detective?"

"I will be able to assist you when you search Spunkmeyer's quarters, correct?"

Boser looked over at the prosecutor who just shrugged. "I don't see a problem, but should you find something that you think might be evidentiary in nature, please let one of the officers handle it for safeguard."

Lydia was pleased with the way the interrogation and the subsequent plans went. She was anxious to call Nancy and share the good news. Back at Dio's condo she could upload the interrogation and email a copy, but she wanted to give her a verbal and see how the first day of the grand jury went. Plus she wanted to talk to someone normal, other than Dio of course.

Dio commended her on her successful interrogation. "You got this guy by the balls, Lyd. And speaking of balls, did he really think he was going to walk away scot-free? He had to help Spunkmeyer. Being around the guy for years, sometimes 24/7. No way, he didn't know. No way is he not culpable."

They discussed the interview and were trying to decide on whether to return to London or spend the night in Germany. Lydia wanted to be present when they executed the warrant on Spunkmeyer's quarters but had no clue how long that might take.

"Hold on," said Dio. "Let me see what I can find out." He picked up his cell and called Boser. "Walter, Dio here. How long do you think it will take to get the warrant for Spunkmeyer's?"

Boser replied coyly, "You want to spend the night with your lady in Frankfurt? I know a cozy little Guesthaus not too far from the autobahn."

"No, Walter, I mean yes, but we are past the cozy Guesthaus phase. How soon?"

"I have someone in court now. We can go early tomorrow if Detective Martinez is agreeable."

Boy was this guy a ball-buster. He acted like nobody has sex, and this is Germany—a randy country if there ever was one.

"Great, Walter, so tell me the name of the Guesthaus and we will see you in the morning." Dio took down the information and said to Lydia, "Boy, that Boser acts as if we're two teenagers sneaking out of our bedroom windows to meet. Kind of silly, if you ask me."

"He's been very helpful, Dio, and he's probably a bit jealous." Dio gave her a look and rolled his eyes. "Seriously, how many hot Latinas do you think are in the BPOL?"

Dio just smiled as they had their driver take them to the Guesthaus. It was about ten kilometers outside of Frankfurt and in a small town called Docbach. Boser was spot on. The food was excellent. The husband and wife who ran the place introduced themselves as Herr and Frau Lippold. She was Czech and he was German. The tiny bedroom had a double bed with the soft featherbeds such places are known for. They ate homemade bratwurst and other assorted meats and cheeses. They each had two excellent local beers, and off to bed they went. After they made love, Lydia lay with her head on Dio's chest.

"Do the Brits have a word for…you know…sex, fucking?

"Shag."

"Shag?"

"Yep, shag."

"Shag, I like that. OK if I use it?"

"Sure, just as long as you don't shag a bloke named Bev or Viv!"

They both laughed and hugged. Lydia changed the subject as only she could. "So you think we'll find anything in Spunkmeyer's tomorrow? Hey, by the way D, can we call him Spunky, like those Scotties? My tongue is getting tired on these names—Minglemeyer, Bodenbender, Messerschmitt. Don't these Germans have any short last names?"

"Kurtz."

"What?"

"Kurtz, you asked if they have any short names and I said 'Kurtz.' It means short in German, but it's also a common surname."

She got up on an elbow and lightly punched him in the chest as she rolled on top of him. "I'll make the jokes, mister you do...oooh!" She felt him getting hard again and raising up, she slipped his penis inside of her. After they climaxed, they fell asleep in that position and when Lydia heard her cell ring, she rolled off of Dio and grabbed the phone, noticing it was 2345.

"Hello."

"Wow, in bed already, Detective? Must have been a long day."

"Oh, Nancy, jeez, I'm sorry I meant to call."

Heichemer cut her off. "It's OK, Lydia. I've been up to my butt in work here too. I had those teens before the grand jury and boy were they a trip, but they did good. Mark Van Hooey sends his regards," she said with a chuckle. "And those two guys from PGA security. You could tell this was not their first time testifying. Very good. And Detective Kiers walked the jury through the evidence you submitted."

"So?"

"Yeah, it was a grounder."

Lydia took her through the events of her day as it pertained to the case.

"Messerschmitt is pathetic. He puts the crime on Spunkmeyer, which we believe, but he takes no responsibility for these deeds himself. I'll be sending you a tape of the interview as soon as I get back to London."

"Where are you now?"

"Frankfurt, the German police are getting a warrant for Spunky's."

"Who?"

"I'm sorry, Spunkmeyer. We're getting a search warrant for his cottage tomorrow and I want to be there. No point flying back to London tonight." Lydia spent the next thirty minutes discussing the interview and answering Nancy's questions. Lydia could tell Nancy was taking notes. Nancy was curious as to how the German prosecutor acted and her take on the crime. Lydia explained how Bodenbender stuck to the issue at hand but implied that neither man committed a crime in her jurisdiction but was visibly shaken by what was done to Jasmin Dollbee. Lydia told her about the Scottish murders and how the story told by Karl was consistent with the story told by Lockie and Hutchinson. She also wanted to be up front and told Nancy what Bodenbender said about extradition and Scotland's right of first refusal.

"So, Lydia, do you think the Scots will want to prosecute these two?"

"If that's the case and they get first dibs, you and I have wasted our time, have we not?"

"I don't see it that way, Nancy, and if you don't mind me saying so, neither should you. We have a job to do. We have to seek justice for Jasmin Dollbee and her family. If the Scots choose to prosecute, so be it. At least we know we did our jobs. Sure, I'd rather they rot in our jails than in their jails. But rot they will. Well maybe not Messerschmitt. You should have seen him, Nancy, when he learned of his suspensions. That upset him more than being implicated in several murders. He just doesn't get it."

"Well he'll get it now. Mr. McDonald notified his attorneys here and in Europe of his indictment. I'm starting extradition proceedings as soon as I can get before Judge D'Emic. The sports stations on TV are talking about his suspension but have not released information about the Dollbee homicide. Don't know how much traction this will get nationally or internationally. Golf is not that big in Germany from what I was told. But here, let me tell you, Martinez. This opened a can of shit for the PGA and The Florida Classic, but they have done their damage control by severing relationships with Messerschmitt."

"Well OK, Nancy. Again, I'm sorry about the late notification. Jet lag, I guess."

Jet lag, Nancy thought, probably more like sex lag.

251

Lydia lay back down in bed and tried to sleep. Dio was on his side in dreamland. So much was running through her head again. Thinking about Karl and Spunky. Thinking about the PBSO and her future with Dio. She knew once this case was completed, she would be able to get an idea of what she wanted to do. She thought to herself, I don't miss Florida, I don't really have any close friends, and my brothers have their own families. I could live here with Dio, travel, and meet people like the Colello's in Edinburgh and the Lippold's here in Docbach. If I get bored, then Dio will find something for me to do. She kept this thought rolling through her half-conscious mind as she finally drifted off to sleep. When she awoke her arms were around Dio's body.

The driver Polizeikommissar Werner from BPOL was waiting when Dio and Lydia left the cozy inn. Frau Lippold made them a breakfast of hard-boiled eggs, fresh rolls and butter, an assortment of meats and chesses similar to what they had for dinner, and a pot of the best coffee Lydia tasted in a while.

"You like?" smiled Frau Lippold.

"*Sehr gut,*" said Dio using one of the few German phrases he knew. "Do you think we can get three coffees to take with us?" She nodded and trotted off.

They finished eating as she bought the coffee and a leather bond check fold. Without looking Dio took out his Amex Platinum and placed it in the folder. Frau Lippold returned and thanked them very much and said to come again. Dio put a fifty-euro note inside the folder.

When they got outside Lydia said, "Wow, nice tip there, D. She must have had a nice ass."

They both smiled as they got into the green and white BPOL cruiser. Werner thanked them for the coffee. It was chilly, and a light rain fell. Lydia looked at the soft leather gloves on her hand and smiled at Dio who was checking his emails.

"Hey, Lyd, we've been redirected back to the Messerschmitt castle. I just got a text from Boser. I wonder what's up."

When they got to Messerschmitt's they were both surprised at the number of police vehicles present inside the compound. There was also an ambulance and a dark blue van marked *Leichenschhaus.* Looking at Lydia, Dio said, "This can't be good." As they exited the car they saw Walter Boser come running toward them, he was in uniform. As he reached them he stopped and looking from Dio to Lydia said, "Karl Messerschmitt hung himself. His body is—"

Before he could finish Lydia pushed by him and ran to the back of the compound where she saw the most activity. As she reached the back of the house, she could see crime scene technicians in white hazmat suits going about their business, taking photos, looking for evidence. As Dio and Boser caught up with her, Boser placed a hand on her arm. As she looked forward about fifty yards, she could see the naked body of Karl Messerschmitt hanging from a tree branch gently blowing back and forth in the breeze. Lydia was shocked and just held her hand over her mouth.

"Was there a note? Did he say anything to anyone?" Boser just held up his hand to stop her. "What about the search warrant? We're still going to search Spunkmeyer's?" Boser looked at Dio with a frustrated look that said, "can you talk to her?" Dio took the hint.

"Lyd, maybe it's best they wait for another time to do the warrant."

"Why?" Turning back to Boser she said, "How much longer before they cut him down and take him away? I assume the blue van is from the morgue." Boser just nodded.

"We have until 1800 hours before the warrant expires so we have time. I need to direct these officers to do what they need to do for this," he gestured toward the body.

"Sure, OK. Mind if I go down and get a closer look."

"Be careful, it's still a crime scene."

"I'll make sure she is," said Dio and they both headed toward to body.

"Dio, cover me," she said as she took several photos with her cell phone. "I'm not sure I can do this, but I am." She got in close and took about a dozen photos. Looking up at Karl's lifeless body she thought this coward escaped justice. People do stupid things in life, don't they? Not wanting to overstay her welcome she and Dio made their way back to the front of the house. Just as they reached the driveway, they saw Doris Bodenbender emerge from a small BMW. She saw Dio and Lydia and bid them a good morning in German, *Guten Morgan,*and extended her hand.

"Messy business, ya," she said nodding toward the back of the house. "Fortunately for me another prosecutor is handling this suicide. I'm here to do a search warrant. Where is Boser? I want to get this over." Lydia smiled at Dio and was glad Bodenbender was as cold as Germans are alleged to be.

As they walked toward Spunky's cottage Bodenbender picked up the conversation. "You know, Detective, it's not like I am not saddened by the loss of life, but after what I heard from Messerschmitt and the way he felt entitled—" she stopped herself and looked over at Lydia. "You know Germans of my generation are still paying for the sins of our grandfathers. The Messerschmitt's and their kind are the old German Uber *Classe* that would have prospered even more if Hitler had succeeded."

Lydia was not interested in the history lesson. She wanted to get into the cottage and begin the search.

CHAPTER 69

Back in Florida the news of Messerschmitt's indictment was still hot news when word of his apparent suicide hit the airways. The PGA of America and The Florida Classic people (who maintained a year-round office) were inundated with calls from the various media outlets. Some of the national networks were also becoming interested. The *Palm Beach Post* ran a picture of Jasmin Dollbee next to the official PGA photo of Karl Messerschmitt. In bold print the caption read: German golfer hangs self after indictment in Jasmin Dollbee's brutal murder.

It took several calls from the PBSO and the state attorney's office to convince the editor to leave the word "rape" out of the headline. McDonald himself had to call the editor in chief and threaten to cut them off if they went to print with the word "rape"in the headline.

Nancy Heichemer called Lydia as soon as she heard, and Lydia assured her the news was correct as she saw the body herself. When she asked about Spunkmeyer, Martinez replied, "We're about to search his cottage now. The BPOL secured a warrant."

"You don't think he's there, do you?"

"I doubt it. According to Messerschmitt he left here as soon as they returned from the states."

"Well I've got to go to court and amend the indictment to exclude the deceased. Justice served, wouldn't you say so, Detective?" Nancy asked in a happy tone.

"Yep, no doubt about it. I only wish he let me put the noose around his neck. I'll get back to you after the search."

CHAPTER 70

The cottage where Dieter lived was about one kilometer from the main house and had its own gated driveway. There were no vehicles in the driveway and no fresh tire marks in the wet gravel. Boser posted the two uniformed officers outside the cottage. He, Bodenbender, Lydia, and Dio entered the small one-bedroom apartment. Dio was surprised no one asked him to wait outside. The uniforms stood by the door with Bodenbender as the group started to search the kitchen and dining area. Lydia and Boser took the bedroom.

The cottage was sparsely furnished—no pictures, the walls bare, and no trophies on a shelf. It appeared as if it were a hotel room, except there was no TV. One of the detectives pointed out a computer and printer cable under a small desk, but the computer was gone. In the bedroom Lydia opened the one closet. There were maybe a dozen pair of slacks—all tan, beige, or white—and about two dozen golf shirts of various colors. There must have been a dozen or so golf shoes and sneakers neatly lined up on the closet floor. Underwear and socks were neatly placed in drawers as were T-shirts and pajamas.

Lydia noticed a small metal box on a shelf in the closet. She looked around and saw that Boser was busy inspecting the bathroom. She reached up and pulled down the box. It had two metal flip locks but was not locked. Inside she found several items: lockets, bracelets, a hair scrunchie, and on the bottom a German driver's license issued to Edletraud Gimke, Dieter's first victim, Scottish drivers' licenses for Barbara Maples and Susan Thorp, the Troon victims, an Irish passport

256

issued to a Doris Spears, two European Union ID cards belonging to two young girls from the Ukraine, and a gold anklet with a golf club charm—Jasmin Dollbee's missing anklet. Without thinking she stuffed the anklet in her pocket just as Boser neared.

"What have we got here?"

She handed him the closed box. "I just took this down from that shelf."

He opened it and examined the items inside. "He must have taken each of his victims' driver's license or ID or some other items. Nothing from your victim as far as I can see"

"Don't you mean *their* victims? Messerschmitt might be dead but he's a part of this."

"Ya, OK, OK, *their* victims," he said shaking his head.

"I wonder how many more there were. Do you think we will ever find out, Walter?"

It was the first time she addressed him by his first name, but she was really finding it difficult to pronounce not only the long names but the even longer names of the various ranks.

Once the search was concluded, Bodenbender addressed Boser, Lydia, and the others. "OK, so we have to do two things here. One, we need to find Spunkmeyer, and two, we need to safeguard these items (pointing to the metal box) and see if we can match them to other victims." Looking at the evidence in the metal box, she sighed, "So it looks like we have at least six other dead girls besides your Jasmin, Detective."

"Messerschmitt said that they never committed any crimes here in Germany, so would it not be better if we took those items to Interpol?"

Bodenbender looked at Lydia and said, "Yes, perhaps you are right, but for the time being we will safeguard these. If at some point they can be connected to another victim, then we will see that they are given to the proper authorities."

They reassembled in front of the cottage after the search was completed and made their way back to the main house.

Lydia could see the elder Messerschmitt talking with several other men, none of whom she recognized.

Frederich Messerschmitt approached her and said, "I'm holding you responsible for this."

Lydia was taken a bit back by this and said, "Holding me responsible? How about your psychotic son and his even crazier caddy? You got some pair of balls, Mister."

Dio and Boser came rushing over to pull her away just as she was getting into Messerschmitt's face. "Easy now, Lyd. Let him talk, he just lost his son."

"His son was a murdering psychopath," she said so everyone within earshot could hear her. "You think he was some kind of *wonderkid* because he could hit a golf ball? Believe me, Herr Messerschmitt," she said with sarcasm, "your son would never have survived in prison in the states. You should be glad he took the coward's way out."

The elder Messerschmitt drew back as Boser said in a firm voice, "Detective, I will not have you talk to Herr Messerschmitt in such a tone. He is a good citizen and just lost his son." Lydia just nodded and turned away. She mumbled to Dio, "The fucking kid did his old man and the world a fucking favor. Let's go find Spunky."

CHAPTER 71

For the next several days Lydia and Dio shuttled back and forth from Frankfort to London. Lydia had to give testimony in the follow-up investigation of Karl Messerschmitt's suicide and once again Dio was only too happy to accompany her in the Gulfstream. Boser and the BPOL had no information on the whereabouts of Spunkmeyer. Lydia kept in daily contact with DCI Hutchinson for updates on the Scottish side of things. The high court of justiciary would decide whether to extradite Spunkmeyer upon his capture. Lydia also spoke to both Nancy Heichemer and Detective Budrow.

"We are pretty much set to present our indictment of Spunkmeyer and start the extradition process. My boss told me a deal was in the working for Messerschmitt, but it did not apply to Spunkmeyer. We may have to take the death penalty off the table to extradite."

"Well the German cops haven't a clue as to where he is and if they do, they're not sharing. This one guy, Boser, is pretty high up the food chain, and he's been somewhat helpful, but since these guys did not commit a crime in Germany, finding Spunkmeyer is not priority one. I am hoping our friend at Interpol can be more helpful tracking him down."

"I'll keep you posted on any new development on this end. The media has pulled back on the Dollbee case since the suicide, so at least that issue has abated."

"OK, Nancy, thanks for the update. Talk to you soon."

No sooner had Lydia ended her call with Heichemer, her cell rang again. It was Detective Budrow.

"Detective Martinez, Fran Budrow here. How are you doing?" Before she could respond Budrow continued. "Listen I spoke to one of the retired constables who handled the accident in 1999 in Troon. I read the report you sent and, lo and behold, Donna Harran lives right here in Jupiter, Florida."

"Go on Fran, I'm listening."

"Well she was a bit vague on the case as it was almost twenty years ago, but she does remember that she thought the object used as a weapon and then used to keep the accelerator down was a wooden golf tee marker."

This would fit with what Lockie told her about the missing tee marker on the twelfth hole that triggered Messerschmitt's collapse. She wondered if it was still kept in evidence after all these years.

"Did she remember anything else, Fran?"

"No, only it was her first assignment in, get this, Historical Crime Unit not Cold Case."

"Yeah, I know, they got a lot of weird terms for things over here. They're a bit behind the times as far as investigations go. Plus they don't have the volume of crime we have in Florida."

"Well I thought you would find it interesting what Harran told me. Don't know if it means anything or not."

"All information is good information, Detective."

"I guess you're right." Changing the subject she went on. "I'm still working the case, but we are all pretty convinced that we know who the perps were. One is dead and hopefully the other will be captured and extradited back here."

Lydia chose not to go into the details of Scotland's right to prosecute. Plus, it's a moot point until Spunky gets captured. She ended the call and told Budrow to keep in touch.

CHAPTER 72

Kurt Gropp was working at his desk when he received a call from the French authorities. The Police Nationale, formerly called the "Surete," has the primary responsibility for major cities and large urban areas. The call Kurt received was from Inspector Denis St. Pierre, a ranking detective Kurt knew through his work with the French authorities.

"Bon jour, Monsieur Gropp. It's your old friend, St. Pierre," he said in a very heavy French accent.

"Bon jour, Denis." Their conversation switched to French as Gropp's French was better than St. Pierre's English or German. St. Pierre's call was in response to the informational bulletin he had seen from Interpol concerning any females going missing during the times Messerschmitt and Spunkmeyer were competing in golf tournaments.

"There was only one tournament here in France that those two played in that I could find, and there are no corresponding crimes of rape or murder." After a brief pause, he continued, "I do recall that during one golf tournament I was working a security detail at Le Golf Club. One evening during the event we had a report of a stabbing of one of the players from the German team. His name was Dieter Spunkmeyer and he claimed in the report that he was attacked by two Middle Eastern types." Gropp knew this story from speaking to Dio and he let St. Pierre continue without interrupting. "I recall a day or two later I was in the station and this woman had been arrested on a petty drug charge. She was yelling how she was almost raped by some foreigner, and the cops did nothing, but now they arrest her on a trumped-up drug charge."

Gropp listened patiently and St. Pierre went on.

"Something rang a bell, so I decided to talk to her. He name was Natalie Gerard. She told me how she was approached by a tall dark-haired boy with a German accent who wanted to pay her for sex. They started to walk to her apartment when she got a bad feeling and told the boy that she changed her mind. She told me that all of a sudden, he punched her in the face and pushed her into an alley." St. Pierre continued. "She said, 'Lucky for me I had a knife in my bag and I was able to get it out, and I stabbed him through his hand as he went to slap me again. The knife went right through his hand and he screamed and ran off, my knife still in his hand.'"

"Did you try to reach out to this woman, Natalie, recently?"

"Oui. Mademoiselle Gerard has been a guest of the La Sante Prison. She is doing five years for a number of crimes related to her *profession*. I took the liberty of showing her a photo of Spunkmeyer and she definitely IDed him as the man who assaulted her. Our statute of limitations precludes any prosecution in this matter, but I believe you will find this information useful for the Scottish and American police. Sorry I could not be more helpful, Monsignor Gropp."

"Not at all, Denis, very helpful. I will pass it on to our American colleague. Merci, Denis."

The called ended and Gropp immediately sent an email to Dio about his conversation with St. Pierre. Gropp knew it wasn't much but at least they knew Spunkmeyer was active in France but fortunately he was not successful. Gropp wondered how many others were not as lucky as Natalie Gerard.

CHAPTER 73

Lydia was getting antsy about the slow pace of the BPOL investigation into the whereabouts of Spunky. She did not know how they operated nor was Boser willing to include her in any planning or operational meetings. He had also suggested that she wait either in London or go back to the states and he would notify her when they picked up the suspect. No way was she going back to the states. She would stay in London with Dio and would monitor the investigation from there. She would call Boser daily for updates, purposely making a pest of herself so at some point he would get tired of her calls and invite her along on a lead. Or so she hoped.

Gropp on the other hand was more giving of information. He even suggested that Lydia speak to St. Pierre herself about the assault in France; she declined but would pass the info along to Hutchinson. It now seemed the Scottish authorities were interested in prosecuting Spunkmeyer in their jurisdiction, as it would show the value of their newly formed Historical Crime Unit.

She was totally enjoying each day with Dio. He was gone most days, but their nights were delightful—either dinner at home or at a fine restaurant. Dio seemed to have a good friend at every restaurant. She noticed that wherever they dined he knew the owner or maître d' and called them by their first name like they were long-lost friends. His outgoing personality was something she envied. It was over dinner one night when Dio's cell phone rang and he excused himself to take the call. When he returned Lydia could see he was excited.

"That was Kurt. Spunkmeyer has applied for asylum in the Albanian Embassy, just outside of Frankfurt. Gropp received a tip from one of the embassy staff that he has been there for several weeks. About the same time as when they returned from the states. Kurt said the Albanians' hands are tied. They knew he held dual citizenship but never thought he would seek asylum at the embassy of his mother's homeland."

Dio told her that Gropp wanted to send agents to watch the embassy, but Boser said he would get the local Landespolizei to conduct the surveillance with instructions to arrest Spunkmeyer should he leave the embassy.

CHAPTER 74

Lydia finished the rest of her dinner and passed on dessert. She was anxious to get back to the condo and call Nancy Heichemer. She also called Lieutenant Cashin and briefed him on the status. He reminded her to keep this latest news to herself and not call the victim's family.

"Why, Lieutenant, you think I would do something like that? *Moi?*" On the other end of the phone, Cashin just shook his head.

"You know what I mean, Martinez. As far as I'm concerned, our case gets closed once this Spunkmeyer is apprehended. I don't care what jail he spends the rest of his life in. Keep in mind the most important thing is he's off the street. And by the way, be careful with this. Let the Germans handle the arrest. Got that, Martinez?"

"You got it, Lieutenant."

CHAPTER 75

When they arrived back in Frankfurt, they were surprised to learn that the Albanian embassy where Spunky was staying was within walking distance of Messerschmidt's Castle Krogberg, about five kilometers (three miles). Without the wrought iron fence surrounding the property, one might mistake the embassy for a country residence.

As they drove past the embassy, Lydia asked Dio to stop the car. Reluctantly he complied. As she got out, he looked around to see if he could spot the German cops in their distinctive green and white VWs. Martinez in the meantime walked to the front gate and looked for a bell or an intercom. There was nothing other than a bronze plaque that she assumed said "Albanian Embassy" both in Albanian and German. She was still looking for a way to get into the embassy when Dio drove closer and hit the horn.

"What are you doing, Lydia? You just can't walk up to the embassy of a foreign country and knock on the door." It was the first time she sensed annoyance in his tone. "What are you going to say if someone answers? Is Spunky there? Can he come out and play? Christ, Lydia, sometimes I think you forget that you and I are both guests of the BPOL, and I don't need to jeopardize that relationship, nor do I want to piss off Gropp and Interpol."

Martinez looked at him and, shrugging her shoulders, got back into the rental. Dio drove off to a location where they were out of view but could see the front door of the embassy. They sat in silence for several minutes and Martinez knew that Dio was upset with her, rightfully so. She knew she had no business doing what she did. But then again she thought, Fuck it. Finally, after about twenty minutes she said, "Hey, D, how about we try to find one of those bratwursts stands? I could go for some processed pork and fries. How about you?"

Dio just looked over at her and smiled, shook his head, started the car, and drove back toward the city. About two kilometers away they found a small diner that the locals called a Schnell Imbus.

"My treat, D, you want a bratwurst with curry like the last time?"

"Yeah sure, Lyd, and some pommes frits (fries) with ketchup. And as long as you're buying, grab me a beer." The diner was empty except for the rather large lady probably in her seventies who was working the counter. Lydia gave her their order by pointing and using her fingers. The large lady said something in German that Lydia did not understand, with the exception of the word *Albanisch*. Lydia assumed she was asking if she was Albanian. She was about to go out and have Dio come in and interpret, but she saw he was on the phone and probably still chaffing from her behavior at the embassy.

"American. Ich been American." That was the extent of Lydia's German.

"Ah so," said the woman with a wide smile. "*Ein moment bitte.*" The woman went into a back room and returned holding a photo, which she handed to Lydia. The old black and white showed a young girl holding a small American flag in one hand. The other hand was held by a beaming JFK.

"*Das ist mich, von ich ver eine machen.*"

Lydia looked at the photo and, pointing to the little girl, asked, "You?"

The woman just smiled and said, "Ya." She continued on in German. Lydia assumed she was talking about how she met JFK when she was a little girl. In broken English she said, "I love JFK. I love America."

Lydia took a picture she had of Spunky and showed it to her. "Does he ever come here?" At first, she seemed not to

267

understand, and Lydia pointed to the picture and then to her open mouth.

"Ya, ya," Lydia held up her hand in a waiting gesture and went out and called Dio inside.

"What did you forget your wallet?"

"No, I showed this woman a picture of Spunky and she seemed to recognize him. I need you to ask her about him in German."

Dio's German was not that good, but he did learn that Spunky eats there often—mostly take-out—but she has not seen him in a while. She did not know who he was or anything about Karl Messerschmitt's suicide. When Dio showed her the story in the German newspaper, *Das Spiegel*, she just shrugged her shoulders. Dio thought she had said she doesn't read the papers.

They drove back to the surveillance spot. Still no sign of the German cops. They wondered what Spunky was planning. They decided they would finish their lunch and wait about an hour then leave.

"Maybe it's better if we let the German cops handle this, D. I'm sorry I've been acting like a rookie trying to make my first arrest."

"It's OK, Lyd. Bribing me with lunch has a way of making me forget your little indiscretion back there."

They finished their lunch and beers and sat for a while. The skies were darkening, and a light rain was beginning to fall. They were about to leave when Dio noticed a tall dark figure exit from the side of the embassy.

"Holy shit, Lydia, could that be our boy?" Lydia reached in the back for the binoculars they brought along and focused on the figure walking away from the embassy in the direction of the Messerschmitt estate.

"It's definitely a man, about six-foot, but he's wearing a hoodie and I can't make out his face."

"What about his hands, Lyd? Look at his hands."

"He's got something in his left hand. Maybe a cane. I can't say for sure." She was now able to focus the binoculars on his deformed right hand.

"Fuck! It's him, Dio. It's fucking Spunky." Her voice showed the excitement she was feeling.

Dio looked around to see if the German cops had finally arrived. "Where the hell are the Germans?"

"This may be our last chance, D. Let's follow him."

Dio put the car in gear and started to drive slowly while Lydia kept an eye on the subject. Dio reached for his phone and was about to press Boser's number when Lydia reached over and grabbed his hand.

"No, Dio, don't. I want this guy. I want to take him down. The Germans don't give a shit, or they would be here."

"Lyd, we have no jurisdiction. *You* have no jurisdiction."

"Bullshit, Dio. We can make a citizen's arrest." Dio knew it would be useless to protest plus he wanted to help her get this piece of shit. As they slowly drove about one kilometer behind Spunkmeyer, Dio handed something to Lydia.

"Here, Lyd, put this in your glove." He handed her a black leather encased object with a heavy metal disc in the top. "It's a slapper. I used to keep it in my glove when I walked a beat. Comes in handy when you need to get someone's attention. A lot of guys carried jacks, which are similar, but are more flexible." He made a whipping gesture with his hand. "You could open a guy's head with one of those. I preferred the slapper, less blood."

"Thanks for the history lesson on dinosaur police tactics." She took the slapper and placed it inside her right-hand glove. At the same time, Spunkmeyer left the road, crossed a fence, and started walking through a field.

"I'll follow on foot. You head toward Messerschmitt's. If my guess is right, he's heading back to his cottage."

Dio wanted to stop her, maybe let her drive and he could follow, but he was too late. She was out of the car before he could act.

"Damn you, Martinez. You're gonna get us both in deep shit." He put the car in gear and followed the best he could keeping an eye on the woman he loved and now feared for.

Martinez followed but kept her distance as Spunkmeyer walked through a wooded area. She could tell by his pace that he was familiar with the route he was taking and was not at all aware he was being followed. Sure enough, he exited the tree line and there stood his cottage. Lydia took out her cell and tried to call Dio.

"Shit, no bars."

Dio had lost sight of her as she entered the forest. His keen sense of direction told him that Spunkmeyer was probably heading toward his cottage on the Messerschmitt's estate. He wondered if he knew his accomplice had given him up and then hung himself. Lydia thought the same thing as she reached the back of the cottage. As Dio approached the Messerschmitt's estate, he reached for his cell and pressed Lydia's number. The phone rang and went to voicemail.

"Lydia, it's me. Back off. I'll call the German cops. Now is the best time for them to grab him. Please, Lyd." Lydia heard her cell but let it go to voicemail. She played Dio's message and sent him a text.

"No, D, I'm going after him. He's in the cottage. Come. Don't call cops yet."

When Dio saw her text, his heart sank. He knew this was not how to play it, but what could he do? He parked the car and started to make his way toward the cottage. He sent a text to Boser: Get local cops to Spunkmeyer's cottage. He's there, hurry.

CHAPTER 76

Lydia was careful not to give herself away. Spunkmeyer did not bother to lock the door behind him and when Lydia entered, she could hear him rummaging in the bedroom closet. She could not resist the temptation and went into the bedroom. Spunkmeyer had the empty metal box in his hand.

Lydia reached into her jeans pocket and pulled out Jasmin Dollbee's anklet.

"Looking for this, Dieter?"

He turned around, not at all startled. "Vell, vell, look who is here. The pretty lady detective from Florida. You came all this way hoping I would do to you what I did to the others. Ya?"

"You're a sick motherfucker, Spunkmeyer, and in a few minutes the entire Lanspolizei will be here to take you away."

Dieter just smirked and she could see the madness in his eyes. "Perhaps, perhaps not. You see the Albanian Embassy has given me sanctuary. I cannot be touched by you or the Germans."

"You're not in the embassy, asshole."

Spunkmeyer reached for the cane he had set against the wall. With a quick move he drew out a ten-inch blade from inside the shaft of the cane. "Yes, but I will be soon." He started to slowly walk to Martinez, like a cat sneaking up on a mouse. She backed away looking for something to grab for protection.

"I am going to slice you open," he said, fingering the blade with his deformed right hand. "But you will not have the pleasure of me taking you. You old crones do nothing for me. I like young, pretty, blonde girls. They mocked me all my life, but I made them pay."

Old crone? Lydia thought. This guy is bonkers.

"What about Karl? Did he like young girls too?"

He stopped. "Karl? Karl was a wimp. He was nothing without me. He would never have made the pros if I had not gotten hurt." He held up his deformed right hand. "See how he died? Like a coward, hanging from a tree because he could not play golf." His voice raised, "I cannot play golf. No, all I can do is carry his bag. You think it was easy for me, growing up in a place where people that look like me are treated like dirt? Even when I was good at golf, I was still a second-class citizen. But not Karl, no Karl was perfect. Karl was handsome. Karl came from money. But not Dieter, no, Dieter was a gypsy. They would mock me behind my back. I was never good enough for the women we met. No, not Dieter, ah but Karl, always Karl. How I hated him sometimes."

"Did Karl help you kill Jasmin? Did he rape her too?"

He started toward her again with the blade in his left hand. "I made Karl put the shoe bag over her head. I told him he could fuck her after I was done. I told him the same thing in Troon, but he got sick. What a [inaudible German]."

As he came closer she raised her gloved hands in the basic defense position and knew she had to rely on the slapper. Just then Dio entered the cottage. Spunkmeyer stopped his advance as Dio instinctively reached for his weapon on his right hip. Of course, he was unarmed.

"Vell, vell, look who has joined the party. I see you brought your Opa along for protection, Detective. I never killed such an old man before, but I guess there is always a first time, ya?"

They made eye contact trying to get a sense of what to do next. Do we just leave him here and wait for backup? That would be the logical thing to do, but they both knew this had to end here. Spunkmeyer started to move forward in the direction of Dio while keeping an eye on Lydia. In an instant he was on him and slashed away as Dio raised his arm in defense. The blade ran across Dio's left arm, but his London fog raincoat took the brunt of the slash. Lydia saw this as an opportunity. She lunged at Dieter and caught him on his right temple with the full force of the slapper. She could hear the crack of his skull, but he was able to spin around and slash at her. At the same time Dio positioned himself on both feet and leaped onto Dieter's back. They both fell forward and landed on the floor, the blade dropping out of his hand. Dio was attempting to land blows on the back of Dieter's neck, but the younger man was too strong and rolled Dio over on his back and started to land blow after blow on his face.

Now Lydia jumped on his back and rolled him off of Dio. As they rolled to the ground Dieter reached into his pant pocket and pulled out a switchblade knife. Flicking it open he tried to stab her in the neck. She was holding his left hand with both of hers, screaming for Dio to help. Dio staggered to his feet, blood rushing from his nose and mouth, picked up a stool, and ran at Dieter and cracked him over the head with the back end of the chair. The cheap wood shattered as Dieter ducked and the chair struck his back.

He got to his feet and was going after Dio. Lydia grabbed on to his leg and he reached down and stabbed her in her hand. Screaming, she let go of his leg. With his leg now free, he kicked at Lydia catching her on the side of her head. Turning away from Lydia, who was struggling to maintain consciousness, Dieter grabbed Dio in a headlock and once again was delivering blows to his face and head.

Staggering and groggy, Lydia got to her feet. Taking a deep breath and mustering the little strength she had left, she once again hit Dieter full force with the slapper, which was now out of the glove. Blood was now pouring out of his nose and he staggered. Reaching out he grabbed her throat with his deformed right hand. He retrieved the knife from the floor and jabbed at her neck with the knife. The blade caught her just below her left ear and she started to bleed. As the blood spurted from her neck, Dio got to his feet. He staggered for a second and looked around for something to use as a weapon.

"Dio, the cane sword," she repeatedly screamed. Dieter had Lydia pinned against a wall and was attempting to push the knife into her, while she was trying with both hands to keep the knife at bay. Both her hand and neck were bleeding and she started to feel her strength sap. Dio did not understand what Lydia was saying. Glancing down he saw the blade of the cane and reached for it. Picking it up he ran at Dieter, who was now screaming in German at Lydia. Just as he was about to plunge the knife into her neck, Dio leaped at him with all the strength he could muster and with a two-handed overhead thrust plunged the steel shaft of the blade into the back of Dieter's neck.

Letting go of his grip on Martinez he turned toward Dio. Blood was oozing from his mouth, and the blows from the slapper opened up a wound on his skull that was also bleeding profusely. He looked at Dio; his face covered in blood. He made one final attempt to move toward Dio with a grin on his face that Dio would later describe as insane. He reached for the blade that was wedged into his neck and, grinning, he fell to his knees. Dio just watched as the last bit a life left Dieter Spunkmeyer as he fell on his face to the floor.

Dio rushed over to Lydia. Blood was spurting out of her neck, her face bruised and battered. Dio placed his finger in the hole to stop bleeding while looking around for something to use. He tore off a piece of his shirt and applied pressure to Lydia's neck. He could see she was in shock and losing blood. Just then two uniformed German cops ran into the cottage.

"Quick, call an ambulance. We need an ambulance, schnell, schnell." One of the cops called on his radio as Dio lifted Lydia's head and cradled it in his arms.

"Easy, baby, easy. Help is on the way. You're going to be fine."

She opened her eyes. Dio could see she was fading. She looked at him and smiled. "You look like shit, D," she said in a faint voice attempting her best snarky smile. "Spunky?"

"Dead."

She just smiled a faint smile and nodded her head. "We got them both, Dio, didn't we?"

"Yes, Lyd, we got them both." Tears were welling up in his eyes. He knew he was losing her.

In a faint voice she said, "I love you, Dio. Please don't let me die."

THE END.

ACKNOWLEDGMENTS

The names of the characters in this novel are either fictional or used with permission. Wilhelm Emil Messerschmitt was an actual person but had no children. Special thanks to Kevin Gropp who was a great help during the editing of the manuscript and Chris Persico who was helpful with technical assistance. Thanks to Ann Quick for the research on Scotland.

The author would like to recognize three characters who passed away during the writing of the novel:

John Whalen—neighbor and golf buddy

Frank Kiers—childhood friend, retired NYPD police captain

Walter Boser—retired lieutenant, commanding officer of the NYPD bomb squad, 1985–1995, one of my dearest friends

May they rest in peace.

Made in United States
Orlando, FL
02 November 2021

10169217R00163